A NEAR-DEATH EXPERIENCE

Darnell prepared himself for the evening, pulled on a robe, dropped his revolver in a pocket, sat in his chair and stared at the cabin door. A small taste of sherry would be no problem, he decided, and opened the bottle on the desk.

The cork was loose, and the bottle appeared to have been opened. He sniffed the contents. Darnell recognized the pungent odor of cyanide, and changed his plans abruptly.

He poured a bit of sherry in a glass, put the glass on the nightstand, then deliberately tipped it over, the liquid flowing over the edge and dripping onto the carpet. He turned down his bed, lay down, still clothed, and covered himself, nothing showing but his head. He clicked off the bed lamp and stared into the darkness. The door was locked, but the extra bolt had not been thrown. A key would unlock it.

The fly, Darnell thought, was now ready for the spider.

THE CASE OF CABIN 13

A JOHN DARNELL MYSTERY

Sam McCarver

A SIGNET BOOK

SIGNET
Published by New American Library, a division of
Penguin Putnam Inc., 375 Hudson Street,
New York, New York 10014, U.S.A.
Penguin Books Ltd, 27 Wrights Lane,
London W8 5TZ, England
Penguin Books Australia Ltd,
Ringwood, Victoria, Australia
Penguin Books Canada Ltd, 10 Alcorn Avenue,
Toronto, Ontario, Canada M4V 3B2
Penguin Books (N.Z.) Ltd, 182–190 Wairau Road,
Auckland 10, New Zealand

Penguin Books Ltd, Registered Offices:
Harmondsworth, Middlesex, England

First published by Signet, an imprint of New American Library,
a division of Penguin Putnam Inc.

First Printing, June 1999
10 9 8 7 6 5 4 3 2 1

For Gary, Pamela, and Stacee,
who were the first to hear me tell this story,
and for Cara and Christy

Acknowledgments

Nostalgically, I acknowledge my father, who told me, when I was a child, the tragic tale of the sinking of the *Titanic*, which occurred when he was just a young man. Hearing his narration of it began my interest in the now-legendary tragedy, and fostered a determination, later, to write about it someday. Real-life persons who were caught up in the events of this story are included in this book. However, except for the historically documented events, their other participation in the story-line derives from imagination, since this book is a work of fiction.

I thank Donald Maass, my literary agent, and Joseph Pittman, Senior Editor at NAL, for their enthusiasm, encouragement, ideas, and support throughout the entire process of publication of my novel. I also express my appreciation for the valuable assistance of NAL's editorial staff. And I thank Shelba Robison and Dan Avery.

Chapter One

London, Monday evening, April 8, 1912

Professor John Darnell smiled as he poked his way along through the clammy opaqueness of the thick, moist fog, using his black umbrella as a walking stick. Predictably, his work as a paranormal investigator always increased with "pea-soupers." How many ghosts would Londoners see tonight? People saw things that weren't there in the fog, and imagined the unimaginable. Darnell could count on a new case whenever London wrapped itself in its mystery shroud. And this was one of those nights.

When two men bumped into him a block from his flat, Darnell jumped back, alert. He saw that one of them, white-bearded, wore a sea captain's brass-buttoned uniform.

The captain said, "I beg your pardon. Do you know where Professor Darnell lives? Can't see a thing in this damn fog."

"What business do you have with him?" Darnell was still cautious, but curious now.

"Business is the correct word," the second man said. "We wish to consult him."

"Consult." Darnell liked the sound of that—a new client. "Follow me," he said. "I'll take you to his place."

Darnell led the captain and the other man, who wore a pin-striped business suit, a gold watch chain and fob crisscrossing his vest. The professor, six feet tall, felt the businessman was at least four inches taller. In minutes, Darnell was unlocking the door to his flat, saying, "This is it, gentlemen. Come in."

"Then you must be the professor," the captain blurted out.

The businessman snorted and stomped his walking stick on the stoop. "You could have told us who you were."

Darnell laughed, led the way into the residence, and pushed open double mahogany doors into a room to the right side of the hall. He stepped over to the fireplace, rubbing his hands in the warmth of the blaze, and said, "Make yourselves comfortable, please."

His usual cold supper of beef, cheese, and bread was laid out on a table by Sung, his houseboy, in anticipation of his arrival. But he covered it with the napkin—that would have to wait.

He heard Sung's step coming down the hall and turned to greet him. "These men are here for a business talk, Sung. We'll have tea, please. Darjeeling. A large pot."

The dark-haired slender man bowed slightly from the waist. "And food?" He glanced at the professor's covered dinner plate.

The professor shook his head. "Just something light. Scones would do."

The servant bowed again, turned, and left the room.

"Sit, gentlemen, sit," Darnell said to his visitors, who were milling about the room. He gestured toward two red leather chairs. Darnell threw off his coat and pulled onto his lean frame the oversized

Chinese silk robe presented to him by Sung as a birthday gift. He poked up the fire, then brought a bottle and three glasses from a nearby cabinet. He put them on a table in front of the men.

"Sherry?" Darnell asked, eyes twinkling. He knew no Englishman could refuse that offer on a night like this, and he was more than ready for his evening glass.

The visitors nodded and Darnell filled three glasses generously. He took in both men in a sharp glance. "Now, what can I do for you, gentlemen?"

"I'm J. Bruce Ismay," the businessman said, bowing slightly before taking a seat. "Chairman and Managing Director of White Star Line. I'm sure you know of us—we have one of the largest fleets of transatlantic ocean liners. And this is Commodore Edward Smith, our most senior Atlantic-crossing captain."

Ismay, a tall man with a slight banker's paunch, graying brown muttonchops, gold watch, and fine tailored suit, exuded an aura of wealth. To Darnell, he appeared to be the kind of client he needed just now—moneyed, and not sparing with it.

The sturdy sea captain, a stocky, white-haired, white-bearded man in a dark blue, brass-buttoned uniform, took the lead, speaking in a rough-edged but friendly voice. "We apologize for interrupting your evening without notice, Professor, but we need your help, and we'll make it worth your while." He removed his cap, stepped forward, and thrust a gnarled hand out to Darnell.

Darnell stuffed his hands deep into the pockets of his robe. "I don't shake hands—health reasons, you know. But there's no need to apologize. I conduct all my consultations in my home."

Darnell was anxious for a new case with a sub-
stantial fee in his consulting practice, which supple-
mented his teaching and lecturing income. A country
manor offered for sale, and perfect for his long-
desired retreat, had caught his eye when he visited
the Cotswolds region in March. A good case could
get him funds to buy it.

Darnell polished his gold-rimmed half-glasses, replaced them on his nose, and peered over their tops
at his guests. "You need my help? Did you lose one
of your ships, in some inexplicable mystery?" He
smiled, looking from one to the other.

Captain Smith shook his head and stroked his
pointed beard. "No. But we've lost a cabin."

The professor's eyes widened. "A cabin? Interesting. How do you . . . ?"

Director Ismay frowned, an irritated look on his
face. "No, Professor. Not missing. But we have lost
the use of it. We can't book first-class cabins with the
number thirteen on any of our ships. You won't believe what we've encountered."

Darnell smiled. "In my work, nothing surprises
me. But are there crimes here? Have you gone to the
police?"

The Captain answered, "There may have been
crimes, and the police have been involved, but to no
avail. We read about you in the *Times*. You investigate psychic phenomena, don't you? The occult,
jinxes, hexes, ghosts, sightings, mysterious events?
Isn't that true?"

Darnell nodded, proud to speak of his work in that
field, so much more interesting than his teaching.
"Yes. I'm the first and only 'paranormal detective.' I
sometimes call myself a 'psychichologist.' It's a term
I invented, but most people can't pronounce it. So
they just call me a ghost-hunter."

"Do you believe in these things?" the Chairman asked.

"No, not all. And I'm not a psychic. I've used logic, my sixth sense, and my experience in investigating these so-called psychic phenomena for ten years now. The public is more fascinated than ever today with ghostly sightings, communications with the dead, and all that. It's claptrap, but it's business for me, and I enjoy disposing of frauds, phonies, and unfounded fears."

"I read that you investigated reports of ghosts in Leeds Castle," the Captain said.

As if on cue with the word "ghosts," the two lamps in the room flickered out, then came on again. The two visitors exchanged glances.

"No ghosts here." Darnell laughed. "That's just our London electricity overload problem. Technology getting ahead of itself, one of the big problems today. . . . Now, the Leeds case—yes. Very strange sightings. It's covered in yesterday's *Times*, but I must confess the reporter exaggerated the circumstances to satisfy the public appetite. Reporters are all sensationalists." He paused. "Well, tell me about your cabins with the unlucky number thirteen. How can I help?"

Ismay nodded at Smith. "You can tell him best, E.J."

Captain Smith fixed unwavering blue eyes onto those of the professor. "White Star Line has some of the biggest and fastest ocean liners in the world, with the latest technology, amenities, and equipment. For a half century there has been no single smudge on our reputation. Until now."

"Go on," Darnell said. In a habitual gesture, he brushed back strands of his long, dark brown hair which fell down onto his forehead. He stepped over to his desk and rummaged about in the strewn papers for a notepad and pencil.

A rap on the door signaled the return of Sung, who brought in a silver teapot, sugar and cream, flowered china cups and saucers. Currant-laden scones were arranged in neat circles on a delicate china plate. For a few moments the men helped themselves to the fare. Darnell waited with impatience for the Captain's story to begin.

The Captain cleared his throat with a gravelly sound. "In the past three months, we've had mysterious suicides of passengers booked in first-class cabin thirteen on three of the ships of the line. Three months and three deaths, all in first class, and all in cabin thirteen." He paused dramatically, taking several sips of his tea. "On one ship, a woman jumped overboard after four days out to sea. Drowned, of course. She was booked in first class, number thirteen."

Darnell raised his eyebrows. "She jumped? Are you sure? Did anyone see her jump, or know why she would do that?"

"Not really. A steerage passenger on a lower deck saw the woman fall, screaming, into the ocean from the first-class deck."

"And the second case?"

"It was on one of our older liners. A man didn't leave his cabin thirteen, first-class again, for two days, presumably with the *mal de mer*. But when the ship's officers broke into his locked cabin, they found it wasn't seasickness after all. He was dead. And when the ship reached port in New York and an autopsy was performed, they determined he had died of poison. Apparently a second suicide."

Ismay interrupted impatiently. "Tell him about

Kapopolous." He fiddled with his watch fob and chain.

The professor smiled. "A Greek? I'm beginning a study of the Greek wars just now." His eyes flicked toward six red-leather-bound volumes on his bookshelf. He had found them on a dusty back shelf of an antique book dealer and was anxious to study them. It looked like that might have to wait now. A new case always took precedence.

Smith spoke in hushed tones. "It was another mysterious case on a third ship. A Greek interpreter was found dead in his first-class cabin thirteen, also locked. There was one shot in his head, and a revolver lay on the floor below his hand, by his bed. The police called it suicide. It looked like a self-inflicted wound, and they couldn't very well interrogate a thousand passengers disembarking in New York." He frowned. "But I wonder whether they took the easy way out."

Ismay stood up, patted his stomach with both hands, and paced back and forth in front of the professor. "Think about it," he said, his voice grating. "Three suicides. Three persons leaving England for America in the last three months, each one booked in cabin thirteen in first class on one of our liners. And not one reaches New York alive. You'll agree that's no coincidence."

"Ismay thinks cabin thirteen is jinxed," Captain Smith said.

"Nonsense!" The professor's eyes flashed. "Jinxes do not exist."

"I knew you'd say that, Professor." Smith looked at Ismay triumphantly. "That's why we're here. We want you to prove that there is no jinx, and dispose of this mystery, once and for all."

Darnell asked, "How do you expect me to do

that?" But before Smith spoke, Darnell felt he knew the answer already.

"You'll embark on our ship which leaves for America on Wednesday." Smith paused dramatically and looked over at the Managing Director, who nodded concurrence. "And you'll be put in first-class cabin thirteen."

"That's only two days. . . . But why not just leave cabin thirteen vacant on all your ships? Wouldn't that solve your problem?"

"No," Ismay said, defiance in his voice. "If we closed the cabins, people would wonder, word would get around. We can't take that risk with our reputation." He paused, looking at Smith. "If it's a jinx, something occult, tell us. Or if there's something sinister killing three of our passengers, as Smith thinks, we have to know what that is. We must know."

Smith nodded.

Darnell looked at first one and then the other of the two men, sizing them up, wondering what financial value they would put on their fears. "All right. If I go, and if I succeed . . . if I live to set foot on American soil . . . what's my reward?"

The Chairman said, "If you solve this problem, get rid of the jinx, and live to tell about it, you'll receive a lifetime first-class pass on any of the ships in our line, for two persons, and the sum of, say, three thousand pounds."

"And if I . . . for whatever reason, do not survive the voyage?"

"The sum of five thousand pounds will be paid to your heirs, or the person or institution of your choice." Chairman Ismay coughed, looking down. "You won't need the passes in that case."

The professor pushed back hair that fell in front of

his eyes. He blew off imaginary dust specks from his glasses, taking a moment to consider. No jinx, of course, he thought. That's superstition. The danger he didn't mind, and the money would come at a good time. The image of his own Cotswold country house amid green fields and a flowing stream nearby flashed into his mind. He remembered his boyhood voyage with his parents from his American birthplace to England, and thought of the opportunity of going back there again. Darnell made his decision.

"I'll do it," he said, "but with several conditions. First, I must receive five thousand pounds even if I survive. You have to admit there is tremendous risk involved." He waited.

The men looked at each other. Smith nodded slightly, and Ismay said, "All right. We agree."

"Number two. Those funds and the lifetime pass are to be deposited in trust with my solicitor with signed instructions before the ship sails."

They nodded.

"And I will take my houseboy Sung with me."

The men nodded concurrence again. "Of course," the Director said. "There are facilities for him—a connecting room."

Darnell smiled. "I do have some other small conditions."

"We're listening," Ismay said. His voice was edgy now, questioning.

Darnell filled a pipe with aromatic tobacco, enjoying his own dramatic pause by lighting it and puffing deeply. He blew smoke into the air.

Ismay wrinkled his nose and waved a hand in front of his nose. He glared silently at the professor.

Darnell enjoyed watching the Captain and Chairman fidgeting in their seats. "First, I must have full freedom of the ship, including the bridge, the engine room, and wireless room."

The heads of Captain Smith and Chairman Ismay nodded up and down in unison. "I would expect that," Smith said.

"Secondly, I'll need complete diagrams of all four ships, the bridge, engine rooms, kitchens, cabins, and service rooms—everything. I'll want a list of crew and passengers on my ship, as well as those who traveled on the other three on which there were the, ah, suicides."

Ismay voiced his agreement, jotting in his notebook. The Captain nodded.

"And finally," the professor said, "I'll need two companions in my cabin."

Captain Smith and the Chairman exchanged glances again.

"Two?" Ismay questioned, folding his arms in a defensive posture and glaring at Darnell.

"Companions?" Smith echoed, eyes narrowing.

"Yes." Darnell laughed, amused at the effect of his words. "One companion will be my new .38 special revolver, together with a box of cartridges."

Smith grinned through his ample beard. "I understand. And the other?"

"You must take special care in delivering my six-volume set of the history of the Greek Peloponnesian Wars to my cabin. It's an irreplaceable 1883 edition. They'll be good company on my return trip . . . I do plan to come back, you know."

Ismay and Smith laughed. "Of course," Ismay said. He patted the vest over his generous mid-section. "We expect you to return, Professor. And as Managing Director of White Star Line I can guarantee every condition you named. I'll have documents drawn and the cash and passes ready for you at once."

Smith said, "And I'll be the captain on the ship, Professor, our newest, safest vessel."

Darnell nodded. "Just one more thing . . . no one aboard except the two of you should know my exact mission. Absolute secrecy is vital."

Ismay said, "My personal assurances, sir."

"The ship leaves the tenth?" Darnell asked absently. "That gives me only two days to prepare for the trip." His mind filled with matters he would need to arrange to embark so soon—speak to his solicitors, tell Sung about the trip.

"Yes, the tenth," Smith said. "I'm sure you've read of our ship's maiden Atlantic crossing, leaving Southampton Wednesday?"

Darnell suddenly recalled the extensive articles in the *Times*. "You don't mean—is it . . . ?"

Ismay nodded, beaming. "Yes, Professor. You'll be on the largest ship in the world. She's incomparably beautiful, and I'm proud of her. Technologically, she's the absolute best man can build. I'm told not to say it—but this is one ship that's unsinkable." He paused dramatically. "She's the *Titanic*!"

Chapter Two

Southampton, Wednesday, April 10, 1912

The docks at Southampton, England, teemed with what looked to Darnell to be half the city's population as the *Titanic* prepared to depart. Although it was almost noon, no sun could be seen through the heavy cloud cover. But the gray and forbidding day did not dampen the spirits of the clamoring people on the docks, nor those of the passengers hugging the rail aboard the towering, majestic ship. There was a festive air, and Darnell knew passengers always looked forward to the parties on the first night out.

Captain Smith, in the full regalia of his dress uniform, stood on the bridge directing the embarkation. Director Bruce Ismay, enjoying his greatest hour of fame, drank sherry with three American multimillionaires in the palatial first-class lounge, boasting of the ship's qualities and innovations.

Professor Darnell and Sung had traveled by boat train from London the previous day and stayed that night at the luxurious Southwestern Hotel in a room next to the millionaire Guggenheim's suite. Guggenheim had nodded at him as they passed in the hall, Darnell recognizing him from photos in the *Daily Mail*.

In the morning, Darnell and Sung had checked into their cabins, Sung staying there to arrange their travel gear. Now, at the ship's railing, five stories above the pier, Darnell looked down at the crowds of people and occasionally waved. He realized, just then, he had no one to wave back, no one to miss him or worry about him on the perilous journey. Colored streamers spiraled down from the topmost decks, and passengers covered their ears as the great ship signaled its departure with blasts from its huge sirens. Stewards were going up and down along the rail offering streamers, little British flags, and champagne.

Darnell became aware of a willowy young woman bundled in a fur coat next to him at the rail. Even in the open air, he could sense her delicate perfume. From his vantage point of thirty-one years, she looked to be in her early twenties, but as she covered her ears with her gloved hands during the booms of the ship horns, her eyes wide, she took on a childlike image.

The sounds reminded Darnell of his first voyage with his family, steaming across the ocean from America to make their new home in London. Ten years old then, it seemed to him the voyage would last forever. Images of his mother and father taking daily walks with him on the decks flashed through his mind.

Looking down at the crowds now, he wondered what this voyage back to his native America held in store, and his eyes glistened. The mystery of the cabins of death intrigued him. And during the round trip he would have two weeks to study the Greek wars in his regimented educational program. The professor often told his students, *"Knowledge is the gateway to reality in an often unreal world."* He took pride in practicing that philosophy himself, whether teaching or debunking ghosts.

The fur-coated young woman at his elbow spoke, interrupting his thoughts. "Exciting, isn't it?" She looked back down at the dock and waved at someone in the crowd.

Darnell nodded, returning her smile. "Yes, indeed," he answered, although his rapid pulse at the moment was more from the intrigue and sense of danger he expected from the trip, rather than from any holiday spirit. Cabin 13 awaited him. But he asked, in politeness, "Is someone seeing you off?"

"My aunt. I've been visiting her, now I'm going back to America." She took out a white handkerchief and waved it vigorously in the direction of the crowd.

Darnell could not tell who waved back—everyone was waving. There seemed to be a lot of little old aunts with white handkerchiefs in the crowd below.

"America's your home?" he asked, again as a courtesy, not really questioning. Her accent marked her as an American.

"Yes. I just love these trips. It's my third one. But this ship is fantastic! So huge. I've never seen anything like it in my life."

The professor nodded. They stood shoulder to shoulder with other passengers lined along the rail—excited young children, gray-haired women and men with the paunches of age, returning from their retirement holidays. He observed all the embarkment procedures—ropes being disengaged, crew members hauling aboard baggage and supplies, and, at last, gangway planks dragged back.

Several crew members carrying black duffel bags over their shoulders ran up to the dock, breathless, their black short coats flapping. They stood arguing with the dock foreman, their fists clenched, as if blows were to be struck. A small crowd encircled them. The foreman was motioning toward the gangplanks and waving his arms. After all the shouting and arguing, however, it seemed it was just too late to let them on the ship. The sailors, resigned to their situation, stood on the dock watching ship's hands securing ropes and railing gates, preparing for the ship to move out. One of the abandoned crewmen gave a parting salute.

"Those poor men—lost their passage. I hope they have enough hands aboard," the woman said.

"Hundreds, I'm sure," Darnell assured her. "They'll get by."

The massive ship's sirens again blasted their warnings of departure, and the ship eased away slowly from the dock. The crowds receded into the distance as the *Titanic* inched its way out through the curving harbor. Darnell was astonished at the size of the *Titanic* compared to another, smaller ocean liner, the *New York*, that they looked down upon as they edged by it.

Suddenly loud, snapping reports came from the direction of the other ship. "Look!" the young woman exclaimed. "We're going to hit that other ship! Look out!" she shouted into the air. Nearby passengers stared at her, then looked below at the smaller liner. It was true. An older woman screamed.

Looking down, Darnell saw that the thrust of the *Titanic's* massive engines had created an irresistible suction, that snapped, one by one, in a series of sharp, explosive pops, all of the half dozen taut mooring ropes holding the *New York* alongside the wharf.

He could see the *New York* was being pulled inexorably into a collision course with the *Titanic* by the suction generated by its huge size, and was within a few feet of the ship. Deckhands ran about on lower decks, shouting, swearing. Darnell could imagine the equivalent pandemonium inside the captain's bridge.

The young woman clutched the professor's arm as, mouths open, they both watched the awesome scene. "Look how close it is now!" she exclaimed.

A stooped, gray-haired woman on Darnell's other side gasped, "Lord have mercy!" He glanced at the woman's face, drained of color.

"Are you all right?" he asked.

"I don't know . . . are we going to crash?" The feeble plaintive voice seemed to express the sentiments of everyone at the rail.

The *New York* continued to drift toward the *Titanic*. Darnell felt helplessly rooted to the spot, and made no move to shake off the hand of his young rail companion or to move away from the rail.

At that moment, Darnell felt the jar of a quick touch on the great ship's engines, no doubt ordered by an alert Captain Smith. The opposing wash from the *Titanic*'s massive triple-screw propellors seemed to hold the *New York* at bay, just feet from the *Titanic*. Two harbor tugboats approached the *New York* from the service docks, smokestacks blowing under full steam, and took sharp action, towing the stern of the *New York* out and away from the churning water of the *Titanic*'s wake, back toward the dock.

Tense moments passed without a sense of time as the collision still appeared imminent. For what seemed minutes the ships' positions were frozen, as if in an oil painting, gently moving along coupled together with the conflicting forces, through the harbor. Some passengers held their breath, watching, while others babbled incoherences in frightened voices. The din of the passenger voices rose to a crescendo, most of them shouting words like, "Look out, look out! We're going to crash!" But at last Darnell could see their ship was, inch by inch, foot by foot, pulling away.

The crowd aboard ship breathed a collective sigh of relief, and nervous laughter and conversation broke out among the passengers up and down the deck. Darnell realized a disastrous ship-to-ship collision had been avoided and wondered how Captain Smith felt at that moment. He was shocked at the slow degree of maneuverability of the giant ship and speculated whether White Star Line had appreciated the significance of that factor in planning the ship's voyage. He knew a difference of only a minute or two in timing could have resulted in a horrible harbor collision, and perhaps deaths.

The young woman released Darnell's arm. "I'm sorry. I didn't mean to hold you so tight. What a scare!" She flashed Darnell a brilliant smile. "My name's Penny Winters."

"And I'm John Darnell. This was quite a way to meet. With a near-shipwreck."

She laughed. "I've got something to tell them about in America already. Who said sailing was dull?" Her expression turned serious. "I wonder if this was a bad omen."

Darnell laughed. "Only if you're superstitious, which I'm definitely not. But there'll be nothing boring about this trip, I'm sure." He smiled, thinking if he told her of the deaths in cabin 13, and the adventure he was involved in, it would convince her without question. He took a lighter tone. "I'm sure we'll be delayed a bit. Would you like some champagne?"

"After that, yes!"

They walked to a portable bar area where men in

crisp white jackets poured champagne into fluted glasses. They took theirs to nearby deck chairs and sat side by side. "Cheers," Darnell said, and they clinked glasses.

Penny Winters smiled. "You Englishmen always say 'cheers,' don't you?"

"It's funny you should say that—I was born in America. Of course, I've lived here since I was a boy." Close up, he noticed how fresh and attractive her face was. "It's a cheery occasion."

"Yes, it is." She paused, taking a small sip from her glass. "Do you have relatives in America?"

"No. It's just a . . . business trip, you might say."

"Someone else is paying for your trip?"

"Yes. And for my houseboy Sung."

"Sung's a quaint name."

"He's Chinese. Came to England ten years or so ago. I was lucky to get him five years ago, when his employer passed on, a foreign-service government minister for the Chinese area—Hong Kong, I believe."

"Sung runs your house for you?"

Darnell nodded. "He cooks—but English style. He's my valet. And he keeps things picked up about the place that the housekeeper misses. He has a cabin adjoining mine."

"First class is awfully expensive on this ship."

"I certainly couldn't afford it. But it's part of my business arrangement." He studied her. "And your fare—your aunt paid it?"

"No." Her laughter carried across the deck. "I inherited money. I'm afraid I fritter it away like this."

Darnell fidgeted, aware he was taking steps out of his confirmed bachelor character. He cleared his throat. "Perhaps—I wonder, would you like to have dinner with me tonight?"

Penny answered without hesitation. "I'd love to. I'll tell you all about America—whatever you don't know already."

"I've been there only once since I was a boy."

They rose together, and sipped the last drops from their glasses.

Darnell said, "Well, I suppose we should find our cabins now. Would you like to meet me in the smoking lounge about five? Dinner is at six."

"Yes, that's fine. Then it's John?"

"Yes." Darnell smiled, remembering how in America his family had called him "Johnnie," which became "John" in England.

They left the rail, strolling into the ship's foyer, past the ornately engraved grand staircase, and beyond it to the first-class cabin hallways. Darnell and Penny Winters parted at a hallway. They touched hands, hers warm and pleasant. Darnell said, "Until later," and watched Penny Winters walk toward her cabin with a graceful, lithe, and sensual bearing. He would have to examine these blossoming feelings of his very carefully.

The hubbub died down and passengers made their way inside now, finding stewards to take them to their cabins. There was the unpacking ordeal to face, as well as finding their way about the ship. Luggage had already been delivered to their cabins, and they were ready to freshen up and get a change of clothes laid out for the gala first dinner at sea.

In his hallway, Darnell met the area steward, a slight, dark-haired man in a white uniform.

"Professor Darnell? I am Mario." He spoke in a Sicilian accent. "Follow me please." They walked down the carpeted hallway, passing original paintings and mirrors on the walls. Darnell shook his head in wonder, noticing solid brass, waist-high, cigar-and-cigarette-disposal stands holding white sand with an impression of the letter "T" stamped into it. It seemed a special sign of luxury.

As the steward led him to his cabin, Darnell thought of the captain's story of the apparent jinxes that had put him on this ship. When they reached his cabin, the number A13, boldly scripted in gold on the cabin door, brought a wry smile to his face.

Mario unlocked the cabin, handing two keys to the professor. "Your houseboy is situated in his cabin, just next to your suite. There's a connecting door."

Darnell stepped inside and viewed the interior of his rooms. He knew immediately this voyage would be filled with a luxury he could become accustomed to very easily.

He crossed the room and peered out of the large outside window overlooking a private promenade deck and the ocean beyond. He inspected the separate sitting room, complete with its electric heater— an ideal spot for his reading. He found his six red-leather-bound volumes of Greek war histories on a desk under a wall reading lamp. Another tall lamp sat behind a plush lounge chair in the corner.

In the bedroom, a full-size, double-poster bed took up less than half the large room. The bottle of sherry he had requested stood on a nightstand by the bed on a silver tray, with several delicate short-stemmed glasses. He felt the thickness of the plush carpets beneath his feet as he walked across the room to inspect the bathroom.

"Just like the *Ritz*!" he blurted to the steward.

"Yes, sir," his steward said. He pointed out some of the features and amenities of the rooms. With a final look about, the steward offered, with a small bow, "If you need anything at any time, sir, just ask."

Darnell decided it was time to start his investigation. "Mario, have you heard any rumors about bad luck, or about the number thirteen? Anything at all about cabin thirteen?"

The steward looked down at the floor. "I am not at liberty to discuss such things."

"Come, man. I'm a friend of Edward Smith, your Captain."

Startled, the man looked up into Darnell's eyes. "There is something, sir—I don't know all of it. A man committed suicide on one of our voyages. In cabin thirteen on another ship. I was on that ship."

"Anything else?"

"That's all I know—the rest is rumors."

"About cabin thirteen?"

"Some." The steward appeared flustered and anxious to get away. "If you need anything, sir, remember to ring for Mario. I'm at your service." He stepped out of the doorway and headed down the passageway.

As the door closed behind the steward, Professor Darnell mumbled aloud, "Knows more than he's telling." He shook his head and rubbed his hands briskly together in happy contemplation of opening his first book that night, with a glass of sherry to sip while he read. But first, the business at hand.

He sat on his bed and opened a bulky, sealed manila envelope with his name on it. He pulled out ship diagrams and layouts from the envelope and examined them. He scanned lists of passengers and crew for the *Titanic* and the three ships with ill-fated, cabin 13 passengers. He circled the names for those in cabin 13 on the other ships—Sally Holstrom on the *Atlantic*; Bertrand Preston, the *Adriatic*; Dimitri

Kapopolous, the *Olympic*. No pattern there. But he felt clues to the cabin 13 deaths must lie in these papers, and careful study could reveal them.

He unwrapped a second small parcel which lay on the nightstand, and his lips turned up at the corners as he saw the .38 special revolver and ammunition. He inserted cartridges into the chambers of the revolver and hefted it in first one hand, then the other. Professor Darnell had found early in life that he was ambidextrous and could write with either hand. And his clay-pigeon target-shooting instruction at Oxford had shown he could also shoot equally well using either hand.

Darnell stacked his books on a spot near the lounge chair and glanced about the rooms. Where to start? He opened the two closets and checked the wood backing of the compartments, finding them firm and solid. He inspected the locks on the window and the inside locks on the door. He walked slowly about the rooms, feeling the walls and thumping them now and again to determine their solidity. His suitcases had already been unpacked by Sung, and his clothes and belongings arranged in dressers and closets. Satisfied with the security of his suite, Darnell tapped on the connecting door to Sung's room.

"Good afternoon, Professor," Sung said, bowing as he opened the door. "Everything is satisfactory?"

"Yes, indeed." Sung looked different somehow in the strange surroundings, and Darnell felt pleased the man was there, a reminder of home. "Now, I want you to enjoy yourself on this trip, Sung. There's no cooking. And the maids will see that the rooms are cleaned. You have your meal arrangements?"

"Yes. I seek out friends. There are Chinese cooks."

Darnell hesitated. "I have to tell you more about

this trip—probably tomorrow. It's not a vacation. Just be alert and watchful at all times. You know the kinds of cases I take. There could be some danger."

"Yes, Professor. I watch. And I have good hearing, too. I can hear a mouse crawling across floor."

Darnell laughed. "I have a dinner date, so I'll be gone quite a while tonight."

Sung raised his eyebrows but said nothing. He bowed low and closed the door.

Noticing his dinner hour approached, Darnell shaved, bathed, and changed into dinner clothes, which Sung had laid out on his bed. He dropped the revolver into his inside dinner jacket coat pocket, shook the knob of the cabin door to be sure it was locked as he left, and proceeded to the ship's first-class section smoking lounge for his whiskey. The professor had long been a creature of habit— whiskey before dinner, sherry after dinner, and a bit more sherry before bed, with a prodigious amount of reading in between. Yet he suspected this trip could change all that. And his step quickened as he pictured the face of Penny Winters.

Chapter Three

Wednesday evening, April 10

John Darnell took a deep leather chair at a table near the windows and was greeted immediately by a waiter.

"Good evening, sir. May I be of service?"

"Yes. Scotch whisky, neat, with a side glass of water." Darnell placed a cigarette in a long holder and lit it, puffing deeply. He sat back in awe and gazed about the luxurious, paneled room. The ship was like a stately English mansion. He admired the shined mahoganies of the tables, the inlaid mother-of-pearl in the mahogany walls, the bright brass rail at the bar, the crystal chandelier, rubbed hardwood floors, and plush carpets.

The great ship was moving at twenty knots an hour, but the lack of any noticeable lateral motion enhanced the comfortable feeling of being in the drawing room of a mansion. He could smell the burnished leather and the polish on nearby brass door rails. Darnell thought, I could get used to this very easily.

The waiter brought his whisky and a crystal dish filled with salted almonds. Darnell sipped the scotch and sat back contentedly. This was his kind of travel.

"Good evening, Professor," came a familiar voice,

and Darnell turned toward the sound. Chairman Ismay stood at his elbow, beaming down at him.

Darnell rose when he noticed the Chairman's companion. It was Penny Winters. "Ah, hello . . ." Darnell said, somewhat flustered.

"Professor," Ismay said, "Miss Winters and I met walking over here. She tells me you two have already met. I just wanted to let you know you're both welcome to dine at the Captain's table tonight. Miss Winters is traveling back to America alone, and I felt the two of you might have some points of interest for pleasant conversation."

"Yes," Darnell said, smiling. He made a slight bow and took Penny's outstretched hand. As he did it, he realized he normally did not shake hands as a greeting, and seldom had dinner with a beautiful young woman in any case. Much was changing already.

She laughed and spoke to Ismay. "We watched that near collision with the *New York* today. . . . How are you, John?"

"I'm happy we're under way." His gaze took in her long auburn hair, the violet eyes, the high cheekbones. She looked even more soft and feminine in her long evening gown, with a fur wrap around her shoulders. Darnell shifted from one foot to another while the three of them murmured pleasantries. He listened to the Chairman's apology for what he called the "incident" at departure.

"That was a slight mishap," Ismay said. "But be assured the rest of the voyage will be as smooth as glass." Ismay patted his vest. He looked with sharp eyes at Darnell and asked in a softer, conspiratorial tone, "And your cabin, Professor? Is it to your liking?"

Darnell frowned. "It is more than satisfactory." He wanted to cut off that conversation, and not open up anything dealing with his true assignment. He hoped the Chairman would remember his pledge to keep the nature of his trip secret. And one person he particularly did not want to know about it was Penny Winters.

Darnell was relieved when Ismay finally left them to each other. But the female companionship itself gave the professor a slight anxious feeling he seldom experienced in his well-regulated professorial life.

He touched his handkerchief to his perspiring forehead and cleared his throat loudly. "Please sit down, Penny," he said. "Ah, may I order you something to drink?"

"I'd just like a sarsaparilla, please. That champagne this afternoon went straight to my head."

Darnell motioned to a waiter and ordered drinks, a sarsaparilla for her, another scotch for him. In the awkward interval before the drinks came, the professor took off his glasses, cleaned them, and laid them on the table. He brushed hair strands back from his forehead and wondered how to open the conversation. Somehow this second meeting, without the framework of the near collision event to discuss, with Penny, as he now thought of her, in her evening gown, was more stressful.

Penny smiled encouragingly.

He said, "Nice day," and realized immediately how inappropriate the remark was, given the cold, overcast weather. At that point the waiter arrived and Darnell smiled with relief.

They sipped their drinks for a moment. The room was buzzing with conversations now, and Darnell began to relax.

"Your name, Penny, is very unusual," he said, adding hastily, "but nice."

"It's really Penelope, named after my other aunt,

in Texas. I was born there. But I live in New York City now."

"Oh, you moved north?"

"My parents were ranchers outside of Houston, just getting by. Then they made a good deal of money selling their land for oil exploration and drilling, and resettled in New York, and I moved with them. I was only sixteen, and I have to tell you it was hard to cope with life in that amazing city. The streets are so crowded with carriages. They say there are over three million horses in the city. And now there are automobiles as well. The buildings are so tall, they're called 'sky-scrapers.' "

Penny laughed in a musical sound and smoothed her long hair. "I was such a child, a real farm girl. I got a stiff neck walking around looking up at the buildings for two weeks."

"Sky-scrapers. I haven't heard that description."

"There's the Metropolitan Tower. And the new Woolworth Building—it's the tallest."

"I've heard that if the *Titanic* were laid next to the Woolworth Building it would be a hundred feet longer, in fact, longer than any building in the world is tall."

"That amazes me, too, especially my being here now, on the ship. It's like being part of history."

Darnell went on. "You'd probably never know I was from America, with my English accent. It was Ohio. My parents moved from America to London when I was only ten years old. . . ." He paused, musing, almost to himself. "They used to call me 'Johnnie' then." He smiled at her. "It's nice to hear you call me 'John.' 'Professor' makes me feel positively ancient."

"London must have been as big a change for you coming from America as New York was for me, moving from Texas." She studied him for a moment. "So you went to school in England?"

"I was really proud to be able to fit into the English schools," he said. "You know—they were so classical and disciplined, compared to those in Cleveland. But I loved to study—still do, and that helped. In fact, I didn't do much beside studying in school, actually, except my trap and target shooting. Never tried out for the cricket team." Darnell described scenes from his early days after arriving in England—his entrance into a boys' grammar school, his classes at Eton, Oxford, and Cambridge. "I was a tall, skinny, freckled kid in grammar school, always with a book, even reading walking from one class to the next."

Penny laughed and touched his arm, resting her hand there momentarily. "I think we all were a bit funny-looking at thirteen or fourteen."

Darnell sipped his scotch. "I finished at Oxford early, at twenty-one, and began teaching. But then everything changed. I solved my first psychic phenomena case, for a judge, a student's father. And I realized my life's main work would be in that field." He smiled, recalling his first investigation. "The *Times* called it 'The Case of the Old Bailey Ghosts.' "

"How exciting! Were there really ghosts there? Tell me about it."

"Maybe someday I can—today it would still embarrass that student's father." Darnell shook his head in wonder that ten years had passed since that first case.

"My father was a minister," he went on. "But he encouraged me to devote myself to my work. Said it was my calling to prove those mystical things weren't true. But, of course, I couldn't do it as a full-time career, at first."

Penny said, "So you teach, too."

"Yes, I took graduate work at Cambridge and I lecture there, and sometimes at the Sorbonne. I have some regular classes I carry in a London private school. But psychic investigations are taking more and more of my time." He smiled. "They pay more. And I enjoy it."

"You like ghosts." She laughed.

He nodded. Talking with her, in another part of his mind, Darnell found himself taking inventory of himself—six feet tall, trim, at 13 stone—182 pounds they'd say in America—in good muscular condition, and with strong facial lines, like his father. He began to feel more comfortable now with Penny.

"Can you tell me about any of your other cases?" Her voice broke through his thoughts.

He thought a bit. "Yes. There's a recent one, a small case. I was called into the Cotswolds region—the beautiful rolling hills country northwest of London— two months ago. A vicar of a small parish there wanted me to look into some strange, midnight organ sounds in a two-hundred-year-old abandoned church by an old churchyard burial site."

"That sends shivers up my spine already," Penny said.

"I spent one entire night in that church. It was in February—very cold then. I huddled in blankets in one of the pews, but didn't sleep at all that night."

"And what did you find out?"

"It was very disappointing. No mystery at all. It turned out to be only the wind blowing through the organ pipes. The wind coming down through the nearby hills seemed to pick up every night between two and four a.m., and it blew in through some drafty overhead windows right down into the organ."

"No ghosts?"

Darnell laughed. "None. The vicar could have solved that one himself, if he'd been willing to spend all night there. I put my fee in the poor box."

Penny glanced about the lounge. "This is such a wonderful ship. Did you know," she asked, "there's a swimming bath on a lower deck? We've just got to go. Imagine swimming in your own pool on a liner in the middle of the ocean. And they even have a gymnasium on the boat deck, with rowing machines, and an electric horse and an electric camel you can ride."

"A camel. The desert brought to the sea."

"There's a squash court, too, and quoits and shuffleboard," she hurried on, her eyes bright.

Darnell said, "I'm afraid I don't know those games." His past academic life, the investigative work, his sheltered routine closed in on him, and he frowned.

"Well, in squash," Penny said, "you hit a light ball back and forth over a net on a court with a long-handled round racquet. It's easy to learn."

"And quoits?"

"It's like horseshoes, only you throw a round ring of rope about this big." She held up her hands, making a circle with her fingers, not quite touching. "You toss it at a peg and try to get it over the top of it." Penny laughed. "They try to invent games to help people pass the time. A week is a long trip."

"I guess I can learn those rules."

"I'll teach you." She rested her hand on his. "It'll be fun to teach a professor something."

"I heard there are Turkish baths, too—separate for men and women, of course." He felt his cheeks flush.

"We'll have to try out everything," Penny said.

She fell silent, as if regretting being too forward, and sipped her drink.

"Definitely, definitely." Darnell nodded, wanting to put her at ease. He thought rapidly, since he would study after dinner, his new acquaintance would not interfere with his plans. He looked forward to the female company, which, other than in meetings or luncheons with the few women instructors at college, had been scarce in his life.

"Let's take a promenade before dinner," Penny said, her voice bright again.

"With pleasure." He held out his arm, she hooked hers in it, and the couple strolled out on the deck toward the grand staircase, chatting, completely relaxed now. They laughed aloud at each other's inconsequential remarks and observations as they strolled along. Penny pulled the fur closer about her neck.

"I heard that the millionaire John Jacob Astor's coming aboard at Cherbourg tonight," she said, "with his new young wife. He divorced his other one. What a scandal! I can't wait to see her. She's only a baby."

The professor smiled. "I think this ship's loaded with millionaires—and scandals. I saw Guggenheim at my hotel."

The thought of the ship's expensive human cargo brought him back to the problem of the "jinxed" cabin 13. The idea had seemed to him, at least for the past half hour, to be not only distant but unreal. But as they walked he became aware again of the weight of the revolver touching his chest in his inside coat pocket and shifting against his body with each step they took. He thought of his original mission and reason for being on the ship—to solve the mystery of cabin 13.

"It's cold tonight," Penny said. She pointed at the dark sea and ice floating in it. "I'll bet that water's freezing."

Her arm in his, Darnell felt her body shiver. That little touch of cold, icy sensation dampened for a moment the gaiety of the evening and the impending luxurious dinner party with the Captain. Darnell knew this was not a simple pleasure cruise, and that he must be on his guard at all times. As they walked past other passengers, he scanned their faces and wondered whether any of them, which of them, might be involved. He was certain there was no jinx, that the ill-fated deaths in the unlucky cabins were too coincidental to be suicides, and that someone on board might be responsible for them.

The thought struck him that his acquaintance with Penelope Winters had progressed very fast. Had she just been at the rail next to him at the departure by coincidence? He shook it off, thinking, It's ridiculous to suspect everyone, especially her—I'll be suspecting the Captain next.

But death had boarded the last three ships alongside the passengers, and haunted cabin 13—that much was certain. And on this voyage, Darnell's career, possibly his survival, was linked inseparably to that fateful number, and to that cabin. With an effort, he dismissed the somber thoughts. They took the grand staircase down to D deck, and Darnell opened the door to the first-class dining room. He followed a wide-eyed Penny through the doorway of the magnificent room.

Chapter Four

"What a gorgeous room!" Penny exclaimed as the host escorted them to the Captain's table. "High ceilings, ornate carved wood paneling—why, it's like the finest hotel." She feasted her eyes on the surroundings and held tightly to Darnell's arm as they walked to the head of the room.

Darnell and Penny took seats side by side at Captain Smith's large, rectangular table. In accord with their name cards, they sat at the right of the white-haired, white-bearded Captain, who presided over the group from one end of the table. Director Ismay sat at the other end.

Twelve people were in the Captain's party, and their conversations, a loud buzz, reflected the festive air of the first dinner after embarkation. The men wore full dinner dress, and the women's gowns were like none Darnell had ever seen—heavy gold-threaded, designer creations suitable for a state occasion.

Penny whispered to Darnell, "Will you look at those gowns? I feel absolutely shabby."

He whispered back, "Nonsense. You're as lovely as any of them," and surprised himself at being so open.

Darnell's feelings were torn. He was anxious for the dinner to be over so he could close himself into his cabin and study the layouts and passenger lists of the ships. He had to get on with his investigation. But he enjoyed being with Penny. He also welcomed the opportunity of hearing the Captain speak about the ship. And, looking around the room and the table, he realized the dinner would give him a chance to study some of his fellow passengers. Was one of them a killer? Laughter across the table brought him back to the current moment.

He said to Penny, "I've been invited to dine at the Captain's table every night. I hope you'll join me."

"Of course I will. I didn't know I was with someone that important," she teased. She glanced around the ornate, wood-paneled room and said, "This is such a beautiful room. Look at that gold and crystal chandelier."

She discreetly felt the tablecloth with her fingers below the edge of the table. "Handmade linen, and exquisite china plates. Just like the Ritz Hotel."

Darnell agreed. "You might say, '*Ritz-y.*' "

He looked about the table with curiosity as well as the touch of ready suspicion and caution he knew he must maintain throughout the trip. On the Captain's left sat a gray-haired couple in fancy but old-fashioned evening clothes. To their left sat a man with jet-black hair, black bushy eyebrows, and a black goatee, all of which Darnell felt gave the fellow a devilish look. The man wore a gold-rimmed monacle, secured by a chain. A young man with equally dark hair, and with an equally large nose, Darnell thought, apparently his son, was at his side. Next to him sat a young couple, holding hands every minute, perhaps related to the older couple sitting by the captain. Bruce Ismay sat at the end, the millionaire Guggenheim next to him, and two older ladies between him and Darnell and Penny.

Captain Smith's gravelly but pleasant voice broke into Darnell's thoughts and subdued the talk around the table. "Welcome, ladies and gentlemen. I know most of you. Let me introduce myself. I'm Captain Edward Smith, and pleased to be your host tonight." He raised his champagne glass. "I propose a toast—I give you the *Titanic*, the greatest ship afloat, and her wonderful maiden voyage. I hope you enjoy your trip."

The guests all clinked glasses, and laughter began again with outbursts as bubbly as the drinks. They sipped from their tall, crystal champagne flutes and introduced themselves to each other.

Waiters with brass-buttoned white coats and navy blue trousers took white linen napkins from the passengers' wineglasses and placed them across their laps. The waiters presented menus to all at the table, and asked for drink and wine orders.

"The waiters almost look like ship's officers." Penny smiled.

The Captain gave special attention to Penny. "What do you think of our ship?" Smith asked. The weathered skin about his blue eyes crinkled with a smile.

"It's a marvel. I'm looking forward to every minute of the trip. Particularly the swimming bath." She laughed.

Smith looked slyly at Darnell. "And you, Professor? Is your cabin satisfactory?"

Darnell ignored the cabin 13 reference. He would have to tell the Chairman and Captain to stop talking about his cabin, if the secret of his trip were to be maintained. "The ship's fascinating," he said. "And, unless you count trips across the Channel, I've only taken ocean voyages twice before—once when I first came to England from America, and one trip back."

"This is the finest ship in the world, Professor. It's a bit larger than our sister ship, the *Olympic*, which had its maiden voyage across last year, so it really is the largest in the world."

As long as the Captain did not discuss cabin 13, Darnell didn't mind him touting the ship. He encouraged his boasting on the fascinating statistics, asking, "How large is the *Titanic*?"

The Captain beamed. "She's half again as large as either the *Lusitania* or *Mauretania*—we're 46,000 tons. For more protection, the *Titanic* has a double hull. That gives us twice the safety."

Darnell searched his memory of the *Times* articles. "I read there's something special about the bulkheads in this ship."

Smith nodded and fingered the black bow tie at his throat, the collar apparently being too tight for his liking. "Our bulkheads are transverse—crosswise the width of the ship. A half-inch thick, most reaching up to D or E deck. They give us sixteen watertight compartments."

Darnell was curious. "D or E? Why not to the top?"

"Couldn't go higher, you know. You wouldn't have the size cabin you have if we used the extra space." The Captain leaned over toward Penny and Darnell as if in confidence, but his voice could be heard across the table. "But the sixteen watertight compartments can be closed electrically, instantaneously, by a simple switch on the bridge."

The young man with short-cropped hair took his eyes off his sweetheart—or was it his young wife, Darnell wondered—and offered a comment from across the table. "That's why they say the *Titanic* is unsinkable."

The Captain smiled. "There's nothing like her ever built." He pointed out a gentleman at a nearby table. "There's our shipbuilder, by the way. The architect of the *Titanic*, Mr. Thomas Andrews."

Mrs. Guggenheim spoke. "Captain, I notice they refer to you as Commodore. What does that mean?"

Captain Smith laughed. "It just means the most senior captain—in more ways than one, I might add, as my white hair would indicate. I've sailed over two million miles in my thirty years at White Star."

"I'll bet you've seen a lot of exciting things," Penny said.

He laughed. "No. I never had a wreck or saw one. Rather uneventful, I'm afraid. Smooth sailing."

"That's the way we like our trips," the elderly man at the end said. His wife smiled with him.

Smith went on. "I retire next year. This will be my last major trip." The Captain's voice seemed wistful to Darnell.

"After two million miles? I guess you deserve it," Guggenheim said.

Darnell changed what he thought was a painful subject for Smith. "The *Titanic*'s smokestacks are huge," he said.

"Funnels, we call them," the Captain said. "One of them is a dummy, for ventilation. I'll let you guess which one."

"I saw the anchors when we boarded," Penny said. "They're pretty big, too."

"Thirty tons each—three of 'em."

"I guess you'd need huge anchors to hold the *Titanic* in place," Penny said.

The Captain nodded, about to elaborate with more

statistics, but looked up then at the approaching
waiters.

The waiters served the first course, a *consommé* of
turtle, along with an appetizer plate of *pâté de foie
gras* and small toasts.

Penny said, "This food's scrumptious."

Darnell nodded but privately would have pre-
ferred his roast beef and Yorkshire pudding. He
wondered if he could stand six days of French cooking, and was already afraid everything would be
doused with heavy sauces.

The monacled and goateed man across from Darnell addressed him during a conversational lull. "I
understand you teach, Professor," he said.

"Yes, Mr. . . .?"

"Professor or Count Fortunio—Dionino Fortunio.
I teach, too—at the Sorbonne. Perhaps I have seen
you there."

"I taught there last fall. John Darnell."

"I know that name, Professor."

The conversation was interrupted by the waiters
serving another course, Dover sole with baby as-
paragus, served individually from a silver tray with
overlarge sterling silver spoons and forks. Darnell
was mollified. This kind of food his English palate
could take.

Penny asked the Captain, "So you've never been
involved in any seagoing catastrophe? A sinking,
anything like that?"

He shook his head. "No sinkings, my dear. Only
a few minor incidents. I started as just a lad on
windjammers—sailing ships, you know. They were
exciting. I got a small command later, and gradually
the vessels assigned me were larger and larger. This
one's the top of the heap. But I'm not material for any

dime novel, like *Disaster at Sea*. The sea has been too good to me. And I love it."

"It's because of your skill as a captain, I'm sure," Penny said, dazzling the Captain with her smile.

Captain Smith fingered his white beard and looked about the table. Darnell saw all eyes were on the Captain, and realized that Smith didn't seem to mind it at all.

At the Captain's left, a silver-gowned elderly woman wearing a double strand of pure-white pearls with pearl earrings to match put a hand on the Captain's sleeve. She spoke in a scratchy voice. "Are we going to set a speed record this trip, Captain?"

The Captain responded with a hearty laugh. "No, Mrs. Straus, the *Titanic*'s fast, but she's not designed for speed like smaller liners. The *Mauretania* and *Lusitania* are sleeker and several knots faster. But we'll make good time. We'll get there on schedule."

The woman turned to her husband, shaking her head. "See, Isidor, I told you it was all right."

In between courses, the Captain looked at his gold pocket watch. "We're heading for Cherbourg tonight to pick up some passengers. They'll be coming out by tender boat about seven p.m."

"I heard we can send messages back to England or forward to New York on the Marconi," Penny said.

"Yes. We have two Marconi operators aboard, and they work all day. They send many messages—Marconigrams, they call them—if that sort of thing interests you."

Penny turned to Darnell. "Yes, I'd like to send one to my aunt."

Darnell nodded. "We both will. My housekeeper would be thrilled. And I'm sure your aunt would be, too."

Waiters brought the final main course, English

grouse, the professor's favorite, and wild rice. They enjoyed a green salad at the end of the meal, continental style. Penny called that custom "amusing." The courses were interspersed with two varieties of white wine.

Chocolate soufflé was served as dessert, and after-dinner liqueurs arrived. As Penny tasted hers cautiously, she said, "Can you believe the elegance of these dinners? If I eat these for six nights on this ship, I'll gain a ton."

Darnell smiled. "We'll work it off in the gym."

The excellent service had moved the dinner along promptly. Diners rose from their chairs now, wished each other pleasant evenings, and drifted off in various directions, some to reading and writing rooms, some to hear music and sip coffee. The Captain shook hands all around, and his table guests dispersed.

Smith told Penny and Darnell, "We're at Cherbourg, and the tender's coming out. The Astors will be boarding."

"I want to see them," Penny said.

Professor Fortunio came around the table to Darnell with an outstretched hand. Darnell shook it, his past reticence abandoned, and noticed the man's hands were cool and clammy. "We must have a talk sometime," Fortunio said. "We have an interest in common, I believe."

"What is that?"

"The occult."

Darnell said, "Well, mine is to poke holes in it."

Fortunio smiled, bowed formally, and said, "Good night."

Penny took Darnell's arm and led him away. "Come on—let's watch the passengers come aboard."

Chapter Five

Wednesday night, April 10

Penny pulled Darnell along, out onto the deck. At the rail, they watched the scene below. The sea air and oil smells from the tender boat wafted up to their deck. Women bundled in furs, men in fur-collared greatcoats, all looking like they were clearly first-class passengers, stepped across to the lower deck from the small boat. Sounds of their voices and laughter, the gaiety of embarking on a great adventure, floated up to the ship's decks above them.

"Look!" Penny's voice showed her excitement. "It's John Jacob Astor and his new wife. She's gorgeous!"

"Can't tell from here." Darnell squinted in the dusk at the people below. He saw a diminutive young woman with long hair, bundled in furs. "I'll take a closer look at her later."

"Not too close." Penny laughed. "I hear he's quite possessive of her. Oh, look—their servant is carrying a dog."

Deckhands on the tender boat passed three large green mailbags and other gear to the *Titanic* crewmen. The bustle of activity created the exciting noise an ocean liner's departure always generated.

Following the first-class passengers, a small group

of what appeared from their clothing and belongings to be steerage passengers boarded from the tender. "They're carrying children. And there's a baby," Penny said. All carried canvas bags and makeshift suitcases or containers. Darnell thought, They probably have all their worldly possessions in those cases.

The boarding was completed within an hour, and onlookers above left the rails. The tender headed for shore, and the *Titanic* moved away, out farther to sea, picking up steam and speed gradually. Darnell and Penny took the staircase back up to the lively *Café Parisien* on B deck where they sat in white wicker chairs at a window table, listening to music. Darnell's thoughts returned to his ships' passenger lists and deck layouts, and he itched to study them. But he could take time for a bit of sherry first. He ordered a half bottle of cream sherry and two glasses. "Something I'd like you to try," he said to Penny.

The waiter filled their small glasses and left the bottle. Penny tasted it. "It's sweet," she said with surprise, "but I like it." They sipped their drinks.

"You were talking about jinxes before," Penny said. "I guess I've had what people in Houston would call a string of bad luck." Her forehead creased. "It started with my father and mother."

"Bad luck? How is that?" He listened closely.

"Their deaths. A railway accident. Forty-one people were injured, but they were the only two killed."

The professor shook his head in sympathy.

"Then a few months after the estate was settled, their New York town house burned down."

"How tragic. And since then?"

"That was four years ago. I took an apartment. A year later, I lost all my jewelry in a hotel robbery when I visited Texas." She paused, frowning. "I'll skip the rest. The worst was breaking up with my fiancé after a two-year engagement."

"That was a long engagement."

"Too long. I think that's why I broke it off. I realized it wasn't meant to be." She smoothed her hair back. "You could say I've been jinxed. But I've had one good turn of luck—getting a first-class cabin on this ship."

"But it isn't fully booked."

She nodded. "I know. My experience was odd. I was originally booked in cabin fourteen, but they asked me to switch to another cabin. And if I hadn't inherited the money, I wouldn't be in first-class in the first place. Anyway I'm here, maybe it's fate. But I'm glad we met, and I know we'll have fun on this floating palace."

"We will, that's certain." The story about her cabin was too coincidental. The Captain must have closed down cabins near 13, for safety. "But your experiences weren't bad luck. It's my work to debunk bad luck and jinxes and superstitions, you know. But I have to admit we've had good fortune meeting each other—I'll go that far with good luck."

Penny touched his arm, rested her hand on it, and smiled.

But Darnell felt a chill thinking of cabins 13 and 14, how close they were, and what might have happened if Penny's "bad-penny" luck had somehow booked her into the "suicide cabin."

After an hour of conversation, Penny and Darnell walked to her cabin. She said good night to him there, kissed him lightly on the cheek, and promised to see him the next day. On an impulse he pulled her closer and kissed her full on the lips. She didn't resist, and felt warm and comfortable in his arms. But she only smiled, said, "Good night," and in moments was in her cabin, the door closed, with Darnell walking down the passageway, smiling, whistling softly.

Inside her cabin, Penny threw herself on the bed and stared at the ceiling. After some minutes, she rose and looked at herself in the dresser mirror.

"Damn!" she said to her reflection. "Now I'm a liar."

Penelope Winters felt guilty of her small lie about inheriting money to travel first-class. That was a pretense she had adopted. She had come to England in second class, but her aunt insisted on booking her return in first class. Penny felt fate had a hand in how it all had turned out.

But why did she have to lie to John? She suddenly realized she would have deceived anyone in first class, wanting to be considered on their level, with all the grandeur and obvious wealth surrounding her. For a cold moment, she felt a chill, and wondered if her present good fortune would last.

The call had come in to her aunt's home two days before the ship was to sail, and she answered the telephone. "Miss Winters?" a man's voice asked. At first she thought it was her maiden aunt he wanted. "No, it's Penelope Winters I want," he said, "not Agnes." He had been polite, asking about her cabin, wondering whether she would mind switching to another cabin, with number 14 in need of repairs. For her inconvenience of switching, "White Star Line will pay you," the man said, "shall we say, a hundred pounds?"

To her, that sounded magnificent. Penny couldn't refuse the offer, the money was over $500, translated into American currency. It would buy her the new type-writer machine she needed in her secretarial office, and let her move into a larger apartment. The money was delivered in an envelope the night before the ship's departure, and she changed the funds into American bills the next morning. Finding that John Darnell was in cabin 13, next door to the one she would have occupied, was a mystery too deep for her to solve.

She said, "Damn!" again, scowling at herself in the mirror. "I'm going to have to tell John that I don't have an inheritance." Having said it, she immediately felt better, and wiped a tear from her eye.

Penny busied herself preparing for bed, removed her rouge with night cream, put her hair up in a bun. She sat on the edge of her bed for a few minutes, looking at the photograph she always carried of her parents, Grover and Katherine Winters. They smiled back at her from the frame on the bedside table. Her eyes again suddenly filled with tears.

After the boarding at Cherbourg, Captain Edward J. Smith walked toward the bridge. His thoughts were filled with nostalgia these days, now on his last official voyage.

He took pride in achieving his position without standing on ceremony. Although his distinguished appearance with white hair and beard, as well as his Commodore status on the line, commanded respect among his officers, he did not hold himself above them, or flaunt his position. He could see himself when he was a young man in the new officers coming along at White Star Line, and remembered how hard it was as a junior officer to make his way up through the ranks over thirty years to his position as Commodore.

After what Smith felt would be the last Atlantic-crossing voyage of his tenure before retirement, he now looked forward with mixed feelings to many years on land—gardening, trout fishing, hunting— doing things he couldn't do aboard ship. He hadn't shared those thoughts yet with others, and his feelings were tinged with regret at losing the sea after a lifetime on it—almost like a death in the family. And now that he had been given the command of the *Titanic*, the greatest honor a sea captain could ask for, he had second thoughts about retirement. He felt he could captain a magnificent ship like the *Titanic* the rest of his life. At New York, maybe he'd talk with Ismay about an extension, at least for a year or two, take her across a few times before he turned in his captain's hat.

Chief Officer Henry Wilde, who had transferred from the *Olympic*, and Second Officer Herbert Lightoller, coming from the *Oceanic*, were conversing on the bridge about their amazing new ship, when the Captain stepped in and said, "Evening, lads."

"I'm hardly a lad," Wilde said, smiling.

"Compared to me, you are." The Captain, wearied after an emotional day, was feeling his years. The near collision, the first dinner out, the cabin 13 matter in the back of his mind made this last trip a bit more strenuous than he had anticipated. "I may be retiring soon," he said, "and you lads can take over these monster ships." He said it to them, knowing it was tinged with a bit of self-pity, really thinking about his possible extension of time, really more testing what they would say than speaking with any conviction.

"White Star can't get by without you," Wilde said. "You belong on the *Titanic*. You two fit well together."

The Captain laughed, pleased to hear it. "We'll see."

"The Cherbourg boarding went well," Lightoller said.

"Indeed," Smith said. "Another ten or twenty million pounds aboard now." Captain Smith assigned values to all the millionaires. Astor was the latest. Smith said, "I'm guessing the fortunes of the first class total a hundred million pounds."

Lightoller whistled.

The Captain glanced at charts and instruments, content they were making good time, if not record time.

"Sir?" Wilde waited, knowing he had to break through Smith's thick thoughts before proceeding.

"Yes, Henry?" Smith rested a hand on his shoulder. Since Wilde's transfer from the *Olympic*, he had become fond of the junior officer, like a son he never had, and as he saw himself thirty years earlier.

"These charts, here, Captain, are my second set. Someone stole the main set."

"Stole them? Who would steal charts?"

"I don't know. I hope this passage isn't jinxed." Wilde frowned. "That near collision this morning," he said, "was just like what happened on the *Olympic* six months ago. You know, when the *Hawke* pulled right into us and tore that gash in our hull." He paused. "That could have happened again with the *New York*, it was that close."

"But it didn't, Henry," the Captain said. He kept to himself his thoughts on the charts, that their disappearance might be tied in to the cabin 13 mystery. "Don't worry about the charts. We have this set, and I have one more in my cabin. And on the *New York* incident—well, we're learning, bit by bit, how to handle these huge vessels. I imagine some passengers would call the *Titanic* a sea monster."

Wilde nodded. "Like the Loch Ness."

Smith glanced idly at wireless notes stuck on a spindle—the ship positions, a greeting from Wilde's wife. He turned back to his chief officer. "But we have to keep maneuverability in mind. Allow more time for turning and stopping. A ship like this moves very slow, especially in the turns."

"And it's so much more powerful it dwarfs other liners."

Smith nodded and stared ahead out at the dark sea. "How's the weather tonight?"

"Just what you probably feel in your bones, sir. Cold, and getting colder. But crisp and clear."

"Well, lads . . ." Smith yawned. "Almost 9:30. I'm off to bed now. Murdoch relieving you?"

"At the next watch."

"Then I'll see you tomorrow." Captain Smith walked to his cabin. He nodded pleasantly at the steward in the hallway. But after closing his cabin door behind him, the Captain felt a wave of sudden weariness. Time was moving too fast lately. Giant ships. Marconigrams. What next?

He had sidestepped Penny Winters' question about accidents at sea, should have mentioned the *Olympic-Hawke* incident. But no need to alarm passengers. He felt what he'd told Wilde was correct— they were learning how to handle her. His officers knew where he stood.

For his part, he wasn't sure he wanted to learn much more of the new technology. Part of him longed for the older, simpler days; part yearned for his retirement; part of him wanted the glory of captaining the largest ship in the world. He sighed, confused with his contradictory feelings. He poured two fingers of scotch into a water tumbler from a bottle he kept in his rolltop desk and gulped it straight.

Then he poured another smaller portion and sipped it slowly, as was his style. He never drank at the dinner table, other than a bit of champagne, only an occasional taste in his cabin, at moments like this one. A private vice, and a small one at that, at my age, Smith thought.

Thirty minutes later, Captain Edward Smith was in a fitful sleep, filling the cabin with his uneven snoring, and not enjoying this night his usual sleep of the angels.

The steward greeted John Darnell at the open door of his cabin. "Hello, Professor. I was just going to see if you needed anything, sir."

"No, thank you, Mario. Not tonight."

"There is something." The steward seemed hesitant. "I was just wondering, sir . . ."

"Yes?"

"Have you had any problem with the cabin?"

"How do you mean?"

"You asked about cabin thirteen . . . the number, I know it is unlucky."

"Not for me. As good as any other number."

"But for other people—the suicide, the other passengers, other ships . . ."

"Do you know any more about that?"

The steward seemed to consider. "Only rumors, gossip. I'm sorry, sir. Forgive me." He backed away, bowing in a continental manner, then turned heel and walked rapidly down the corridor to the end, rounded the corner, and was gone.

The professor let himself into his cabin, wondering again at the steward's remarks. The man must know something about the other ships. Darnell guessed that gossip about those events might have spread within the ranks of the crew who moved from one ship to another, although the facts might be hushed up for passengers. He would have to force the steward to tell him everything he knew. Captain Smith could use his influence on that. Mario seemed to have a fear of the Captain.

Darnell knocked on the door of Sung's room. "Good evening, Professor," Sung said as he opened the door. A single light burned next to Sung's bed, and a book lay opened on the bed. "Just reading."

"Did you have a good dinner?"

"I ate in the kitchen. A Chinese cook I met said it was all right. They fix their own kind of food there."

"Great." Darnell paused. "I want you to ask your friend if he has heard any rumors about this ship, or any other White Star Line ships."

"Rumors?"

"Stories about jinxes, suicides, deaths."

"Sound mysterious. I ask."

"Very well. Good night, Sung." Darnell closed the door. Exhilarated but weary with the day's happenings, he changed into pajamas and stepped into Persian slippers and pulled on his silk dressing gown. He poured a glass of sherry. The events of the evening swam in his mind, but his interest now was in the cabin 13 jinx Ismay had hired him to dispel.

Darnell bent to the business at hand. On deck, at dinner with Penny, he was John, in an unaccustomed role. In his own room again, cabin 13, he felt more himself again—the professor of occult psychology, the "psychic detective"—and he was ready to concentrate on his assignment. He was concerned about his contact with Penny Winters. It was diverting, and he wouldn't want to give it up. But he couldn't let his guard down, or forget his main mission.

Darnell spread out the deck layouts of the *Titanic* on his bed, each deck separate, side by side. Pulling a chair up to the side of the bed, he studied the designs, while sipping his sherry. At one point, he went to the desk and brought back a large magnifying glass he used to study the first-class cabin section. Gazing through the magnifying glass, he thought of how Sherlock Holmes was always portrayed using one, and smiled. He folded up the *Titanic* layouts and took out those for the other three ships, one by one, and studied them in the same fashion.

He saw that cabins ordinarily could only be entered through the single door. In other cases, as in his own cabin, there was entry also through the single large window overlooking the promenade deck, if it were unlocked, and from an adjoining room designed for a valet or maid's quarters. Inspecting the cabin earlier, he'd concluded the doors were secure. So the logical conclusion was that access to his cabin could only be by the occupant allowing someone to enter it or by possession of a key. The thought occurred to him that a closet was a place of concealment. He looked inside it again, and double-checked his water closet and bath area.

He looked over the deck layouts of the three other vessels and pored over the passenger and crew lists for the *Titanic* and the three other ships, circling names of passengers whose names he had heard or who had sailed on more than one of the four ships on these crossings. Out of the two thousand who had sailed on all three ships, he counted fifty-two passengers and crew members who had been on more than one of the ships. It seemed natural for crew members to have served on more than one of the ships, given the way crews were shifted.

Some of the crew members that stood out were Captain Smith and his Chief Officer Wilde; Fourth Officer Boxhall; Pietro Amado, a cook, who had been

on three of the four ships; Floyd Nordroff and Bill
Blatts, stokers, on two ships; Jack Phillips, one of
the two Marconi operators; several stewards, including his own steward, Mario Sandrini; a barkeep;
restaurant waiters; several members of the *Titanic*
band; one of the crow's nest lookouts; the ship's
doctor; a headwaiter; a gymnasium attendant; and
the chaplain.

After his work, he checked locks on the window
and door, inserted a key in the door lock, turned it,
and set a chair in front of the doorknob. He decided
his cabin was about as secure as he could make it,
and that it was certainly safe enough from a casual
intruder.

The professor tried to delve into his Greek war volumes. But he finished only a half dozen pages. His
mind was elsewhere, fixed on the cabin 13 mystery—
and Penny Winters.

Although the weather was chilling, Darnell felt
an uncommon lassitude that night, and lay on his
bed, feeling the slight hum of the ship's engines in
the ship's bowels through his mattress. He stared
dreamily at the ceiling, but as he lay there, an idea
formed for a way of apprehending a killer—if he was
on board the ship. He would see the Captain about it
the next day.

Chapter Six

Queenstown, Thursday, April 11

After a quick breakfast, Darnell stopped by the bridge to see Captain Smith. He found him with two junior officers, making preparations to take on passengers at Queenstown, Ireland. "I need an hour or so of your time, Captain," Darnell said. "When can you do it?"

Smith consulted his watch. "We reach Queenstown at noon. And we'll need to get the passengers settled in. How about after lunch, say, fourteen hundred? That's two p.m., you know."

"Will you come to my cabin?"

The Captain nodded. "Two p.m., your cabin." As an afterthought, he said, "Mr. Lightoller can give you some time now. He's going off watch."

Darnell stepped over to the pleasant second officer, Herbert Lightoller, and mentioned the Captain's offer of his time.

"Very happy to help you out, Professor. You've got some questions, I'm sure. Perhaps you'd like a 'cook's tour.' "

Darnell smiled. "You've obviously dealt with landlubbers before. We can talk as we walk about, if you will."

They left the bridge and strolled the deck.

"Are we trying to set a speed record?" Darnell asked.

Lightoller smiled. "This ship could never do that," he said. "We're too big. It takes one of those sleek, smaller steamers to set crossing records."

"But I suppose you want to see what she can do? A brand-new ship and all."

The officer shook his head. "I'm not particularly interested in that. In fact, we run full speed ahead most of the time. But I know Chairman Ismay spoke to our engineer about opening up more boilers later."

Lightoller took him to the wireless room, which fascinated Darnell. They chummed with the two wireless operators, Phillips and his assistant Bride, each enjoying Darnell calling them both "Sparks," the new name for the job.

"It's a strong installation," Phillips said with pride. "We've got backup batteries supplied by Marconi. Course, most Marconigrams are just personal greetings sent by passengers back home or ahead to their destination. No earthshaking messages."

Bride told him, "We spell each other, and serve twelve-hour shifts. We take turns sleeping on the cot in the side room. I've never seen such volume of messages that say nothing at all."

Darnell watched as Harold Bride sat alertly but unmoving for minutes at the wireless key, blue sparks flickering under his fingers on the key, sending messages back to Ireland, turning over the notes one by one as he finished them.

"I can see why they call you men 'Sparks,' " Darnell said.

Phillips smiled. "Not enough sparks to start a flame. But we work steady, and you can see 'em flying."

"Some ships close down the wireless about midnight so the men can get some sleep," Bride said, "but we're too busy. Everyone wants to send a Marconigram from the *Titanic*."

Lightoller took Darnell on a tour of the engine room to show him the huge furnaces firing the boilers to produce the steam power. Darnell marveled at the continuous feeding of the furnaces by the burly stokers, who perspired liberally as they shoveled, their glistening bodies gradually becoming covered with a film of black coal soot.

"We should get back up top," Lightoller said. "Queenstown's coming along."

"Yes. I want to find a friend of mine to see the boarding."

As they retraced their steps to the upper decks, Darnell asked, "Could you show my friend and me the third-class section after we pull out again?"

"Gladly. Meet me on the boat deck at thirteen hundred hours."

Darnell left him on the promenade deck and quickly found Penny Winters, who told him she would most likely be there. "We're due into Queenstown soon," he said. "Want to watch the boarding together?"

She smiled and took his arm. "Of course. Cherbourg yesterday, Queenstown today."

"And then the open sea for a week."

"I know. Isn't it wonderful? I mean—there's so much to do on the ship. A week isn't too long at all."

In Penny's company, Darnell could feel his professorship peeling off a layer at a time. There was something infectious about her enthusiasm. He thought, *If this were only a holiday trip.* Sighing, he took her arm and walked toward the bow.

* * *

The *Titanic* stopped at Queenstown a few minutes past noon. The tender boat, *America*, brought out the new passengers, mostly young Irish immigrants going to the United States with their cloth suitcases, bare belongings, and their dreams.

Darnell and Penny watched them board from their vantage point on the first-class promenade deck. "I'd say there are about a hundred," he said.

Penny clutched his arm. "They look so poor, yet seem so happy. I've never seen so many smiling faces, such great expectations in their eyes. You can see it even from here."

"I'm sure they've brought all their worldly goods with them," Darnell said. He shook his head, seeing the worn suitcases, the duffels slung over their shoulders, their hands holding their younger children's hands tightly. The older children, many of them barefoot, followed along, helping parents with the load, carrying sacks and baskets of belongings.

Irish dealers in clothing, souvenirs, and artifacts also boarded the ship briefly, offering expensive garments and wares for sale to the first-class passengers. As they watched, Darnell and Penny saw them gradually reboard the tender to return to shore. They stood at the rail and watched the tender recede in the distance.

This was the last stop before heading across the Atlantic. Darnell felt a pang of isolation as the great ship prepared to steam out to sea, its sirens blasting, leaving behind the last sight of land its passengers would see for a week.

He could feel Penny shiver next to him, and imagined she had similar feelings.

Darnell said, "They're all aboard. Now we'll move on."

"I'm glad we saw them come aboard. I'd really like to see their quarters."

Darnell smiled. "I anticipated you. Officer Lightoller said he'd take us down there at one o'clock." He glanced at his watch. "We can find him now on the boat deck."

Up one flight, they located the officer. Darnell introduced Penny to him, and Lightoller led the way back down various staircases to the lower decks and into the third-class area. As they approached down the passageway, they heard the cultural music emanating from a large hall.

"It sounds delightful," Penny said.

Lightoller nodded. "Third class is largely occupied by immigrants going to America to seek their fortunes, or just to escape poverty in their homelands."

They stepped inside the door, into the hall.

"No windows," Penny said.

"We're below the waterline here," Lightoller said. "These steerage outfittings may not look that inviting to you, but to these people, it's luxury. Few ever saw a real water closet before coming aboard the *Titanic*."

"But everyone seems happy."

Darnell said, "They have the looseness and gaiety of simple folk. It looks like they'll enjoy the trip as much as anyone in first class."

They stood listening to the cultural songs of the Irish, Italian, and Greek groups, who took turns playing. Heavy Greek men danced about lightly on their feet within a circle of friends, who clapped and laughed and encouraged them.

"The dance is lively," Darnell said to Penny, "and yet there's something serious and somber in it—an ethnic memory of ancient times." He thought of his volumes of the history of Greek wars.

Penny nodded. "They carry on their traditions. And in the old country, sometimes traditions, like in their songs, have a sadness that goes back to their glory times."

"Maybe their songs will change when they reach America—their land of dreams. Well . . . I have an appointment at two. You have some things to do this afternoon?"

Penny said, "Yes. You can find me on the promenade deck about four."

They retraced their steps up the winding staircases and took their leave of Lightoller. Still filled with the emotion of the morning, Darnell took her in his arms and kissed her, holding her longer than necessary. "Then I'll see you at four," he said breathlessly. As she walked away, he took a deep breath. Now to see Captain Smith.

The Captain knocked on the door of cabin 13 at two p.m. sharp. Darnell glanced up and down the empty passageway after ushering Smith into his cabin and before closing the door.

Pouring sherry into glasses, Darnell spread out his notes on the desk. "Look at this," he said, pointing out the passengers and crew who had sailed on the previous three vessels and were on board the *Titanic*. "I'm convinced your problems with cabin 13 on your three ships have been caused by human hands—not by a jinx. It's my opinion your three suicides were really three murders, and the murderer could be aboard the *Titanic*."

"Murders! Now, just a minute, Darnell."

"Murders, exactly. I suspected it immediately. I know what you're thinking—Ismay's 'jinx.' But I never entertained those superstitions at all, and I don't think you did, either." He showed his list to Smith. "These are the only crew or passengers who have been aboard more than one of the four ships."

"You think a passenger or crew member is the murderer?"

"Yes. The woman thought to have jumped overboard could have been *thrown* overboard, and I believe she was. Her bad luck was to be an innocent occupant of cabin thirteen, which the murderer chose for his own reasons, I don't know why, yet. Maybe to create some idea of superstition. Your second so-called suicide was thought to be seasick and then found to have died of poison. He obviously could have been murdered. Poison in a drink, for example. The third man shot, with a revolver found on the floor, could easily have been another murder. Murders—*masquerading* as suicides."

The Captain scowled. "God, man! You're telling me we could have a murderer on the ship right now. If the passengers heard this . . ." Smith's voice trailed off as he looked around the cabin, as if the walls were listening to them. "There's something you should know. A set of our navigation charts was stolen. We have an extra set, but it sounds like someone is trying to create havoc aboard this ship."

Darnell nodded. "There may be more of that. He's expanding his mischief from murder to thievery—it usually goes the other way around. I'll be his most likely target for any violence, in this cabin with his favorite number, thirteen. I'm like the fly waiting for the spider to drop by for tea. But everyone should be on guard."

Smith sat silently for a moment and bottomed-up his sherry glass. "You wouldn't have any scotch over

there, would you?" He nodded toward the bottle
and glasses on the sideboard.

Darnell shook his head. "Sorry, just sherry. Captain, I'm going to need to lean on your knowledge
and your authority. The first thing is this—is there
any reason for you, or anyone, to suspect anyone on
that list?" He pointed to his notepaper.

Captain Smith looked it over, frowning. "The
Blakes—the only couple on all four ships. They're
opportunists. They sell doubtful assets and services
to other passengers—real estate, jewelry, stocks and
bonds, sometimes in the thousands of dollars. It's le-
gal, but sometimes I have to warn some of the more
vulnerable passengers against them. Yes, the Blakes
are afloat about half their lives. That's their style.
They're the spider types you were talking about.
Someone could easily have a grudge against them
for losses. But I don't know whether they'd be able to
kill anyone."

"What about the crew? Any of them on the list.
Would you know of any motives to do harm to the
line itself?"

He mused. "Well, two or three of them have had
run-ins with higher officers or management, and
disappointments. Herbert Lightoller was dropped
to Second Officer on the *Titanic* from first on the
Oceanic. He's anxious to captain his own ship, but
the board feels he's too young for that. I think they
expect a man to have a white beard to get a ship." As
if to demonstrate, he pulled at his own beard.

"The others?"

"MacDougall, a purser, was disciplined for dip-
ping into the whiskey a bit too much. He says he's a
teetotaler now, but I don't believe him. I've caught a
whiff on him more than once. Then there's Sandrini—
that's your steward. I almost fired him because of

missing jewelry in cabins he served on two different ships. There was no evidence, of course, or he'd be gone. But I can tell you he's scared to death of me. And almost any stoker or cook would have a complaint—they've wanted higher wages for years." He thought a moment. "The ship's doctor—Burton— I see him on your list. He floats back and forth across the Atlantic all the time. Examined the two, ah, suicides, other than the drowning case. He's above reproach, except he drinks more scotch than is good for him."

"He's a drunk?"

"No, I wouldn't call him that. He lost his wife and daughter last year, and that's enough to start any man drinking. But aboard, we seldom have anyone seriously ill—usually just a case of providing something for seasickness. And he's been a loyal official for years."

"Anyone else?"

"Professor Fortunio. Dionino, I think the first name is. He also calls himself Count Fortunio. He sat at my table the first night out, opposite you. I must say, if anyone looks the type, he does. But he's a professor, like you." Smith smiled. "Does that take him off the suspect list?"

"No. He books passage frequently?"

"He was on two of the other ships. Maybe he was listed as part of a traveling group on your log. It's not a foolproof list."

Darnell pushed hair back from his forehead. "Who has ready access to the first-class cabins, and specifically cabin thirteen?"

"The pursers, stewards, maids. I have a master key. Ship's Chief and First Officers have master keys. Also, the *Titanic* had a recent short shakedown cruise, and a passenger may have kept a key from that trip."

"No one else?"

"Unless a key was stolen. But most of our first-class passengers on this voyage are very wealthy, millionaires many of them." He paused, in thought. "If you're serious about this murder business . . . well, it could have been another passenger on one of the other ships, someone who'd make friends with the passenger in thirteen to get into it when the time came . . ."

Darnell finished it. ". . . for the murder."

"Exactly. There are many shipboard friendships—romances, too, you know." Smith looked down at the floor.

Darnell's thoughts flicked to Penelope Winters. Shipboard friendship, romance? They met conveniently at the rail. Too conveniently? He shook the thought out of his head—it was impossible.

The captain interrupted his thoughts. "So what do we do now?"

Darnell folded his arms and stared straight ahead. "Two things. First, I want your authority to talk to any of these people on my list, interview them, so to speak, and any others I want to."

Smith frowned. "We can't upset our passengers. You can't tell them what you're investigating. It'd sweep through the ship in hours."

"No, nothing like that. I'll handle it discreetly. I'll tell them, as a professor, I'm writing a paper about the *Titanic*'s first voyage, and want background and opinions. But I'll size them up while we're talking. I can tell a lot from demeanor and attitude, the language of the body."

"You'd use utmost discretion." Smith tugged on his beard.

"Of course. Just give me your card, with a note on it referring to me and the project. For an introduction."

Smith pulled out a card and scribbled on it with a pen, signing his name with a flourish. "What's the second thing?"

Darnell stood, signaling their talk was about over. "Simply this—I may stir things up a bit with the interviews, in fact, I want to. Then we watch, we watch carefully, and we wait. Eventually the spider will come for me, the fly. I'll leave myself open as bait, as the target, and hope to draw him in."

"Spiders eat flies."

Darnell smiled grimly. "But this fly has an advantage over the killer's other victims."

"What's that?"

"I know he's coming. And I'll be ready for him."

Smith scowled. "Or . . . her," he said. "It could be a black widow spider."

Darnell wondered what the Captain meant by that, whether it was a veiled warning to beware of Penny. He would not tell the Captain he'd thought of that already and dismissed it.

After Captain Smith left the cabin, Darnell carefully packaged up all his notes. The short list he returned to his wallet. The remainder, and his charts and lists, he locked in his steamer trunk. Then he went in search of Penny. He would not begin his interviews until tomorrow, and the day was young. His step quickened as he hurried down the corridor.

Chapter Seven

Thursday afternoon, April 11

Darnell was pleased to find Penny on the promenade deck within a few minutes. Otherwise, searching the giant ship could take hours. He saw her strolling, caught up with her, and hooked his arm in hers.

"Want some company?" he asked.

"Always."

He felt better seeing her smile, and could not believe the Captain's suggestion or his own fleeting thoughts of this gentle woman being a killer. After a quick walk down the deck and back, they took to chairs. When a steward passed by, Darnell ordered pots of hot tea.

"Lemon?" she asked, pouring the steaming tea into cups. "It's better for you than cream."

"Really?"

" 'Vita-mines,' you know. They're talking about that a lot right now."

He agreed, with reluctance. He watched her carefully as she added lemon, dropped in two lumps of sugar to offset the sour taste, stirred it carefully, and handed him his cup. Tasting the tea, Darnell concluded that English style, with clotted cream, was much better. He'd arrange to get his vita-mines some other way.

"This ship is like an American men's club," Penny said. "All leathers and woods and brass. And the smell of cigars."

Darnell smiled. "You speak as if you were a member of one—a men's club."

"No, not in America. They don't allow women, of course. But my father took me to his club once or twice—just to look, you know—and again for a visitor's luncheon."

Darnell mused. "This ship is beyond luxury. It's almost self-indulgence. Mostly Americans in first class on this crossing, you know, and I might say, the cream of wealthy business and society families. They expect the best, and they're certainly paying a pretty penny for it."

"A pretty penny." She laughed.

Darnell laughed with her. "You are a pretty Penny."

"Thank you, sir—you got out of that easy."

They sat and talked until it was time for dinner, then dressed and dined together. Afterward, that night, a cold one, they walked briskly on the promenade deck, arm in arm and in their heavy coats, stopping at the rail occasionally to gaze out at the moonlight reflecting in the mirror of the sea's surface.

"These winds are icy cold," Penny said, frowning, bundling her fur about her. "Why didn't they take their maiden trip on the *Titanic* in June?"

Darnell laughed. "Well, if they had, we wouldn't be here, would we? But there's no wind, really. It's from the speed of the ship. If we were completely stopped—which we'd never be in the middle of the ocean, of course—we'd see it's totally calm."

In those moments, the black sea brought back dark

thoughts to Darnell of the murders on the other ships, especially the woman who had jumped—or had been thrown—into the unrelenting sea. He enjoyed his time with Penny, but part of his mind wondered about those victims, and his duty to find the killer.

After escorting Penny to her cabin Thursday evening, Darnell retired reluctantly to his own cabin. He couldn't invite her there, because of the danger. But he thought of being with Penny in her cabin. It would be exciting—but he wasn't sure how far his courage would take him. There was an innocent air about her, and recent inexperience on his part.

He examined his cabin carefully, looking for anything out of the ordinary, but found nothing. If cabin 13 had a jinx, it had yet to show itself to him.

He spoke to his valet, Sung.

"I see or hear nothing suspicious, Professor," Sung said. "But I watch."

Yes, watch, Darnell thought. Because it would come. The spider was toying with the fly.

Chairman Bruce Ismay stopped by Captain Smith's quarters at nine p.m., Thursday, and rapped sharply on the door. Smith opened it shortly, standing there in his white socks, no shoes, no tie. He scowled, but his facial muscles relaxed when he saw the visitor was the Chairman. Privately, he considered Ismay somewhat of a nuisance. Ismay sometimes acted like a crew member or officer, with some authority, but other times wanted special, first-class-passenger treatment.

"Not disturbing you, I trust," Ismay said, stepping into the room past the Captain, without waiting for an invitation. He strode past him and took a chair. "Some things to discuss."

Smith said, "I was having a bit of a nap. I'll take the late watch tonight, give the lads some time off."

"Very democratic, I'm sure." Ismay looked about the cabin, inspecting it.

Smith knew what Ismay was thinking—not as sumptuous as his own cabin—but Smith didn't mind. He'd had much smaller cabins in his career. It was comfortable and quiet, and equivalent to a first-class cabin on any other liner. That, he liked. He cleared his throat discreetly. "Something on your mind, Bruce?"

Ismay rose and paced about the room. "About the arrival time—Wednesday morning? Could we make it to New York by Tuesday night—nip it within a week?"

Smith stiffened, frowning. Now what? Wanting to set a record? With this monster? He sat without answering.

Ismay ignored the Captain's apparent annoyance and asked, "We're going twenty or twenty-one knots, sometimes twenty-two?"

Smith knew that Ismay was perfectly aware of the speed. He saw a game going on now. "Yes, about that."

"Could we do a steady pace a bit higher? Five days of steady steaming at, say, twenty-three knots, twenty-four hours a day? By my calculations, we could pick up at least half a day—steam in Tuesday night late instead of Wednesday morning."

Ismay stopped, sat in a chair opposite the Captain, and bore into Smith's eyes with his own. "Well, what do you think, E.J.—can you do it?"

"All due respect, Bruce, I think you're a bit balmy. We're running close to our top cruising speed now, and this isn't summer, you know."

"Meaning what?"

"Lower visibility. We have to see where the hell we're going. It's bloody black out there at night."

Ismay fumed. "Well, during the day, then—twenty-three knots in the day, twenty-two at night?"

Captain Smith seethed inside, but knew his limits with the Director. "We're not in any contest—at least, none I know of. No records to break, right?" He stopped, short of blowing off completely.

"No, no records. But it would be pleasant to beat the *Olympic*'s speed."

Smith bit his tongue. "I'll talk with the lads. You want more speed in the day, will accept a bit less at night. I'll think about it." He knew he was committing to nothing at all.

"Why don't we ask your men to fire up more boilers?"

Smith jumped to his feet. "Goddammit, man! I'm running this ship. You're just a passenger, and I'll appreciate it if you keep away from my officers."

Ismay smiled broadly, apparently pleased to have broken through the Captain's ice. "Calm down, E.J. Just some suggestions." He stood and gazed sternly at the Captain. "But we're agreed on the main points, aren't we? Fire up another boiler or two. Beat the *Olympic*'s speed. Right?"

Smith said nothing, and Ismay turned and left the cabin. Smith stood looking at the closed door for a long minute, then burst out, "Bloody, dammed-blasted meddler!" He stalked over to his dresser and poured a stiff jolt of scotch into a tumbler and tossed it off, then poured another and clenched it in his hand, staring at it. "Cold day in hell before I go for a record."

Chapter Eight

Friday morning, April 12

During the morning, Darnell dedicated his time to Penny, although his mind was on the interviews he would commence that afternoon. He enjoyed visiting the swimming bath with her, having learned to swim in college and never losing the ability.

He said to Penny, amused, "This is the first time I've swum since college—and here we are, hundreds of miles out into the ocean, in an ocean liner's swimming bath."

They played squash also, and Darnell happily lost every game to his companion, who seemed to be quite good at it. Hitting little balls about with racquets was not a skill he had felt worth cultivating. They tried the other deck games, took promenades about the deck, had lunch and sat bundled up afterward in deck chairs. They gazed out on the unending vista of the gray sea.

Penny wrinkled her brow. "Did you see those ice floes yesterday?"

"Yes. We'll see some of that, even though Captain Smith said we were on the southern route. The spring weather breaks the ice up and it floats down here."

"I'd love to see an iceberg!"

He laughed. "Not too close to it, I hope. It would probably weigh a half million tons—more than ten times as big as this ship."

"It would be like a skyscraper."

"But most of it's under the water."

They sat contentedly and sipped their tea.

After a while, making a show of looking at his watch, he excused himself, offering her his stock reason for the interviews. "I'll be interviewing some passengers," he said, "for a paper on the *Titanic's* first trip."

"Interesting . . . so you'll be busy this afternoon. But we'll see each other at dinner?"

"Of course. And the week is young. Dancing tomorrow night, chapel on Sunday."

"Wonderful."

"There might be a boat drill," he thought aloud. "They usually have them on Sundays, I understand."

"On the *Titanic*?" Her eyes twinkled. "It's *unsinkable,* they say."

"Nevertheless . . ." But Darnell didn't finish his thought. He knew his conservative nature from a professor's viewpoint could sometimes dampen a bright conversation. Instead he just said, "Let's take one last promenade as I plan my project."

As they walked, Darnell formulated questions he would ask the passengers and crew. What he'd like to do was just blurt out at them, "Why did you kill the passengers in cabin thirteen?" That might jar one of them into an indication of guilt. He knew that was impossible, that he must find another way, but smiled at the thought.

"Why are you smiling?" Penny asked.

He looked into her eyes. "Just happy to be with you," he said, knowing he was not being completely honest with her, and he could not tell her the entire truth until it was all over.

After seeing Penny to her cabin, Darnell began his interviews. Selecting the easiest first, he met with the purser, MacDougall. He concluded the man had not reformed from his drinking habit but was not a killer. He talked also with an innocuous cook, stokers, two clearly guiltless waiters, a ship's lookout, band members, and others, and dismissed them as suspects.

The most likely suspect, based on outward appearances, seemed to be Professor Dionino Fortunio, the monacled, clammy-handed, black-bearded man who had shared dinner with Darnell, Penny, and others at the Captain's table the first night out. Even Penny remarked later that Fortunio looked strange to her.

"Professor Darnell." Fortunio beamed as he opened his cabin door to him. "Come in. This will be suitable for our talk, yes?"

Darnell glanced about the room. "If anything, your cabin is even more comfortable than mine."

"You're in . . . number thirteen, I believe?"

"Yes. The unlucky number." He watched Fortunio for a reaction, anything that might show a knowledge of the deaths.

"I hope you have no—superstitions." Professor Fortunio laughed, his deep voice going up and down the scale.

Darnell answered with vehemence, "Not in the least." But Fortunio's laugh brought a private thought—are laughs Italian, German, French? Musical, guttural, melodic?

"Sit here." Fortunio gestured toward one of the chairs next to his desk. "There's a pot of tea here."

"Professor," Darnell said, "Captain Smith may have told you, I've been commissioned to do a special paper for a college at Cambridge on the crossing. You know, psychological aspects of the maiden voyage of the largest ship in the world. Any paranormal aspects, that sort of thing."

Fortunio's eyes narrowed as he said, "Paranormal, yes, there are definite signs of that. My field is not psychology, as such, but it is close."

"What is your specialty?"

"I deal in problems of the mind, and I am a mesmerist."

"Mesmerism? That's hypnotism."

"Exactly. It's a new field, at least the way I practice it. I use it to explore people's problems, to help cure them."

"Psychological problems."

"Yes, in a sense. Mental blocks. Habits. Fears. Dreams. I use suggestion, and autosuggestion."

"And on the *Titanic*—or any ship—do you practice it?"

He shook his head. "No. But I do watch the people. As on this ship—there is artificial gaiety, of course, but underneath it all . . ."

"What?"

"It escapes me, precisely—but uncertainty, a fear of the unknown." He smoothed his black hair back with both hands, then clasped them together about his midsection. "That near accident at Southampton. It unnerved many people. It reminded me of a similar event when I sailed on the *Olympic*, another White Star ship. It pulled a smaller ship into its side, and the smaller one tore a gash in its hull. The *Olympic* is the same size as the *Titanic*, almost a twin."

"They're behemoths, no denying it." Darnell paused, focusing on the incident on the *Olympic*, one of the ships on which a suicide was reported. Darnell asked, "So are you a frequent ocean traveler?"

"About every month or two, lately, I go some-where, yes. I serve as—how do you say—a consul-tant on a special patient. Sometimes I stay long, two months once, but mostly two or three weeks."

"Did you experience any other events on your White Star Line trips—other than that accident?"

"No . . . except I heard rumors on the ship—about a suicide."

"On the same ship?"

"Yes. The *Olympic*." He removed his monacle. "The steward said . . . yes, I believe it was cabin thir-teen. The same as yours." Fortunio smiled. "A super-stitious number, and one that has produced a death. I trust you're not disturbed by the coincidence."

Darnell nodded. "Quite. Now, is there anything you can tell me about that incident? It might help my study."

Professor Fortunio's forehead furrowed. "A man was said to have shot himself. That's what my stew-ard told me. Stewards seem to know everything that goes on. They attributed it to a nervous breakdown, and his financial losses on some new investments."

"And you?"

"Frankly, as one skeptical professor to another, I did not believe a word of it. To me, it sounded like foul play, although I did not see the scene."

Darnell studied the man's face, what he could see of it behind the beard and mustache. "Professor, could a man, or woman, be mesmerized—hypnotized—into doing something violent to themselves or others?"

Darnell sensed defensiveness as the man folded

his arms across his chest. "You mean, say, shooting themselves at a certain hour, by posthypnotic suggestion?"

"Exactly. Yes, could that be done—could you do it?"

"You cannot force a person to do something against his or her deep sense of morality. Now, if a person were already a killer . . . well, theoretically you could plant a suggestion for him to kill a certain person in a certain way." He smiled broadly, showing large white teeth and a gold cap in an upper molar. "But I can assure you, I've never tried that."

After leaving the professor, Darnell headed along the passageway and up to A deck and the ornate reading and writing room where he had scheduled his next appointment. As he walked, he mulled over Fortunio's comments. The Italian professor seemed to be toying with him, was well-informed regarding events in cabin 13, and was a mesmerist. And sailing on at least one of the three ships put him high on Darnell's suspect list. Could he have hypnotized the man into killing himself? And, if so, why? Mesmerism was an inexact science but had strange power.

The two gray-haired women representing his next meeting sat together at a writing table—sisters, Marybelle and Carrie Trent—two spinsters, the Captain had said, who traveled extensively on a large bank balance. "Old maids," Smith had called them.

After the introductions, Darnell pulled up a chair to the writing table and sat opposite them, so he could view both of them at once. The ladies turned their correspondence facedown on the table. The thought crossed his mind—two old ladies going about killing people for sport. Darnell covered a smile and cleared his throat. After explaining his supposed mission, he said, "You were both on the *Adriatic* in February, I understand."

"Yes," they both answered together, then looked at each other and smiled.

"We always travel together," Carrie added.

"Distressing trip, though," Marybelle said.

"Quite so," her sister echoed.

"In what way?" Darnell felt a revelation coming.

Carrie looked at Marybelle and spoke up, as if for both of them. "The ship was much smaller than this one, of course."

"Aren't they all?" Marybelle said. "But that wasn't the problem."

Carrie nodded. "We were in cabin twelve—and you won't believe what happened in the cabin next door to us."

"Right next door," Marybelle echoed.

Darnell said nothing, nodding encouragingly.

Carrie went on. "A suicide. They said he took poison."

"You didn't agree?"

Carrie sniffed. "Not at all. We met that young man in thirteen. He was nice—he helped us open our window once when it was stuck. That man couldn't have taken his own life."

"Why not?" Darnell leaned forward, and the two sisters leaned toward him also, as if conspiring with him. "How can you be so sure?" he asked, looking from one to the other.

"Men don't take poison," Carrie said with assurance. "Poison's a woman's thing, a woman's way out. A man might hang himself . . ."

Marybelle tacked on, ". . . or shoot himself . . ."

Carrie went on, ". . . but we know Mr. Preston

wouldn't do any of those, don't we?" She looked at her sister.

Marybelle nodded. "He was too happy. He was going to America to be married. Now, who would commit suicide under those circumstances?" Her face clouded over. "We've never been married—Carrie and me—but we've seen honeymooners on our ships, and he was just like one of them, only his fiancée wasn't with him. He showed us her picture. A delicate, pretty face."

"Yes, very pretty," Carrie said.

"Did the man say anything else to you that showed his state of mind, that his life, wasn't, say, all peaches and cream?"

Carrie said, "Just a word or two about losing money on something. A bet, an investment, I don't know. But being in first class, it didn't seem important."

"Nothing more?"

"No," they chorused.

"So, then," Darnell said, standing, "how are you both enjoying this trip?"

"We're just hoping . . ." Marybelle said.

". . . nobody dies this time," Carrie finished it, pulling her shawl around her with a shiver.

Her sister nodded. "We took cabin thirty-four, this trip, just to make sure we weren't anywhere near thirteen. Not that we're really superstitious . . ."

". . . just cautious," Carrie added.

Marybelle echoed it. "Very cautious."

Chapter Nine

Friday evening, April 12

Darnell returned to his cabin in time to change for dinner. He took the stairs to the dining room to meet Penny Winters.

She smiled as he approached. "It's nice to see you," Penny said. "I had a lonely afternoon."

Darnell smiled sympathetically and took her arm. They walked over to a small table near the window.

"We'll take our own table tonight," Darnell said. "I don't feel like small talk at a large table."

The waiter came as soon as they were seated. After a quick glance at the menu, they gave him their order.

"I'm starved," Penny said. "Since you were busy this morning, I went to the gym, tried the rowing machine and even rode the electric horse and camel—they're so funny-looking. Then I took a dip in the swimming bath. And had my hair done."

Penny paused. "And you? How's your interviewing going?"

"Some crew members, one professor, and two old maids." He laughed. "Not very exciting so far."

"You're writing this paper for your college?"

Darnell disliked lying to her but felt the necessity

of it. The truth would be harder for her to believe, and not safe to know.

"Our library has a section for reports on foreign travel," he said. "Sort of a travelogue. This trip would have great interest—biggest ship in the world, maiden voyage, a great adventure." He was satisfied that he didn't lie directly but still was uncomfortable about not telling her everything. Later, when the time was right, he would.

"It's certainly an adventure for me." She smiled.

The waiter poured their tea, presented a tureen of soup, ladled it into their bowls, and offered rolls to them. As they ate, Darnell and Penny talked spiritedly for an hour. After their meal, they took a stroll on the deck.

He said, "Sorry, I have to visit the bridge and talk with some of the officers."

Penny kissed him on the cheek. She put her hand on his arm and said, a tease in her voice, "Don't fall overboard. I guess I'll do some reading tonight."

The scent of her delicate perfume was intoxicating, and his resolve weakened. He walked purposefully toward the bridge, fortifying his determination with each step. As he recalled Penny's words, his mood dampened, thinking of the woman who had indeed fallen overboard—the first of the three suicides, or murders.

Second Officer Herbert Lightoller was in charge of the helm. First Officer William Murdoch stood nearby, engrossed in charts.

"Am I interrupting?" Darnell asked as he entered.

The young man shook his head. "E.J. said you'd be here. Anyway, this ship pretty well runs itself if you point it right." Lightoller smiled.

Darnell doubted Lightoller's humble words. The

largest ship in the world needed the best officers it could get. The incident at Southampton proved that.

"Captain Smith said some of the officers and crew transferred over from the *Olympic* for this voyage. Did you need more officer coverage here since this ship was so large?"

"Mostly we needed experienced men. E.J. brought Chief Wilde over from the *Olympic* where Henry was also Chief," Murdoch said. "I became First Officer, same as on the *Olympic*. But Lightoller became Second instead of First, as on the *Oceanic*."

"A bump down." Darnell glanced at Lightoller, who stared straight ahead.

Murdoch went on. "We're duty-bound to White Star. Where they send us, we go." He paused and looked at Lightoller. "But I don't think any of us wanted to step down, or even across. Would've been a plum for me to be the *Titanic* Chief." He shook his head. "Maybe next trip."

"Wilde had the greater experience on the *Olympic*," Lightoller said. "It's almost a twin of this one. Sister ship, isn't she? So we understand the reasons for bringing Wilde over. Passengers deserve the most experienced personnel. It's the way of it."

Darnell noticed Lightoller had not used the word "best," and felt tension in the air. He changed the subject. "How is this trip going? Any problems?"

Lightoller grunted. "Not unless you call missing binoculars a problem. And I do."

"What happened to them?"

"That's what I'd like to know. They were for the lookouts. They use them for sighting other ships, ice floes, that type of thing. The glasses just disappeared."

Murdoch said, "They were on the manifest. But no glasses."

Darnell was puzzled. "So what do you do now—what will your lookouts do?"

Lightoller cupped two fingers around each eye. "They'll use the eyeball system. Our lookouts have good eyes."

"Are we likely to see other ships?" Darnell gazed out at the open sea through the window glass.

"Not on our route," Murdoch answered, "unless at some distance—five or ten miles."

Lightoller said, "The binoculars weren't the only thing."

Darnell guessed his words—Smith's report of missing charts.

"Some of our charts were taken," Lightoller said.

"Disappeared," Murdoch said. "Into thin air. Tuesday night they were there, Wednesday morning gone."

Darnell looked about the room. "So, how do you manage?"

"We had an extra set. These." Murdoch tapped the papers in front of him. "And I'm not letting these out of my sight."

Lightoller said, "The Captain said we could help you, Professor . . ."

Darnell nodded and chose his words carefully. "On your other crossings, have either of you been aware of any unusual incidents?"

"Unusual?" Lightoller took off his cap and scratched his head, then ran his fingers through his hair.

"Anything out of order—peculiar, mysterious . . ." He was going to use "psychic" next, but Lightoller interrupted him.

"Like a suicide?" Lightoller's pale blue eyes squinted as he stared ahead at the sea.

Darnell nodded. "Tell me about that."

Lightoller glanced sidelong at Murdoch, who was busy with the charts. "I'm sure Captain Smith has told you about the woman who jumped overboard?"

"Yes. Were you there?"

"I was Chief on the ship. It was the *Atlantic*. We were about four days out from Southampton when the woman jumped. I understand she was in her thirties and should have been in good health. No apparent reason. It was late at night, early morning actually, only a handful of people on deck, those who couldn't sleep. Another woman on a lower deck saw her go by, plummeting down to the ocean, screaming. The scream stopped immediately when the woman hit the water. She went under at once—that's what the witness said. And didn't come up."

"So she screamed." Darnell remembered Captain Smith relating the incident to him four days earlier, at his flat.

"Yes. Of course she was gone before we could do anything. If you hit the water out here sixty feet down from the deck to the water, with a ship going twenty-two knots an hour, you're as good as dead. There's no way for us to turn back. A junior officer threw a life saver down, but she never even surfaced."

Darnell asked, "Ever see another suicide, Herbert?"

Lightoller shook his head. "Didn't really see this one. Heard of it in the morning." He paused. "I wondered about the scream—do you scream when you jump? But a woman could have decided to jump, and changed her mind on the way down, or just got scared at the last minute."

Murdoch looked at the two of them and cleared his throat. "Professor," he ventured, "I don't want to pry, but Captain Smith said you specifically wanted cabin thirteen. I wondered about that. The woman was in that same cabin number on the *Atlantic*—thirteen. Isn't that an unlucky number?"

"Just call it superstition. Lightning never strikes twice in the same place. That should make it perfectly safe." He wondered if they'd see through that fog.

Lightoller frowned. "But according to the Captain, lightning's already struck three times in that cabin number. Three suicides. You could see a purser about changing cabins."

"No thanks," Darnell said. "Not on the trip over. Coming back—yes, I will."

Murdoch went back to his work. Darnell and Lightoller walked through the wheelhouse to the exit.

Darnell said, "So, there were no other strange occurrences?"

Lightoller frowned. "The Captain said there were three incidents in cabin thirteen. But . . . well, there's a rumor, among the crew, of a fourth incident—a young girl falling overboard earlier last year on another ship of the line. Which ship, I don't know. The crew tells lots of tales, not all true."

"How young was the girl, and what cabin was she in?"

He shook his head. "I really don't know much about it. Everything was rather mysterious. But the story is, she was in her teens."

Darnell pushed. "Is there anything you're not telling me?"

"It isn't pleasant." The officer lowered his voice. "The rumor was, she was—how can I say it—involved with some men when the accident occurred, when she fell overboard."

"Did Captain Smith know of this?"

"I don't think so. It's just a rumor, and I don't repeat them. Not my place. I'm not even sure it's true. But I'll see what I can find out, if you're interested."

"I am, very. Well, thank you both."

Darnell left them to their work and returned to his cabin, for a fleeting moment wishing he were on a vacation cruise, free of concern, such as he would be on his trip back. He resolved to be more cautious for the remainder of the trip.

The disappearances of the binoculars and charts bothered him. But the revelation of the mysterious fourth death concerned him even more. It could have been the first one in the series, if it happened the year before, and if it was connected to the three deaths reported as suicides.

As he walked to the cabin, he determined to warn Sung about the need for greater safety precautions. The way his valet's cabin adjoined his, Sung was equally exposed to whatever danger might come.

Darnell was sure danger would come to him on this voyage. It was just a matter of time. But he had to keep Sung out of danger. He patted his .38 special revolver he had taken to carrying at all times in his inside coat pocket. It gave him a certain comfort.

Chapter Ten

Saturday morning, April 13

After breakfast with Penny, Darnell excused himself and headed for the infirmary for his first appointment of the day, to interview the ship's doctor, Gareth Burton. He thought over Captain Smith's comments about the doctor's tendency to drink too much, and decided to probe that topic.

The doctor sat in a glassed-in office farther back in the infirmary rooms. He seemed to be studying papers on his desk.

A nurse at a small front desk in the outer office asked, "Are you the professor?" and Darnell nodded. Through the glass, he saw the doctor look up and motion him to come back. Stepping into the office, Darnell shook hands with him, the doctor's big, clammy hand feeling moist in his. He wondered why the doctor was nervous. He also noticed the clutter in the office and wondered if the man's drinking had dissipated his professionalism.

"Sit down, Professor. Captain Smith said you have some questions about ships on the White Star Line? Something about a paper, about some accidents?" The doctor leaned back in his leather swivel chair and stared bleary-eyed at him.

As he seated himself, Darnell noticed a photograph on the doctor's desk of the doctor and a young girl, probably the man's daughter. He glanced obliquely about the room, seeing a box of odds and ends on a shelf opposite the desk, containing a sextant, a model ship with a broken sail, and a square box bearing the word "Nest," all half-covered with sailor's togs, scarfs, and gloves strewn on top. Were they the daughter's things, or flotsam and jetsam accumulated in the doctor's frequent ocean travels?

Darnell eyed the doctor. He knew he had to break through his wariness about the suicides, perhaps some feeling of medical failing in treating them. "You examined two of the, ah, accidents—as you call them—the gunshot death and the poisoning. I merely want to get your impressions."

Burton said, "Remember, doctor's confidentiality."

"You can tell me everything—both the Chairman and Captain have authorized my inquiries, I might even say, ordered them."

Burton's face reddened. "Damned intruders. Can't even leave the medical profession to itself." He sat fuming for a moment. "All right, dammit, let's get it over with."

Darnell cleared his throat. "Let's take the poison death first, on the *Adriatic*. Was it a suicide, in your professional opinion?"

"Of course it was. The cabin was locked." The doctor ticked off other points on his fingers, which Darnell saw were trembling. "Number two, the symptoms indicated poisoning. The residue in the glass beside the bed was found, later, to contain poison. There wasn't anything I could do—he was dead when I found him. The autopsy in New York indicated the death was caused by the poison. It turned out to be cyanide."

"But why would he kill himself? He was going to be married, I understand."

Burton snorted. "How should I know? Maybe he changed his mind, couldn't go through with the marriage. It happens."

"It was in cabin thirteen."

"Hmm? Oh, yes. Thirteen."

"And the Greek interpreter who supposedly shot himself? Also cabin thirteen, that time on the *Olympic*."

"Seems to be an unlucky number." The doctor smirked.

"But did you examine him?"

The doctor drummed his fingers on his desk. "All these questions . . . well, of course I examined him. There was one shot in the right temple. He died immediately. The revolver was on the floor below his right hand. The New York police officially called it suicide, when the ship docked and they took a look at him, and hauled him in to the morgue."

"And you agreed with them?"

"I think the evidence speaks for itself. A locked room, one shot, the gun lying on the floor. Of course he shot himself."

"What about the woman who jumped overboard from the *Atlantic*?"

"I heard it was pretty clear. She jumped."

"Did you examine her cabin?"

"No. The Captain did that."

Darnell studied the other's face and asked, "You couldn't assist any of them?"

The doctor's eyes narrowed. "Are you suggesting I was derelict in my duty in those unfortunate happenings? I couldn't save them. I couldn't pump a dead man's stomach, cure a man of a gunshot wound to the head. I can only save lives occasionally, and I can't prevent suicides."

"No. But your, ah, presence, was, shall we say, unfortunately of no help."

The doctor stared down at the desk. When he looked back, Darnell saw tearful red eyes and a scowl. "You don't know how hard it is to be a ship's doctor. No facilities. Dealing with people who are seasick, who fall and twist an ankle, who want painkillers for headaches, powders for an upset stomach. I'm just a damn pill dispenser." He stood, paced back and forth, then again slumped heavily in his chair.

He went on, "I never know where I'm going to be next. They shuffle me around from ship to ship. Some captains don't want me." The doctor blew his nose. "So this is my life. Not altogether thrilling, is it? And then if I drink a bit, they don't like that, either."

"Can you control your drinking?"

Burton grimaced. "I think that's a personal question . . . yes, I do. It doesn't affect my work."

"Where did you begin your medical career, Doctor?"

"What? In Southampton. Then when I got into a spot of trouble there—well, never mind that. That was long ago. With all the sailings leaving from there, I saw a chance to become a ship's doctor."

"You move about from one ship to another?" Darnell persisted. "You examine two different suicide victims. Why?"

"Coincidence. Unfortunate—your word. They move me around. Maybe just my usual dumb, bad luck, of which I've had a long run lately. I don't know."

"A lot of bad luck. Your wife and daughter died last year."

"Yes—I have to find my comfort in a bottle now." He stood. "Now, can we end this? It's very painful, and I've got some exciting announcements of new pain pills to read."

Darnell decided he would get nothing more from Doctor Burton, at least at this time, and took his leave. He glanced back over his shoulder at the door and saw the doctor resting his head in one hand, taking a whiskey bottle out of his bottom desk drawer with the other. He's either a thoroughly beaten man, a man whose best friend is a bottle, Darnell thought, or a damned good actor.

When Darnell returned to his cabin, he found Sung putting away clean clothes and organizing the professor's personal things. The valet smiled. "Hello, Professor. Just finishing."

"Don't rush. We haven't seen each other much on this trip."

"The young lady—she is very entertaining?" The valet lowered his eyes, looking down at the floor, a smile on his lips.

Darnell's cheeks flushed. "It's the interviews—well, yes, I have spent time with her. She is very, ah, entertaining. But I'm wondering about you, Sung. Have you made some friends?"

Sung bowed slightly from the waist. "Thank you, yes. A cook. He has been in the galley on White Star Line ships for twelve years. Sailed on many ships."

Darnell sat at his desk. "Could he tell you anything about the deaths?"

"There are many rumors among crew about cabin thirteen. Say the woman was pushed, not jumped. Say other two suicides, the men, were not—as seemed."

"They're saying they were murders?"

"The cook does not use that word. The crew just say, not suicides. Cook tells of another death on a ship last year."

"The fourth death! Again I hear of that!" Darnell shot to his feet. "Take me to see your friend—I must talk with him."

Sung nodded. "I take you."

Minutes later Sung led Darnell into the galley on D deck. Darnell breathed in the delicious smells of the food being prepared for the dinner hour. He discerned aromas of roast beef and chicken in the air and, as steam tables were opened and closed and lids of pans lifted, identified familiar smells of carrots and onions. The sparkling steel implements and white uniforms, the placement and organization of the kitchen operation was like nothing he had seen before. The luxury of the *Titanic* showed even here, in the lowly galley.

A Chinese man of about Sung's age looked up from his work in surprise as they walked over. Sung spoke to him in Chinese. "He speaks no English," Sung said to Darnell. "I translate."

Darnell nodded, and smiled at the man. "Tell him I wish to ask a few questions."

Sung spoke words in Chinese to the cook, then turned back to Darnell and said, "All right."

"The fourth death. I want to know everything he knows or has heard about it, even if he doesn't know whether it's true."

Sung spoke rapidly, the other seemed to ask a question, and Sung went on, then the cook spoke at length.

Sung turned to Darnell. "Cooks talk of *first* death, you called fourth. They hear story from crew, who hear from other crew. Rumor. It is dangerous, they say, to ask too much. It was a girl, not yet twenty.

Excuse word, please—is ravished. Then jumps overboard."

"Wasn't the death investigated?"

Sung relayed the question and, after a response, looked from the cook to Darnell again. "It was, how you say, hushed up. Don't know why. All he knows now."

Darnell nodded. "All right. Tell him to ask around, see if he can find out any more, let you know."

Sung spoke some words, and the cook said what might have been one of the few English words he knew, "Yes."

Darnell shook the cook's hand, pressing a five-pound note into it, receiving a wide, gap-toothed smile in return.

Back in his cabin, Darnell spoke to Sung of his other concerns. "Other things now. Special duties, Sung."

"Yes, sir."

"My instincts and what the crew says tell me the three deaths were murders. Thirteen—it might be to establish a jinx."

"I understand."

"We're almost halfway through our trip. If the killer is on this ship, he'll want to try something soon. In this cabin."

"Try to kill you, too?"

"Exactly. I'd be just another cabin thirteen jinx victim on his list. But I want to stimulate him—or her, whoever it is—to act on my timetable, not his own."

"You want to set trap."

"Yes, I want to entice whoever it is to act before he's ready, to show his hand. I'll need your help to do it."

Sung bowed slightly and said, "Of course. Say what I must do."

"I plan to spend quite a bit of time out of my cabin, talking with passengers, having meals and entertainments with, ah, Miss Winters. Tonight there is a dance."

"Yes, sir."

"Watch for intruders around the cabin, anyone walking up and down the passageway. Observe but don't interfere."

Sung nodded.

"And tomorrow evening being Sunday, there'll be other activities, the evening chaplain's service, some poetry readings. I expect if he sees we're gone, the killer will choose tonight or tomorrow to visit cabin thirteen, in the early or late evening."

"What do we do, Professor?"

"I want to let him try what he will. You and I will both plan to be away from the room until late, say midnight. You can be with the cook, and I'll be at the dance tonight with Miss Winters. Tomorrow evening we'll be at the chaplain's service. He can see me out of the cabin. If you're gone also, he'll feel the cabin is deserted and try to carry out his scheme."

"You bait the trap? And leave trap door open?"

"Yes, Sung. And I'm the bait, but I know he's coming, and he doesn't know I know. That makes it a trap."

Chapter Eleven

Saturday afternoon, April 13

Darnell headed for the first-class lounge for his next appointment with the Blakes at two p.m. Smith had warned they were the predatory type, preying on unsuspecting passengers with shady investment deals. He knew the Blakes had sailed on at least two of the other voyages. Darnell felt that they were possibly involved in some way with the three deaths. Lost investments? A motive for suicide—or for murder? He'd told Smith, "Under the right circumstances, someone who lies and steals could kill. Crime shrinks the conscience and eventually destroys it."

As he walked through the lounge he found the Blakes speaking with a gray-haired woman. She said to Warner Blake, "I don't know—I'll talk with my daughter. She handles my money for me."

Blake and his wife Delia shook hands with the woman, urging her not to "pass up this opportunity." When Darnell reached them, Blake stood and offered his hand. "Oh, Professor," he said in a brisk tone, "we're almost completed here. We'll be ready for our two-o'clock meeting in a moment. Won't you join us for a tonic?"

Blake's smile reminded Darnell of the jaws of a

shark. If he accepted, he would be able to watch these sharks try to devour another small, defenseless fish. "Well, if it won't interfere with your meeting."

Blake introduced him to the woman, a Margaret Worthington.

"Sit down, sit down," Blake said, his voice high-pitched. "Delia and I have looked forward to chatting with you. Mrs. Worthington is interested in some Australian silver-mine bonds."

"Well, I don't know . . ." the woman said. "As I said, my daughter. . . ."

"You bring Sarah around tomorrow," Delia Blake said. "If she handles your finances, she'll love this investment. Silver, you know, always holds its value." She fingered an ornate silver bracelet, as if to demonstrate the fact.

Mrs. Worthington nodded, rose, and hastily excused herself. The two Blakes turned to Darnell, Blake with a broad smile.

Delia Blake smiled also but with her lips only. There was no warmth in her eyes, cold and inhuman, reminding Darnell of the cold, shiny marbles and agates of his boyhood games.

He took a chair facing Blake while the other motioned to the waiter and asked, "What would you like to drink, Professor?"

"Sherry would be fine," Darnell answered. He nodded at Delia Blake, and she gave him another broad, cold smile.

"You don't travel frequently, do you, Professor?" Blake tried a smile. "We haven't seen you before, aboard ship."

Darnell shook his head. "No. This holiday is unique. I decided it was about time I visited my original homeland."

"You were born in America?" Delia Blake raised her eyebrows, looking surprised and interested.

Darnell sensed the interest shown him was in what they felt was potentially a large bank balance. Everyone in first class seemed to have one. "I came over many years ago, when I was just a lad. My parents resettled just outside London. I took my university training in England."

As he spoke he studied them, imagining what they were thinking. As predators, they would have as their first premise that anyone crossing in first class must be well-off. He felt they were also sizing him up, in his case, as a wealthy American returning for a luxurious stay in New York. He'd let them form their own conclusions.

"And you teach?" Blake asked.

"Yes. I lecture at Cambridge, the Sorbonne, and some small private schools."

"I imagine you're in need of sound investments for your excess funds." Blake's eyes glistened, reminding Darnell of a cobra eyeing its prey.

Darnell smiled at the words "excess funds." Not likely in his case, but he wanted to draw out these people rather than shut them off. His interest was to determine their connection with any of the three deaths. "Perhaps," he said.

"Bonds? Stocks? We offer a full line of very attractive investments. Even jewelry—perhaps for your young lady?"

A shiver went up Darnell's back as he realized they had been watching him with Penny. Would that put Penny in danger?

He tried to ignore their comment. "I don't see how you can sell investments on a ship. You must travel continually."

Blake nodded, laying a hand on his wife's arm.

"We haven't stayed on land more than four weeks at a time for the past year."

"Do your customers all come from aboard ship?"

"Entirely. But we do the trades, the money transactions, on land in between voyages. And we can communicate by Marconi wire now. For example, we could buy an issue for you today and confirm the price to you by tomorrow morning." As Blake talked, he thumbed through a sheaf of papers and handed a sheet to Darnell. "Here are some of our favorites."

Darnell glanced at it but asked, "You must have some interesting experiences, cruising the ocean as much as you do."

"No. Just business."

"I heard—I'm sure you have, too—of the suicide on the *Atlantic*. You sailed on that ship, I believe."

"Well, we heard rumors." Delia Blake's eyes were cold.

"She jumped overboard."

"Yes, that was it," Blake said. "The word went around."

"She had investments, they said. Bonds found in her cabin that proved worthless when examined later."

"Not worthless." Blake's voice rose to a higher pitch. "Just worth a bit less . . . less than she paid."

"So you sold them to her?"

"Yes, but we had sold many people those bonds. She bought some." Blake touched his forehead with a handkerchief, picking up beads of perspiration.

Darnell let him think a bit. "Did she complain? Threaten to go to the authorities?"

Blake bristled. "If someone loses a few pounds on an investment, they have to be adult about it. We'd simply placed some funds in diamond-mine bonds for the woman. She jumped overboard, and some people thought she may have had second thoughts about her funds. But there was no foundation for anything beyond that. It was a sad case—buyer's remorse, perhaps, or a nervous disposition."

Delia Blake shook her head. "And the investments were sound when we sold them. The bad news came, well . . . very soon."

"She didn't threaten you?"

Blake's voice rose again, and his eyes bulged. "No," Blake said. "And if you're thinking we had anything to do with it, that we're responsible for her death—well, we're not. She just took things too hard. She jumped."

"I understand." Darnell could see Blake was angry and under pressure—but why? Guilt? Fear? He saw Blake would admit nothing about the event other than it being a suicide. Maybe he had argued with the woman—he showed he could have the temper for that. Darnell thought of the Shakespeare line, "He protesteth too much."

"Were you aware of the other deaths on ships you were on?"

Blake's eyes narrowed. "Again, rumors, yes. We had no more information than that." He cleared his throat, fidgeted with his papers. "But back to your position. We'd like to help you enhance your bank balance, as we do for many of our clients."

Darnell nodded. It was over. "I'll look over your investments list and let you know," he said, rising.

The Blakes looked relieved at his departure, despite their avowed purpose and business of trying to sell securities. He may have been getting too close to the quick.

Blake promised, "We'll talk with you again."

But Darnell felt another meeting was the last thing

they wanted. They knew he would investigate them further. And he knew they were holding something back—something that could do them harm. He was convinced of one thing—they were thieves with white collars, and maybe killers as well. Love of money and evil deeds often went hand in hand.

Chapter Twelve

With an hour or two before dinner preparations, Darnell again reviewed his plans of the three ships and lists of the passengers and crew on more than one of the voyages. He decided he had done all the interviewing he needed to do at this time, and should now follow through on making it easy for the killer to invade the cabin. Tonight was the dance.

He freshened up, changed into his black tie and tails for the celebratory Saturday night dinner, and headed for Penny's cabin to pick her up. He whistled a light tune he'd heard the ship's band play earlier on deck.

The dinner, at the Captain's table, was a great success, as far as the Captain was concerned. He told more tales of the sea and again extolled the many features of the ship. Darnell observed carefully the Count, who again sat at the table that evening, but who showed no sign of nervousness after their interview. He realized a man who was a mesmerist by profession could certainly control his own feelings, with something of a personal mesmerism, self-hypnosis.

After dinner, Darnell and Penny joined in the evening dance, she trying to teach him the new steps, he having trouble picking them up—the polka, the waltz, the badger's gavotte, the two-step, and the quadrille. Darnell stumbled and slipped, stepped on her toes, and she laughed about it, but he valiantly tried every type of dance. Finally he said, "Let's sit the rest of this out." They took a nearby table and watched the others dance. They sipped champagne from crystal flutes.

"I see I'm going to need dancing lessons," Darnell said with a sheepish grin.

"You're getting better, and I'll teach you," she said, smiling. "It just takes a little time. It'll give us time to be together."

"You feel good in my arms," he said, and regretted it.

But Penny said, "Yes, and you in mine." Her cheeks were pink and her eyes glowed.

He cleared his throat. "You'll teach me after we reach port? In New York?"

"Yes. You *can* stay, can't you?"

"I'll stay as long as I can, but I do have classes. . . ." He reviewed his schedule in his mind. Nothing until May tenth, except one class which a substitute was handling. "Yes, I know I can manage a holiday."

"You mean a vacation."

"Holiday is what we call them—we *English*." He laughed, thinking of his childhood in America, and how much, as an American, he had become an entrenched Englishman.

"Our voyage is almost half over," Penny said with a wistfulness in her voice.

"It's been fun."

"New York is fun, too. I'll take you to see the tall buildings, like the Woolworth. And the Statue of Liberty. The sky-scrapers."

"And the dance studios."

Penny laughed. She looked about the room. "Many

of these people will part in New York—except those who are married, of course, and families."

"And us. We'll be together, for a while." He was already looking forward to two weeks in New York. He'd cable the school when they docked, or send a Marconigram from the ship.

"It's almost midnight," Penny said.

"Cinderella's bedtime?"

"Yes. Will you walk me home?"

They walked to her cabin and Darnell kissed her long, held her close, inhaling her perfume. He couldn't bear to leave her.

"Would you like to come in, John . . . for just a minute?" Penny's eyes were closed. She opened them and looked directly into his.

Darnell nodded, and followed her into her cabin, closing the door behind them, turning the bolt. She found his arms again in the dark, and their breath came heavily. Darnell felt his heart racing, his chest pounding, as unaccustomed feelings washed over him in waves. His hands roamed over her body. He pulled off his coat with one hand, and Penny dropped her coat in the direction of a chair.

Ambient illumination from the deck sifted in, in shafts of yellow light through space between the window drapes, and they saw each other removing more and more clothing, kissing in between each movement as they did so. Soon they had disposed of all their clothes with all their inhibitions, and found the bed. Darnell tossed back the counterpane.

His urgency brought them together hotly, boldly in the dark, with all pretense of society thrown aside. He spoke her name over and over, "Penny, Penny," as their bodies joined. "Penny!"

"I love you, John. Love me, love me!"

After their first frenzy, the two lay close, holding

each other, sighing, kissing, then again joining in the dark in mutual ecstasy. Afterward, Darnell could feel the slight hum of the ship's great engines against their glowing bodies through the mattress as they lay, their desires satisfied, yet still sighing, touching, exploring each other's body, kissing.

"I don't know what came over me," Darnell said. "I had no idea I was going to . . . it's just that you're so wonderful."

"I do love you, John."

"And I love you. More than you could know, Penny. We're part of each other now."

"Yes. And for always. Nothing can ever part us."

They held each other tightly, as if someone or something was trying to separate them, even now. "I don't want to go," Darnell said.

"I know, but go to your cabin now, darling. On ship, we have to keep up appearances. But after we reach New York . . ."

"We'll be together, forever."

As Darnell strode to his own cabin, his shirt collar loose, his tie askew, he began whistling a light tune, then stopped, remembering it was after one a.m. He smiled. Soon he'd be in New York. With Penny. The thought blazed across his mind.

What a change in his life four days had brought, what wonderful days lay ahead. But he broke his stride and stopped in the corridor as he realized, it wasn't just two weeks, as they had talked about earlier. She was to be with him always. He'd ask her to go back to London with him, to be his wife. He'd ask her tomorrow. The spring in his step as he walked on belied the late hour, and another low whistle escaped his lips.

Darnell's thoughts were shattered when he opened

his cabin door. He heard a muffled sound in the
dark, and stepped to one side, letting a shaft of light
from the passageway fall into the room. In the stream
of light, he saw a body on the floor.

"Sung! What happened?" He clicked on a lamp,
closed the door, and knelt at his servant's side. Blood
had dripped down onto the carpet from the back of
Sung's head.

Sung groaned. "Someone hit me."

"Are you all right? Can you sit up?"

The valet demonstrated that he could, by pulling
himself into a sitting position, holding his head with
one hand. He touched it and brought his bloody fingers down, looking at them. "Blow was hard, like
gun barrel."

"You saw him?"

"No. I come into your room, turn off all the lights,
and sit facing your door. I wait to see what happens.
But someone hits me from behind. Must have come
in from door in my room. All goes black."

Darnell hurried to the water closet and brought
back a wet, cold cloth. He gently cleaned Sung's
wound. The cut was not serious but was accompa-
nied by a swollen, discolored bruise on the back of
his head. He brought Sung a glass of water, examined the wound again. "The bleeding's stopped. But
you'll have a beauty of a bump there tomorrow."

"Had them before. In China. But never learned to
like them." Sung smiled, but winced with pain.

"Someone must have a key to your door, and came
in behind you. Probably has a key to my door, too.
We'll put the extra bolts on tonight." Darnell helped
Sung through the connecting door into his bedroom
and saw him into bed. "I'll look in on you in the
morning." He locked and bolted Sung's outer door.

He inspected his own room but saw nothing out of

place, and bolted his door. Perhaps the intruder had been scared off, he thought. If so, he'd be doubly careful when he returned. But not tonight. Darnell would make it easy for him next time. He would plan their next encounter.

He knew the next night, Sunday night, would test his plan. He'd make sure Sung was not in danger this time, make sure he was somewhere else. Then let the killer come again.

Chapter Thirteen

Sunday morning, April 14

Sunday morning broke brightly. The sun's rays flashed across the ocean, flickering on the waves. Although most days felt much the same as the others, Sunday evoked a different mood on the ship. There were religious services in the morning, games and contests later on deck, even in the cool air, and in the saloons. A festive air would pervade throughout the day.

Darnell burst forward with enthusiasm, his one thought of Penny, remembering the night before. He shaved, dressed quickly, and strode to her cabin, where he had arranged to meet her before breakfast. When she opened the door, he swept her into his arms.

"Close the door," she said softly. "Oh, John."

"I need you."

She put her fingers on his lips. "Not now, my love. We must wait . . . until tonight."

Darnell held her close, they kissed fervently, but finally he stood back. "All right, then." He smiled. "How about some breakfast?" He realized he was ravenous. Love made him hungry for more of everything in life.

They ate a hearty breakfast and attended chapel,

holding hands throughout the service. Like a couple of love-struck kids, he thought, breathing her fragrance, and smiled at her, proud she was sitting near him. He looked about the room, wondering if others could tell they were in love.

Captain Smith came up to them after the service, a tall man next to him, a diminutive dark-haired woman on the man's arm. "Oh, Professor, step over here and meet someone."

Penny turned her head slightly and whispered in Darnell's ear. "John—it's her. Mrs. Astor."

Smith said, "Professor, I'd like you to meet John Jacob Astor and his bride. Mr. and Mrs. Astor, Professor John Darnell and Penny Winters."

Mrs. Astor moved forward first, smiled, and put out her hand to Penny. "It's so nice to meet someone close to my own age," she said. "I hate to say it, but, well, the average age in first class is a bit high. Call me Madeleine."

"I saw you board at Cherbourg, Madeleine," Penny said. "Are you having a good honeymoon trip?"

Young Mrs. Astor blushed. "Yes, I guess the first year is the honeymoon."

John Jacob Astor took Darnell's outstretched hand firmly in his steel grip. "Very pleased to meet you, Professor." His tone dropped to a confidential level. "The Captain has been telling me of your, shall we say, extracurricular interests."

Darnell shot a glance at Smith but said to Astor mildly, "I have a small consulting business on the side."

"Ghosts, eh?" Astor's eyes twinkled. "I was wondering—in our new country estate, there have been rumors, you know, legends about ghosts."

Darnell laughed. "No decent country estate could

do without one or two. Sometimes people are disappointed when I show them they don't exist. Takes away the glamour."

"Glamour in ghosts?"

"I guess you could say, in your line, even stocks and bonds can have glamour—that dark green, parchment paper; the gilt edges; pictures of dead queens and kings."

Astor nodded. "Money does have its own mystique, of course. But it shouldn't be the life goal of the average person. Making money is a speciality in itself, just as your field is special. But I always say a man can live as comfortably with a million dollars as if he were rich." A smile played about his lips.

Captain Smith said, "Mr. and Mrs. Astor will be joining me at dinner tonight, John, as you and Penny will. We'll see you then."

The man said, "Good day," and Penny and Mrs. Astor tore themselves away from their newfound friendship. Madeleine Astor told Penny, "We'll talk more tonight."

"What a thrill!" Penny said as they walked out on deck. "Wait 'til I tell my aunt."

"Why don't you do that now? We'll send a wireless."

"Wonderful."

Reaching the wireless room, Darnell glanced through the round glass window in the door and rapped twice. Phillips looked up from his work and smiled, nodding as he saw their faces, and Darnell opened the door for Penny.

"Sparks," Darnell said. "My, ah, friend Penny here would like to send a Marconigram."

Phillips wiped his brow with a handkerchief. "Can't just now. The wireless machine has been broken for several hours. Bride and I have to fix the bugger."

"What a shame. . . . When do you think you'll be back in business?"

"Try us late this afternoon or tonight." He stooped down under the table, applying a wrench to a bolt. "We'll get her going again. All those to send." He pointed at a stack of messages, then looked at Darnell. "Bloody strange, this breakdown. It almost looks like—well, like someone jammed up the works intentionally. But who would do that?"

Darnell said nothing. But he had his opinion.

"Can I fill one out now and leave it?" Penny began to answer her own question, reaching for a pad and pencil.

"Of course, ma'am. I'll put it on top of the pile." He winked at Darnell. "Special news—an engagement, perhaps?"

Penny blushed. "Well . . ."

"I know how it is aboard ship. Romance is everywhere." He winked at Darnell again, who smiled back.

"Do you find those things in your outgoing messages?"

Phillips nodded at Darnell. "Two engagements from second class already this trip."

Bride looked up from the other side of the table. "Could you give us a hand here, Jack?"

Phillips stepped around the table. Penny had finished her message and put it on top of a pile. "Thank you so much," she said, and received a bright smile.

Phillips' head ducked down behind the machine table again. "Let's get this bloody thing working, Harold. And, from now on, we lock this door at night, even if we're sleeping in there."

* * *

Afterward, Darnell and Penny took part in the quoits contest, but he failed to circle a single peg with the ten rope rings provided to contestants, while Penny won two prizes with perfect tosses.

"I played horseshoes with my father in Texas." She laughed. "Quoits is an American game, with an English name."

Darnell nodded. "For either country—I'd need a lot of practice." He reflected that his only sports skills were swimming and pistol shooting, learned in college. Since then, his energies had been almost totally devoted to his teaching and delving into paranormal matters, as his second career slowly flourished. Now Penny had changed his life in some small ways and some very significant ways. He looked at her with new eyes, and she held his arm even tighter as they promenaded the deck.

They enjoyed a leisurely lunch together, and Penny excused herself afterward, "to freshen up." He knew that meant a hairdo, and a selection of a dress and jewelry for the special dinner that night.

At the double swinging doors leading to the promenade deck, they found they were alone for a moment and kissed lingeringly. Penny turned back in, toward the grand staircase, and Darnell watched her go.

On deck, he strolled leisurely for a while, his mind contemplating events that could occur in the next day or two. He reached an area where first-class passengers could gaze down at the second-class deck. The noise and laughter of the children in second class, drawn into prominence by the games and prizes, broke through his thoughts briefly.

Not many children were booked in the voyage's first class, occupied largely by the very wealthy and prominent American businessmen and their wives, but second class had many young children. It seemed there were about twenty of them below.

"All right, Jim, see if you can beat this," one called out, and tossed the rope ring at the peg. The other laughed as the ring bounced beyond the peg and almost went over the side.

"My turn," the other shouted.

The scene brought back memories of his trip over from America with his father and mother. Dim thoughts of the games he played aboard, one or two ship's companions of his age. Was it Barnie? And Craig? What had happened to those children of long ago? He shook his head.

Darnell returned to thoughts of the adventure that could await him that night, an effort to entice the murderer back to his cabin. What was the American expression—give him enough rope to hang himself? He would inform the Captain, and Sung was aware of his plan. Darnell felt he was in control of the situation, except for one thing—his concern for Penny.

He could not bring Penny near his cabin, for fear of her safety. And he still felt reluctant to tell her what was really happening on this voyage. He didn't want to bring her into it.

Darnell stopped by the Marconi wireless room to see whether the system had been repaired. He found Harold Bride, the junior operator, at the wireless desk. "What's the word, Sparks?" Darnell asked, knowing Bride relished the title. Darnell enjoyed his freedom of the ship, being able to talk with the operators.

The sandy-haired, shirtsleeved man looked up at him, an annoyed expression on his face, and frowned, eyes squinted into slits. "It's not been a good day, Professor. We're way behind in our Marconis—the mechanical problems. Got it partially

fixed, then it went down again. And now ice reports by wireless from other ships are interrupting
everything."

"Ice?"

"Field ice," Bride said. "Floaters, you know. The
water was warmer this spring, breaking up the ice
faster. We had one warning Friday. But today
we've had five already." He waved notepapers at
the professor. "Listen to these: 'large icebergs' . . .
'ice field' . . . 'heavy ice' . . . 'bergs and growlers.'
Our course is taking us right into the ice."

"Smaller field ice isn't particularly dangerous, is
it?" Darnell asked.

"Well, not for a ship this size. Oh, we might have
to slow down. The bergs, of course, are a different
thing. The small bergs—growlers, they call 'em—
can be a bit dangerous because you can't see them
very far ahead. But it's really the big buggers you
have to watch out for. I heard those dark ones at
night are most invisible."

"I know someone who'd love to see an iceberg.
What do you think of that?" Penny's musical laugh
when she had said the word rang in his mind.

"I'd rather meet up with the Loch Ness monster
myself!"

Darnell thought a moment. "I suppose the Captain knows about the ice warnings?"

"Yes. Even Chairman Ismay does. We've had six
warnings. Phillips saw Captain Smith hand the
Chairman one of the Marconigrams we delivered.
He stuffed it in his pocket."

"What did he think?"

"He said something like, 'Thank you. Ice is common this time of year.' Sounds like him . . . no disre-
spect, sir."

"None noticed." Darnell smiled, but wondered at

Ismay's confident attitude Bride had noticed. He also wondered, Where did confident and reckless cross lines?

The chief wireless operator, Jack Phillips, stepped into the room from a small alcove, rubbing his eyes. Darnell saw a cot in the alcove, blankets askew.

"Hello, Professor." Phillips yawned. "Sorry. I've been napping."

"We haven't been to our own cabins to sleep for two days now," Bride offered.

Darnell nodded sympathetically. "Lots of messages."

Phillips spoke. "These bloody greetings people are sending. Hundreds of them. Back to England. Forward to America. It's all we can do to handle them. And then we keep getting interrupted by those ice reports from other ships."

"Then the wireless breaks down today." Bride ran a hand through his tangled hair. "We fix it, then it goes down again. And it still isn't working right. I think we've got hours of work ahead of us. What do you say, Jack?"

"We'll have to get back on that job now," Phillips said. He frowned. "There'll be hell to pay if we don't get these bloody important messages out for all these bloody Aunt Susies and Uncle Joes!"

As Phillips looked at Darnell, he remembered Penny's message. "Oh, of course, we sent the 'gram for Miss Winters. I didn't mean that."

"I understand. Thank you." Darnell took his leave and completed the short tour he had started about the ship. At the bridge, he spoke with Second Officer Lightoller. "Making good time?" he asked.

"Not bad. Not setting any records. But we're close to full steam."

"Are you watching the Marconigram reports? Wireless said there's ice out there."

"Yes. Some field ice. It's a bad month for it. It might be better if we were fifty miles south. But our lookouts are posted."

"The Captain and Director Ismay know about it?"

"Yes. They don't seem overly concerned. So I'm not."

Chapter Fourteen

Sunday evening, April 14

The dinner that night took on a party air at the Captain's table with the hosts George and Eleanor Widener, the Astors, publisher Henry Harper and his wife, along with Ismay, Penny, Darnell, Isidor Straus and his wife, and Sir Cosmo and Lady Duff Gordon. The hour was early, but the April sky was already dark.

Captain Smith, in great form, again told more of his sea stories and extolled the features of the great ship for newcomers to the table. Darnell felt it was becoming repetitive, like watching a play night after night from the wings.

"Smooth as glass, isn't it?" Smith asked.

Lady Duff Gordon responded, "Hardly any motion at all."

Darnell realized that only the distant slight rumble of the engines deep in the innards of the ship showed it was moving at all. He thought of it as a floating hotel.

Penny and the new Mrs. Astor, an unspoiled and enthusiastic young woman, sat next to each other and talked happily of fashions and the sights in London. They had New York in common, yet shared different views of the city life because of their stations.

But he knew they both had something else in common now, their love for a man. He moved closer to Penny, just to feel her bare arm touching his.

Penny noticed the movement and smiled at him. Then she turned back to Mrs. Astor.

"You must enjoy the party life in New York," Penny said to Madeleine Astor. "All the glamour, the music, the dancing."

Madeleine frowned. "I did at first. I was swept off my feet by it, really. And our trip to Europe has been the same what you might call 'mad whirl' of parties. Meeting people in very high places." She paused. "But, Penny, I'll tell you something I'm going to have to tell my husband soon . . . I'm tiring of it. I'm carrying our baby now, and she—or he—occupies my thoughts."

"Your motherly instincts are only natural. Every woman has those deep-down needs." Penny glanced at Darnell, who was now engaged in conversation with the Captain.

"Money can bring many things, and I'm sure our child will benefit from that. But the strength of a good father and devotion of a good mother can't be replaced." She smiled. "I'm very young, I know that, but I'm learning."

Later, Penny told Darnell she was always aware of the gap in their stations, now that Colonel Astor had brought his new wife into the exalted levels of wealth and position, but Mrs. Astor had never given Penny any feelings of being beneath her.

The dinner was to Darnell's liking—barley soup, filet mignon with green peas and creamed carrots, followed by Waldorf pudding. "Real English fare," he said to Penny.

"It could even be American. We have that in common."

Champagne and white wine, a Bordeaux, were served during the meal, and a claret came with dessert. Penny said, "No red wine for me. It's going to my head." She ordered black coffee.

After dinner, on the quiet Sunday evening on which there was no dancing, passengers found quiet pursuits, many retiring early.

Penny and Mrs. Astor parted with effusive promises to meet again later in the voyage. Astor said to Darnell, "You and Miss Winters must come visit us sometime."

As Penny and Madeleine stood and talked for a moment, Count Dionino Fortunio came over from another table to Darnell's side and bowed curtly. "And how is your little investigation going, Professor?"

"My research—"

"Come, let us not deceive each other. The polite fiction of your supposed psychological 'paper' does not conceal your true purposes from a discerning eye."

"And what does your eye see?"

He smiled mirthlessly. "I've thought back on questions you asked. You are looking into the death of the man in cabin thirteen on the *Olympic*, yes? What they called a suicide."

"Do you have more information on it? I recall you termed it foul play."

"A true professor—answering a question with a question. No, no more information. But I am sure you will have no trouble solving your, ah, case. And I must leave you now." He bowed again and turned abruptly away, walking toward the exit.

Penny put a hand on Darnell's arm. "I don't like his looks. What was that all about?"

"I don't know. Ego. Or something more sinister.

He may see it as an intellectual challenge." He gave her a reassuring smile. "Count Fortunio is simply a bit hard to fathom."

Darnell hooked his arm in Penny's. "Let's go for a promenade on deck." He walked arm in arm with her to the exit.

"It's really icy out here," she said. They looked down at ice floes drifting past. "Where's my iceberg?" she demanded, giving Darnell a saucy look.

Darnell put his arm about her shoulders. "Harold Bride said he'd rather see the Loch Ness monster."

She laughed. "He's a Scotsman, I suppose."

"Yes. And the boys said they sent your message."

"My aunt will be pleased." But Penny frowned. Something had been bothering her all night as she sat amidst the vast wealth at the captain's table. "John . . . there's something I have to tell you."

Darnell looked into her eyes and saw concern there. "Anything you say will be music to my ears."

She cringed. "I doubt it." She stared out at the sea as she spoke, avoiding his eyes. "When I told you I had an inheritance, that I was traveling on that money—well, that was wrong. It was a lie. I'm just a secretary in a law office. My aunt in England paid for my trip home."

Darnell smiled reassuringly. "Penny, you could be a cleaning lady in the Woolworth Building—I wouldn't care. I love you. And remember, I'm no Colonel J. J. Astor myself, just a college professor." He pulled her to him and pressed his lips on hers. "Whatever we are, we are each other's. We're a pair, you and me."

"A pair of lovebirds," she said. "I don't know why I got carried away in that deception." She thought a minute. "And one other thing, someone at White Star Line called and asked me to move from cabin fourteen to my present cabin—something about re-furbishing it. They paid me a hundred pounds."

Darnell knew the reason, Smith or Ismay clearing the way for cabin 13, probably on both sides. And it brought home to him his own deception, not telling her of his true mission and the mystery of cabin 13. He could not reveal that yet, but he would say what he could.

"Penny, there's a special reason for my trip. I can't tell you the details, I'll just say it's a case. You know about my consulting work, my paranormal events investigations."

"Ghosts!" she exclaimed. "You mean there are ghosts on the *Titanic*? John, how wonderful!"

"Shhh. Now wait, I didn't say ghosts. Let's just say, it's a case. And please don't mention ghosts to anyone. I don't want J. J. Astor saying we frightened his new bride, carrying his child, with ghost stories."

Darnell took Penny to her cabin, wanting desper-ately to stay, yet his plan for that critical evening had to be executed. They kissed and embraced for long minutes until he was able to tear himself away. He was anxious for the ship to reach New York so they could put their lives together.

When he returned to his cabin, his steward, Mario, was standing in it, the cabin door open. "What is it, Mario?" Darnell, surprised and alert, looked about the room.

"Just checking to see that everything's shipshape, sir," he said. "If there is anything else you need, sir, let me know."

As soon as the steward closed the door behind him, the professor locked it and inspected the cabin, closets, windows, the door to Sung's room. He knew Sung was in the cook's quarters, staying away from his cabin, as planned. Everything seemed to be secure.

He prepared himself for the evening, pulled on a robe, dropped his revolver in a pocket, sat in his chair by the desk, and stared at the cabin door. He drummed his fingers on the desk. A small taste of sherry would be no problem, he decided, and opened the bottle on the desk.

The cork was loose, and the bottle appeared to have been opened. He pulled out the short cork and sniffed the contents. It had a bitter odor, not the usual musty, sweetish smell. Darnell recognized the pungent odor of cyanide, and changed his plans abruptly, realizing the killer had planned another apparent suicide by poisoning. He decided instantly he would play along with it.

Darnell poured a bit of sherry in a glass, put the glass on the nightstand, then deliberately tipped it over, the liquid flowing over the edge and dripping onto the carpet. He turned down the blankets on his bed, removed his shoes, and placed them in plain view next to his bed. He lay down in the bed, still clothed, his revolver in hand in his pocket, and covered himself with the blankets, nothing showing but his head.

He clicked off the bed lamp, the only light in the cabin, and stared into the darkness. The door was locked, but the extra bolt had not been thrown. A key would unlock it. Only a thin shaft of light crept into the room between the window coverings.

The fly, Darnell thought, was now ready for the spider.

Chapter Fifteen

Sunday night, April 14

Captain Smith retired early, before 9:30 p.m., leaving Second Officer Lightoller at the helm on the bridge. "If there are any problems, rouse me," he told him.

Lightoller nodded. "Murdoch comes on soon."

Jack Phillips and assistant Harold Bride worked feverishly sending the piled-up Marconigrams ahead to the station at Cape Race, Newfoundland, which received their messages. It had taken them seven hours to fully repair their devices, and messages had stacked up on their desk.

"We'll never get these all sent," Phillips complained to Bride. "Fast as we send them, another batch comes in."

" 'Hello, Mother. Having a wonderful time. See you on Wednesday.' " Bride put on a falsetto voice, reading the one he held in his hand. "Really important stuff, eh?"

At eleven, Phillips' work was interrupted by a persistent message from the *Californian*, saying heavy ice had drifted into the shipping lanes. The *Californian* said they had stopped, surrounded by ice floes. The ship was so close, the Marconi Morse code message blared into his earphones, startling him and angering him. "Dammit," he said, and tapped back

angrily, "Stay out!" He called to Bride, who had
wearily lain down on the cot in the next room,
"Don't these people know I've got messages to
send?" Bride, sound asleep, gave no answer.

On the moonless night, the ocean presented a dark
and forbidding aura, brightened only by the intense
starlight, the glow of lanterns lining the decks of the
ship, and lights in the comfortable saloons and cabins. High in the *Titanic*'s crow's nest, two young
lookouts stared ahead at the smooth, black ocean.
They had begun their watch at ten p.m., and the cold
was getting to them by eleven.

"Shouldn't be so cold—no wind tonight, except
what the ship's stirring up," Fred Fleet said. "It's like
a bloody, black painted sea out there. I wish we had
our binoculars."

His partner, Reggie Lee, nodded. "Calm as a pond.
The glasses would help."

Fleet scowled. "They say they weren't put aboard,
but I think some bleedin' idiot stole 'em. On a night
like this, we really need 'em every minute. I like to
scan with 'em."

Lee grunted, slapping his gloved hands together.
"Damn, but it's cold."

"It's iceberg air," Fleet whispered. His breath
made a small silver cloud in the night air. "I c'n feel
'em out there. Caught the scent of 'em before—just
like this. It gets in your nostrils. There's bergs out
there, take my word. The buggers are near invisible
in a calm sea, no waves, y'know. But they're out
there. Maybe you can't see 'em, but you can smell
'em."

"You can smell bergs?" Lee laughed. "Not bloody
likely."

Fleet scowled. "Bleedin' right I can. I'm smellin'

'em right now." He fell silent for several minutes as he stared ahead into the impenetrable darkness.

Lee fell in with his mood, saying nothing.

Shortly, Fleet broke the silence, muttering, "You're right about one thing, Reggie—it's goddamn cold out here." He stuffed his gloved hands in his jacket pockets.

Lee smiled. "Cold for us. But for them in their cabins, it's cushy enough. Them, with their thick pillows and blankets. Sippin' their toddies down there, while we're freezing our arses off up here, watchin' out for 'em."

"It's the job, mate. And don't complain too much. We see it all from up here. Top of the world. A view they'll never have, comfortable as they are."

Down in cabin 13, not quite as comfortable as lookout Lee imagined, Professor John Darnell lay in his bed, still fully clothed, alert, his revolver in hand, waiting for his adversary to return. After carefully planting the poison, the killer would want to be sure his victim was dead. That was vital to the killer's purpose of establishing the cabin 13 jinx. Darnell was to be the fourth suicide. And, beyond that, no one knew what could be next. Darnell was ready, and his pulse was racing.

Elsewhere on the ship, Sunday evening had worn on without unusual incident. Earlier, passengers sang hymns for an hour in the chapel with every seat filled, until the service ended at ten p.m. with the final hymn, the popular "Nearer, My God to Thee." Beyond that, there was little else to do on a Sunday night except retire early. There was no evening dance. But in the first-class smoker lounge, through special permission this night, a few men nursed their whiskeys, smoked cigars, and played poker or bridge, and could be expected to be there until the early hours of the next morning.

In the bowels of the ship, engine room stokers sweated in 100-degree temperatures. Above, on deck, only a few passengers stood at the rail, bundled in their heavy coats, collars turned up at the neck. They stared at the sea, watching their breath vaporize in the freezing air. But most passengers sat snugly in their cabins, some propped up in bed, reading, and enjoying their luxury. Captain Smith dozed, snored and snorted at the cusp of waking in his cabin, forewarned that Darnell's plans might trigger some action that night, and ever alert for the overriding duty of captaining his ship.

Earlier, Darnell had instructed his valet, Sung, to stay away from his cabin, and Sung had joined a late party in the cook's quarters. Now Darnell was alone in his darkened cabin, wide-awake, listening, knife-edge alert.

A few minutes after eleven p.m., Darnell heard the slight, whispery sound of a key turning in the door lock and the soft click as it unlocked. He gripped his revolver. This is it, he thought. Now we'll settle this damnable jinx, once and for all.

A shaft of light from the corridor slanted into the room and framed the bulky figure of a man in the doorway. Darnell kept his eyes almost closed, in slits, to appear asleep—or even dead—from the poisoned sherry he supposedly had drunk earlier.

The man closed the door behind him, the room dark again. He struck a match, bringing a flicker of light to the cabin. He stepped over to the bed and inspected the upended sherry glass and the spilled wine on the night table, and his lips curled upward.

He reached toward Darnell's neck, as if to check for a pulse.

Through narrowed eyelids, Darnell recognized the familiar face, saw the sneer on the man's lips. He bolted up and shouted, "Hold it right there, Doctor!" He leveled his revolver at the man and sprang out of bed to his feet—just as Burton's match burned out, plunging the room into darkness once more.

The doctor exhaled, "Damn it to hell!" and flailed at Darnell in the sudden darkness, knocking his gun to the floor.

Darnell lunged at him and barreled him against the table. The table crashed against the wall, and both men hit the floor hard. Stunned, Darnell stumbled over the table and struck at the other in the dark. His fist smashed into the doctor's chin, Darnell's knuckles cracking loudly with the blow and sending a jar of pain up his forearm. He gasped as the intruder grabbed his throat with both hands, choking him. "I'll kill you," the doctor grunted, "you meddling bastard!"

Darnell tried to draw his breath and clawed at the large hands. With a wrenching turn, Darnell broke the doctor's grip, and pounded him about the face. "Looks like . . ." he gasped, "your plan . . . is jinxed." He heard a crunching sound as his fist connected with the doctor's nose, and he felt warm blood spew forth on his hand. But the doctor caught the professor a sharp blow in the eye. Darnell saw a flash of lights in the black room, and his knees buckled.

Just then the cabin door flew open and the dark room was brightened by the hallway lights. Sung charged into the cabin and grabbed the doctor's shoulders, pulling him backward off Darnell. Darnell recovered his senses and struck the man's jaw as hard as he could.

Burton collapsed. "Stop, stop," he groaned. He pressed a sleeve to his bleeding lips and felt his front teeth. One eye was already puffed up, closing rapidly.

Sung clicked on a light. "Who is this?" he asked Darnell.

"The ship's doctor—Doctor Gareth Burton. And I have an idea why he's doing this." He retrieved his revolver and trained it on the doctor. "Just lie there, and you won't be hurt." He looked about the cabin and told Sung, "Rip down that sash from the window."

Sung jerked down the drapery sash, and the two men tied the doctor to the bedpost.

"I'm glad I came back," Sung said. "Felt you needed me."

"Another of your premonitions, Sung?" He felt the fear and concern in Sung's voice and put his hand on the servant's shoulder. "It'll be all right," he said. "You came just in time. Thank you, my man."

Darnell pointed his revolver at Burton and placed the gun in Sung's hand. "I've got to see the Captain now. Keep this gun pointed at him. Stay a safe distance away—in that chair. And I'll be back as soon as I can."

With that, Darnell grabbed his overcoat and dashed out the doorway, down the corridor. He wanted urgently to see Penny and tell her about it all but knew he must find the Captain first.

On deck, Darnell rushed to the bridge. "Where's Captain Smith?" he asked First Officer Murdoch. "I have to see him."

Murdoch tipped his cap to the professor. "The Captain's in his cabin, getting some sleep. I'm on the watch."

Darnell stood there momentarily, wondering whether he should rouse the Captain to tell him about Burton.

Suddenly a repetitive ringing of bells clanged through the room, and Sixth Officer Moody picked up the bridge telephone connected to the lookout station. "Yes?"

"Iceberg!" Darnell heard the words squawking from the speaker. "Iceberg dead ahead! Iceberg dead ahead!"

James Moody said, "Thank you," and hung up the phone. Eyes wide, he turned to Murdoch. "Iceberg dead ahead, sir."

Murdoch reacted immediately. "Take her to port! Hard-a-starboard!" he shouted. His voice boomed through the wheelhouse. Almost in the same breath, Murdoch ordered, "Full speed astern!"

Moody moved the control lever to starboard and relayed the message over the phone to the engine room, then yanked a lever to the down position. The great ship hesitated, shuddered, and seemed to struggle, reacting to the conflicting orders. Murdoch sweated in the cold air, waiting for the ship to respond. But the movement toward port to avoid the iceberg was imperceptible. The full-astern order took power from the propellors, making the directional change excruciatingly slow. Murdoch and Moody stared ahead, watching the iceberg inexorably come into view.

The ten seconds that passed seemed like ten minutes to Darnell. He found he was holding his breath, his pulse racing, as he stared ahead, unmoving, at the monstrous blue-black shape seeming to bear down on the ship. Then the ship struck the iceberg. A tremor, a distant grinding rumble began as the ship inched by the iceberg, and Darnell expelled his breath in one loud exhalation, saying, "We're hit." It seemed to him the iceberg had moved, scraping the side of the liner, but, in fact, the liner had passed alongside the immovable, monstrous iceberg.

Murdoch removed his cap and wiped his brow. He said, "Most of the berg's underwater. I'm afraid that sound was the ripping of our plates below our waterline."

Ice chunks fell on the forward deck as the ship grazed the iceberg. The *Titanic* continued its tortured, forward movement until the full effect of the commands took hold, and it gradually came to a virtual halt, only drifting forward slightly.

Murdoch touched a warning button and announced, "Closing watertight compartments." In a half minute, he threw the switch. He stared glumly at a stunned Moody.

Captain Smith burst through the doorway. "Good God! Did we hit something?" The Captain wore no tie, and his usual neat appearance looked disheveled—his hair mussed, his shirt unbuttoned, a greatcoat hanging loose about his shoulders. Then he said, "Iceberg?" But it seemed he knew it already. The Captain's brow was deeply furrowed.

Murdoch grabbed his arm and took him to the window. "Come, look out here." The two stared back at the wash of the ship. Murdoch pointed at a huge, dark shape and involuntarily shuddered. "There's the berg—it's a black one. I've heard them called black bergs, blue bergs, clear ice. Point is, you can't see them, especially in this flat water, with no waves . . . must be a hundred feet wide, twice or three times that tall."

"Tell me what happened," Smith demanded quietly.

Murdoch said to Smith, his voice quavering, "I

took over from Lightoller at ten p.m., and at 11:40, all hell broke loose. It happened so fast—only took ten or twenty seconds. Lookout Fleet shouted, 'Iceberg dead ahead!' over the telephone. I gave the orders— 'Hard-a-starboard'—away from the berg, you know. Then, 'Full speed astern.' My fault. My responsibility." Murdoch rested his hand on a brass control handle and seemed to gather his thoughts.

"Go on, man," Captain Smith urged.

"I tried to avoid the berg," Murdoch continued. "But it was the wrong thing to do, especially to go with 'astern.' I know that now. We lost momentum. The bow came around to port, all right, but slow, really slow. I thought at first we'd missed it. I was holding my breath. But she couldn't turn fast enough with the rudder off. We must have grazed the berg under the water level." Murdoch clenched a fist and pounded it into his other palm. "I don't think I handled this right at all." He removed his cap and ran his hand through his hair.

"What's done is done, lad." Smith rested his hand on the other's shoulder. "You reacted with your best instincts—no time to think. Did you close all the watertight doors?"

"Yes, sir."

"The lookouts didn't see the berg, didn't tell you in time?"

"In the water, that color of berg, it was nearly invisible. They saw it at the last second, called us as soon as they did. They have no binoculars up there."

"Were the lookouts hurt?"

"Not that I know of. They were secure enough— we didn't hit it head-on."

"Head-on might have been better," Smith muttered, more to himself than the other man. The Captain gripped the First Officer's arm. "But it's time for other actions now, my boy." He pulled out his gold nautical watch and checked the ship's time—11:50. "Stop all engines."

Murdoch repeated the order aloud and pulled the brass control handle. Deep below in the sea, the three huge propellors stopped churning. The great ship shuddered, and continued gliding slowly, majestically, trying to halt.

A bellowing, shrill sound came next as the engines shut down and the boilers sent steam shooting up through the three giant funnels into the frigid air and darkness that surrounded the ship. The sound was deafening, and showed no sign of stopping or diminishing.

Murdoch stared into the Captain's eyes. "What now, sir?"

"We need to see how sound the ship is. Get the ship's carpenter. And I have to see Tom Andrews— we'll inspect the damage together." He looked at Lightoller and Boxhall as they burst into the wheelhouse.

The Captain asked Darnell, "Did you see it hit?"

Darnell nodded. "Yes. I was looking for you, to tell you something . . ."

"There's hell to pay now."

Darnell said, "Yes . . . but, ah, I had some other news."

Smith seemed not to hear the remark and said, "Andrews designed the building of the ship—he'll know."

"Andrews will know . . . what?"

"How she stands. Thank God Tom's aboard. If anyone can put this thing right, he can." Smith buttoned his shirt, pulled his arms into his coat and buttoned it, and pulled his cap tight on his head. "We've got a rough time ahead of us tonight, Professor."

"I know your mind's totally on the ship, Captain," Darnell said, "but you need to know one thing—I've caught the killer—at least I've got a man who tried to kill me."

"The killer?" A puzzled expression flashed across the Captain's face, then one of comprehension sank in at last. "Oh . . . cabin thirteen. Then who is it?"

"Burton, your ship's doctor."

"Burton? Doctor Burton?" He frowned. "Ridiculous. I can't believe that. Why . . . ?"

"I don't know why, yet. He's in my cabin, tied up."

The Captain looked at his watch again. "No time to do anything about that now. We'll have to investigate, later, of course."

"He tried to poison me."

Smith's forehead furrowed. "One of our cabin thirteen deaths was by poison, that's true."

"Right. I'll just keep him in the cabin until you have time."

"Fine, fine. . . . Where's that carpenter?" he asked a junior officer as he returned from a search for him.

"On his way, Captain. And Mr. Andrews should be here soon. But, sir . . . I took a quick glance but didn't see any water below. Maybe the doors are holding."

Smith grunted. "We'll see. Thank you, lad."

Darnell spoke softly to Smith. "Captain, how serious is our ship's condition?"

"Serious enough." Smith gritted his teeth, his jaw stern. "Some damage to the hull, maybe small, we hope. Some water's pouring in, for sure. We'll see about repairs." He shook his head. "I don't know— we'll have to inspect her before I'll know any more. I don't think a cursory inspection could reveal the complete picture. Andrews is best qualified to know."

Darnell thought of Penny and felt pangs of concern. He had to get to her soon. He spoke urgently. "Captain, I've heard it said that the *Titanic*'s . . . well, unsinkable."

Smith nodded. "Practically unsinkable, yes, under normal conditions. But in this kind of situation, I just don't know. Andrews will." He paused, then spoke in a low voice. "Some watertight compartments may be flooded."

Darnell pressed, his heart racing. "To caution my friend, Penny Winters, about what to do now—what should I say?"

Smith returned Darnell's intense stare. "Tell her to put on warm clothes, her life jacket, and wait for officers to instruct her. She should be prepared for anything." Smith's grim, cold frown looked out of place on his usually complacent face. "I'm afraid, Darnell, it's going to be a damnably long, hard night."

Chapter Sixteen

Monday morning, April 15

As he ran from the wheelhouse, Darnell brushed past Chairman Ismay, wearing pajamas topped with an overcoat, heading in. Smith will give him the worst news of his life, Darnell thought. He raced across the deck and down the grand staircase steps to Penny Winters' cabin. He pounded on her door.

Penny opened the door, yawning. "Oh, John— what's happened?"

Darnell stepped in and closed the door behind him. "Trouble, Penny." He took her in his arms, held her close, kissed her, then stepped back.

She said, "Tell me honestly. Does it have to do with your case—your real purpose in taking this voyage?"

"No, Penny. It's the ship itself. It has struck an iceberg. You've got to get dressed right away."

Penny rubbed her eyes. "An iceberg? Is there danger? Why get dressed?" She searched his eyes for answers.

"Penny, we have to get up on the boat deck. I was on the bridge and saw the collision. It damaged one side of the ship—how badly they don't know."

"What did the Captain say?"

"He told me you should get dressed, putting on

warm clothes and your life jacket, and take instructions from the officers."

"A life jacket! My God! Is the ship going to sink?"

"Captain Smith said be prepared for anything."

Penny put her hand on his. "What do you think, John? Will it sink?"

"They're talking about repairs, but life jackets could mean abandoning ship—in lifeboats."

Penny looked about the room, thinking about clothes.

"Warm clothes, and your life jacket."

"We need to stay together, John."

"Yes. Now get dressed."

She whirled, went to a dresser, and grabbed underwear, long stockings. From a closet she took a thick dress, a sweater, and her fur. "I'll just be a minute." As she tossed her robe aside and ducked into the other room, he caught a glimpse of white skin through her nightgown and memories of the night before surged.

He sighed and turned his attention to finding her life jacket in a chest at the foot of the bed. Waiting for her, he could see the Captain was right—the long night was beginning.

After Penny dressed, Darnell strapped the life jacket on her and they hurried up to the boat deck. He found Second Officer Lightoller walking briskly toward the bridge. He stopped him with his hand on the officer's arm.

"This is Penny Winters, Herbert. I think you know her. Can I count on you to take care of her if I don't return right away? I have some things I must do."

"Of course, sir." Lightoller nodded. Turning to Penny, he said, "Sit here in this deck chair, miss. I'll be back as soon as I meet with the Captain."

Satisfied, Darnell held Penny briefly in his arms, promised to return as soon as he could, and he and Lightoller turned toward the bridge. Darnell looked back at her, and she smiled.

Passing by on the boat deck above the forward deck, he heard the sound of distant laughter. Someone called, "Throw me some more ice." Darnell looked down and saw men and older boys from second class on their deck. He and Lightoller watched for a moment as they played with chunks of ice from the iceberg, kicking them around, as if in a soccer game.

On the first-class deck, they saw a passenger take a chunk of ice into the smoker lounge. "Want a souvenir?" one said, holding out the ice. One passenger examined a chunk intently, as if to see what it could be made of other than ice, and put his tongue on it. There was talk and laughter.

But their laughter blended with new sounds of confusion among the few passengers who came on deck as the two men strode by them. Most questioned each other, or addressed Lightoller. "What happened?" Some asked Darnell the question, but he shrugged his shoulders and continued on his way.

"Better they find out from an officer," he said.

Lightoller stopped to speak to a woman passenger and told Darnell, "I'll catch up with you." As he hurried on, Darnell heard him say something to her like, "No need to worry."

Darnell thought of his valet, holding a revolver on Burton. He had to check on him soon. He decided to see the captain on the bridge first, then go quickly to his cabin, get a life jacket, decide what to do with his prisoner, and go back to see about Penny. He'd have to work fast.

When he reached the bridge, Darnell heard Thomas Andrews, the ship's architect, talking to the Captain. Smith stared at him, listening intently. "From what I've heard," Andrews said, "the iceberg grazed the ship below the waterline on the starboard side and damaged the steel plates of the first few watertight compartments. Water must be pouring into the compartments. That's our problem, Captain, and I have to tell you it's a devastating one."

Captain Smith glowered. "I know it's serious, Tom. But we locked the compartments down—won't that stop it? And can we repair the damage? Tell me something I don't know."

Andrews stared back at him. "The carpenter's making his inspection. But the only way to be sure is to see for ourselves. Let's go below—there's no time to waste." He turned, his loose coat flopping about his shoulders, the Captain following.

Professor Darnell fell in step behind them as they left the bridge. Andrews ignored Darnell's presence and led the way in a rapid tour below decks. Smith looked back at Darnell. "Come with us," he said. "Maybe you can carry word back."

When they reached the extreme lower forward holds and looked down into them from the stairwell landing, they heard rushing water pouring in.

"Damn," Andrews said, his frown deepening. "I don't like the sound of that, or the looks of it. It's worse than I thought."

As they entered a passageway and walked back through it, the captain said, "The squash court's swamped already."

They glanced in the post office room and saw that mail was floating in six inches of seawater and sloshing against the walls. Darnell caught the briny scent of the ocean, which made the reality of it all that much stronger.

"It's filling fast," Andrews said. "I've got the sense of it. Let's get back to the charts." He retraced his steps, the Captain and Darnell a few paces behind.

As they began their ascent, Darnell looked back down the long corridor and saw seawater inching forward, following them. Reaching the boat deck after some minutes, they burst into the wheelhouse. Andrews pulled out bulky sets of ship's blueprints.

Lightoller watched Andrews pore over the charts. Lightoller asked Darnell softly, "How bad is it?"

Darnell said, "The water's coming up fast. The mailroom and squash courts are flooded."

Lightoller shook his head. "We're in for it."

Andrews spread his blueprints out on a high table and turned to pages showing lower decks, boiler rooms, and watertight compartments. He gave Darnell a grim look, turned to Smith and spoke with deliberation. "E.J., this ship is designed for maximum buoyancy. She'd float even if several watertight compartments were filled. But plates in five compartments are damaged, and water is pouring directly into them from holes in the plates. The first compartments are filling fast. When one fills, it will flow over into the next."

Smith frowned. "Incredible! Can't we do repairs?"

Andrews shook his head, his face white and drawn. "Too many plates damaged, E.J. Gradually, all sixteen compartments will fill, one by one—you know, the domino effect. *Titanic's* bow will be dragged down. She'll sink by her head. There's already a forward list to her."

"Damn! So our famous 'watertight' compartments aren't watertight at all." Smith scowled, his face reddened with anger.

"Ordinarily the buoyancy would be sufficient, but not under these conditions, not when the bulkheads stop at E deck. To be safer, they'd have to go all the way to the main deck, to be capped off. As it is . . ." He stopped.

Smith stared at him. "Let's have it all, Tom."

"This ship, E.J.—our magnificent ship—is dying!" Andrews struck the table with his fist, hitting the corner. A drop of blood from his hand fell onto the charts. "It'll sink, and take us with it."

After a shocked silence, the Captain found his voice. "How long, Tom . . . how much time do we have?"

Andrews ran a hand through his tousled hair. "Based on what I've seen . . . we've got two hours, give or take. That's all."

There was a stunned silence on the bridge following his announcement. Darnell realized the stark reality of the ship's imminent death was beginning to sink into their consciousness, just as it was into his own. The bleak expressions of the Captain, the officers, and Andrews told Darnell the story. Their faces reflected their individual emotions—blends of amazement, dread, and resignation as to their fate. An abandonment of this ship on the high seas was unthinkable, but now very real. Penny—he'd have to tell her. But she'd already imagined the worst, even as he told her of the iceberg. *"Will it sink?"* she had asked.

Fourth Officer Boxhall expelled his breath in a half sigh, half sob, and said, "Mary, Mother of God!" He leaned on a chart table for support. "It's the end, then."

Smith stepped to Boxhall's side and gripped his arm. "Steady, boy. It's our duty to think of the passengers now."

Darnell stared at Smith, recalling the Captain, himself, bragging his life at sea was uneventful. The Captain had said he'd never faced a foundering of any of his own ships, never had a serious accident of any kind. Darnell wondered if the white-bearded, grand old captain of the line would be up to the task of dealing with a sinking ship. The next half hour would tell that tale.

Smith's brusque voice jarred Darnell out of his thoughts as the Captain barked orders to his officers. "Turn out all the stewards at once. Have them arouse the passengers, get them to dress warmly, with sweaters and coats, and put on their life jackets. Then get them up on the boat deck, as soon as humanly possible.

"Murdoch," Smith urged, "prepare to swing out lifeboats on the davits. You take the starboard side, and Lightoller will take port. Get the boats filled and lowered." He paused. "Women and children first, you know—but we must avoid panic at all costs. Tell the women it's a precaution. They can think it's for safety for themselves and their children to be off the ship during repairs, if they like. Otherwise they won't want to leave alone. Any questions?"

Murdoch hesitated, but in a moment said, "We've never had a drill, sir. Handling those davits can be tricky."

"Then this will be your drill and everything, all at once."

"What about the men, sir? What should we tell them?" Lightoller's expression was bleak.

"Just say they'll go in later boats. You can say that. The women will feel better about it when they hear that."

"Captain?"

"Yes, Herbert?"

Lightoller spoke again, with some hesitation. "Sir, we have only sixteen lifeboats and the four collapsibles—there isn't enough room for everyone."

Captain Smith growled, "I know, Herbert. Dammit, man, I can count—our lifeboats hold less than twelve hundred if filled to capacity—only half of our passengers and crew . . . but who would ever have thought we'd need more?" He wiped his brow. "Tell the men there'll be later boats. Just do your best."

Andrews stared out the window at the dark sea, his face ashen and drained. "Some of us wanted more lifeboats," he muttered to himself.

Darnell left the officers to their duties and ran back to his cabin. The ship's list to forward and starboard was now noticeable to him as he took the stairs, throwing him slightly off balance. But his mind shifted from the ship's problem to his own special one—the criminal in his cabin. He had left Sung there alone with him much too long. And Penny was alone, on deck. Darnell grimaced. Too much happening all at once.

As he reached his cabin, Darnell knew something was amiss, and he had a strange feeling everything had gone wrong. The door stood ajar. He pushed the door wide and looked at the sole occupant of the room. Sung lay on the floor, unconscious.

Dr. Burton was not in the cabin. The drapery sash hung loose about the base of the bedpost.

Darnell moistened a cloth with cool water, knelt down, and applied it to his valet's face. "Sung! Sung . . . are you all right?"

The valet groaned and opened his eyes. "The doctor. He worked hands loose somehow, hit me." Sung sat up and looked around the room. "He's gone!" He put a hand to an ugly-looking blue bump on his forehead and winced.

"Take it easy," Darnell said.

"Doctor said he felt sick, asked for water—I made mistake to give to him." Sung held his head with his two hands. "But your gun—it went under bed when I fell." He knelt down, reached under the bed, brought the revolver out, and handed it to Darnell.

Darnell pocketed the revolver. "Hold this cloth on your wound," he said. He brought Sung a glass of water. "Drink a little."

The valet complied and set the glass on the floor. "What now?"

Darnell put his hand on his valet's shoulder. "Sung, the ship's going to sink."

"Sink?" He stared wildly at Darnell. "The *Titanic*?"

"Yes. It hit a huge iceberg, sustained a big gash— water's pouring in." Darnell stood, impatient now to move on. "Get dressed—heavy clothes and strap on your life jacket. If we get separated, go to the boat deck and wait for word as to what to do. Penny is up there. All right?"

"Yes—but the doctor?"

"I'll have to find him and deal with him. Right now we have to be ready to abandon ship. They're going to be lowering boats. In two hours we might be adrift in the ocean, and this ship may be gone." But as he said it, he realized it was unlikely he and Sung would be in a boat at all. Women and children first.

"Professor . . . something I should tell you," Sung said, looking down at the floor.

"Yes?" Darnell's thoughts were about Penny now. He had to get back to her before they loaded her into a boat.

"I cannot swim."

"Damn." Darnell's thoughts swirled—he should never have brought Sung on this hellish trip. And Penny—he hadn't expected to fall in love with her. Now he knew he was responsible for their safety, both their lives, as well as his own. And he knew, whatever else happened, he'd have to save them. "Don't worry, Sung," he said. "We'll manage."

He strapped on his own life jacket on top of his overcoat, stuffed his revolver in a pocket. At his desk, he dipped his pen in the inkwell and wrote some words quickly on notepaper, blotted it, and put the sheet in an envelope, and in his coat pocket.

Sung returned from his room at that moment, working with his life jacket snaps over the top of his coat. "I'm ready."

"Then let's go," Darnell said. He took one last look around his cabin before he and Sung charged out the doorway. An ironic smile came as he saw the number 13 on the door. Unlucky number, indeed. They ran down the hallway toward the stairs and up to the boat deck where, he hoped, Penny still waited for him.

Chapter Seventeen

Monday morning, April 15

Doctor Gareth Burton rushed down the first-class passageway toward his cabin. As he passed a steward, the man said, "You're hurt, Doctor," and ". . . there's been some trouble on the ship."

"Trouble?" Burton stiffened and covered his puffed eye.

"An iceberg, sir, we hit one." The steward stepped closer and spoke in a softer voice. "We're supposed to reassure the passengers, tell them to dress and go on deck, you know, with their life jackets on. Like a drill, or something."

"But . . . ? Out with it, man!"

"But the ship is going to sink. I heard that from someone I believe—not just a rumor. And it'll be women and children first. I must go on now."

The steward continued down the corridor and knocked on a cabin door, calling out, "Passengers are requested on deck. Dress warmly. Bring your life jackets."

Burton rushed on to his own cabin. He rummaged in his closet and found an old dark blue crew coat and dungaree pants. He pulled them on, changed to sturdy sailor shoes, and took a blue stocking cap

from a box on a shelf. Odd articles he had accumulated over the years. His mouth twisted into a smirk,
seeing the box containing the crow's nest binoculars.
He pulled on the knit cap and surveyed the result in
a mirror—he could pass for a crew member.

Suddenly weary with it all, he felt a wave of his
familiar depression wash over him. He sat on the
side of the bed and tried to pull himself together.
He held his head in his hands, the shambles of his
life, now that he might also lose it, flashing through
his mind. His thoughts were producing a blurred-
red uncontrollable rage, and one clear thought came
through—he must kill the prying, accusing, meddling Darnell.

The face of his wife, who died of consumptive
tuberculosis when the Line sent him away on a voyage, haunted him. That was followed by images of
his daughter Emily—her long blond hair, tiny freck-
les on her nose, crinkles around her smiling brown
eyes, and her laughter's music. Yet Emily, the one
bright spot of his life, blamed him for her mother's
death, and pleaded to live with her American aunt.
Tears came as he remembered saying good-bye to
her, in her cabin, aboard the ship bound for America.

Now he jerked himself back to reality. He couldn't
bear to think of any more of that now, there was no
time. He steeled himself to what he had to do, deal
with the meddling professor. His own life was ruined, but he could take others down with him. Take
them down—yes! At the thought, he laughed—a
crazy, twisted laugh. Down into the sea! Had his
stealing of charts and binoculars caused the crash?
What a delicious irony!

Burton jumped up and tore out of his cabin. He
must get into a lifeboat. As he ran by an open cabin
door, he saw long dresses and coats lying on a bed.

Suddenly, he had an idea to disguise himself, ran into the cabin, closed the door, and pulled on a long dress, a woman's coat, and a black veil. He whirled around and was again running down the corridor in moments. Women and children first? He could follow that rule.

Now that Captain Smith had inspected the ship and heard Andrews' final opinion, he knew calls to other ships for help were essential. He hurried to the wireless room and found both operators, Phillips and Bride, ready for instructions.

"Send calls for help," Smith said. "And keep sending them. Don't be proud—tell them we're sinking. And let me know what ships you reach, where they are . . . and exactly how far away they are."

"It's true what we heard," Bride said, "that she's sinking?"

"Yes, lads. Tell them we only have an hour or two."

Phillips sat at the transmitter, finger poised. "I'll send CQD, the regulation distress call."

"Exactly. This is our latitude and longitude." He handed a sheet of notepaper to Phillips and turned toward the door.

Even before the Captain had stepped through the doorway to leave them to their work, Phillips began clicking out the standard distress call, CQD, followed by the *Titanic's* call letters. CQD—CQD, over and over.

As Darnell and Sung raced to the boat deck, they heard stewards running through the halls of the first-class section, knocking on cabin doors, shouting, "Emergency. Open your door."

Then as passengers opened doors and peered out,

the stewards repeated the same message, over and over, "Put on warm clothes, please, and your life jacket, as a precaution, and come to the boat deck." When passengers asked questions about the safety of the ship, the stewards answered, "No immediate danger."

Darnell shook his head at the politeness. "Please, save your own life," is how he interpreted it. Polite to the end, that's the way it would be, he knew, in first class, for both the crew and the passengers.

Just as Darnell and Sung reached the boat deck, they saw a rocket shoot into the dark night sky, flaring brightly high above their heads. Passengers let out shouts of wonder and fear at the wailing sound and the brilliant white flash above the ship. Darnell and Sung stood in the crowd and watched it burn, illuminating the ship and bathing the night sky with an eerie, ghostly light.

"They're signaling another ship," Darnell told Sung. "One must be near enough to see a rocket." His own words gave him hope.

A group of men stood near the rail behind a rope strung up to indicate a waiting area for them. He could see the women separately gathered closer to the lifeboats. "You stay here with these men," Darnell told Sung. "I'll be back soon."

He pushed forward through the growing crowds and the steady buzz of their talk about the ship. He heard snatches of conversation as he hurried by: "What's happening?" ... "Will it sink?" ... "Where's Mary?" ... "Isn't it unsinkable?" ... "Oh, my jewels!"

He reached the lifeboat deck where he had left Penny only to find she was not in sight. He searched for her for minutes with growing panic. He saw one lifeboat down in the water, holding only a small number of passengers. Crewmen pulled on their oars to move it away from the ship. He looked sharply at the passengers in the boat, but from the distance, he could not identify Penny as one of them.

At last, Darnell found Lightoller and grabbed his lapels. "Where's Miss Winters?" he demanded.

"Be calm, sir," the officer said. "She's right over there." He pointed to a group of women lined up to board the next lifeboat. Penny stood slightly apart from them. "She passed up the first boat—I couldn't get her into it."

Darnell rushed over to her. "Penny, you're still here."

"I couldn't leave without you, John."

"But you'll have to. Only women and children are going in the first boats. You should have gone in that one." He swept her into his arms and kissed her lingeringly. He held her tight, now afraid to let go. The conflicting feelings disturbed him. He had fallen in love for the first time and so soon had to say goodbye to her, perhaps never to see her again. But finally Darnell said, "You must board the next boat. I'll follow, of course, in a later boat." He couldn't help but think of Smith's words to his men on the bridge. Orders for deception, and now he was taking part in it.

"But what are you going to do now?" Penny's arms still held him in a tight embrace. She touched her cheek to his and spoke, her voice quavering. "Maybe it's women and children first, John. But I don't want to go without you."

Darnell grimaced. This was the difficult part— lying to her. "You'll go now—but I'll come along later. I promise. Don't worry. Right now I have to help out any way I can. There are many things to do." One, he thought, was to find Burton, before he killed again. He steeled himself not to break down in front of her.

Darnell turned toward the boats and walked her to a short line of only a few women, standing in front of the third boat.

Officer Lightoller was loading the women into it, one at a time. He spoke to a woman at the head of the line. "Just step into the boat, madam. It's perfectly safe."

A sailor in the boat helped the woman into it. Each woman in turn stepped into the boat. When Penny reached the lifeboat, Darnell said, "I won't say good-bye—just good night, for now."

Tears filled Penny's eyes as they kissed once more. "Good night, then. I . . . I love you, John."

"I love you, too." Darnell took from his pocket the notes he had written in his cabin and thrust the envelope into her coat pocket. "This is important, Penny."

She looked startled at his seriousness, but, hearing the officer urge her to move on, turned, and stepped across the two-foot gap between the ship and the lifeboat, and down into it. She looked back at Darnell with concern after she was seated.

"I love you," he called to her. She held a hand up in reply.

The sailors cranked the boat out on the davit, connecting lines lowering the boat slowly down to the ocean. With the list of the ship in the other direction, lifeboats had to be lowered from a height of sixty feet above the ocean and at an angle. It took several minutes to lower the boat. Darnell watched the procedure. When it hit the water, oarsmen pulled the boat away into the darkness. Darnell leaned out at the railing and waved to Penny, but was not sure whether she saw him. A deep, uncontrollable sense of loss swept over him. He swallowed hard, taking a deep breath. Now he must keep a sense of purpose.

Darnell stood at the rail, looking at the lifeboat Penny was in until he could see it no more, then headed back to the bridge. As he walked by groups of passengers, he heard a woman's high-pitched voice. "I'm not going in that boat—the *Titanic* is safer than that little thing." He shook his head in dismay.

He noticed the nature of the crowds—it seemed to be all first-class passengers, mostly well-dressed, women with their jewels on, and a few apparent second-class businessmen and students. No steerage passengers at all that he could see at this point, none appearing to be Irish or Italian or Southern European immigrants had yet reached the boat deck.

Another rocket fired, soaring into the sky with a surge of white light, making the sky momentarily bright as day. Distress rockets, Darnell knew, were one of the last resorts of a dying ship. The flaring of the rockets in the dark sky cast an umbrella of light over the ship, but as they died out, the returning gloom was even more foreboding than before.

As he reached the bridge, Darnell brushed against Chairman Ismay, who was leaving it. Ismay's clothes were disarrayed, his collar and tie loose. He seemed dazed, looked at Darnell blankly, and said only the words, "What a tragedy," as he hurried through the doorway.

Darnell glanced at the ship's clock—almost one a.m. He entered just as Captain Smith spoke to Officer Pitman. "Are the stewards getting the passengers on deck?"

"Yes, sir. But mostly only from first class so far. We're into the second class notices now."

The Captain scowled. "Dammit! Someday ships this big should have some way to notify everyone at once."

"A ship's telephone in every room, sir?"

"Something. Loudspeakers in the passageways. Why the hell not? It would save lives." Smith turned to Darnell. "Have you seen to the safety of your lady friend?"

"Yes—she's in a boat."

"My officers tell me we can't get people to take this seriously enough. The first boat was practically empty."

"I know. I saw it." Darnell frowned, puzzled. "Why not wait until they're full before lowering them? You could save more."

Smith scowled. "It takes time, dammit. We're lucky if we have only another hour and, maybe, fifteen or twenty minutes beyond that to uncover another fourteen boats, swing them all out, lower them under almost impossible conditions with this severe list. And then we have to deal with the four collapsible boats, get them loaded, too, and lowered into the water. We're listing more and more to the bow. Yet people still aren't convinced they need to go, and we can't wait for them."

"I heard one woman say the *Titanic* was safer than a little lifeboat. She wouldn't get into it."

"Exactly." The Captain took off his hat and wiped his brow, perspiring despite the cold weather. "But later . . . well, it'll be different later, when the truth strikes home."

Another rocket went off.

"Is there a ship near enough to see the rockets?" Darnell peered out the window at the dark sea.

Smith stepped to the window. "My men saw a light, ten, maybe fifteen miles away, in that direction.

It could be the *Californian*—they wired us earlier about ice, said they were stopping. It might be stopped there, that light might be theirs. But we can't reach them by wireless now—they probably shut it down for the night. We're hoping the rockets will stir them."

Darnell spoke with hesitation. "Dr. Burton escaped from my cabin. I don't expect to find him in all this turmoil, but I'll keep looking."

Smith dismissed the news. "His justice is waiting for him, as well as the rest of us." He paused, seeming to size up Darnell, then spoke. "There's something else you can do to help me."

"Of course. Name it."

"We don't have half enough officers to do what's needed in the next hour. I need someone to notify the steerage passengers of the disaster. They may have seen water moving up, but most of them may not know what to do. Get them to put on their life jackets and come up to the boat deck. Tell them to tear down the stairwell barriers if they have to. Here, take this gate key. You may need it."

Darnell nodded. "I'll try—but when I went down there, I noticed most of them don't speak English, and I don't speak any foreign languages." He thought, My classic Latin and Greek won't help me with this.

Smith rested a hand on Darnell's shoulder. "You'll find a way to communicate. They may not have much chance, but if we don't try at all, it will be just too late for them. You know how few boats we have. A little over an hour now, from what Tom Andrews said. So you'll need to start at once, if you go."

Darnell nodded. "I'll do it."

Smith put out his hand. "Thank you, John. I know

this isn't exactly in your line of work—but you'll save lives."

He shook the Captain's outstretched hand and said, "I'm on my way." As he left the bridge, he wondered whether he would ever see the captain again.

Darnell knew his way down to steerage from his tour of the third-class area earlier on the voyage. He shoved his way down the stairs through crowds of second-class passengers moving toward the boat deck. After ten minutes of struggle, he reached the third-class areas and unlocked a barrier. He found utter turmoil there. Many steerage passengers had crowded into hallways and stairwells, and he had difficulty passing them.

He saw others still sitting in their cabins, talking in foreign tongues. He could hear the sounds of prayers. One older woman repeated, *"Madre de Dios,"* over and over again.

Larger groups congregated in the dining room. They seemed to be waiting for instructions, although water in lower stairwells was creeping up, just a few feet below their deck, and could be seen by those near the stairwells. The immigrants were schooled in taking orders, and they patiently waited for them, seeming to expect everything to be all right when help came from the authorities.

Darnell ran from cabin to cabin, pounding on locked doors, throwing doors open that were unlocked, urging passengers to get dressed, to get their life jackets on. But he saw the futility of it, since most could understand nothing he said, and did not respond. He needed interpreters.

He burst into the dining room and shouted above the din of voices, "Does anyone understand English? English? Anglo? *Ingles?*" He shouted it several times until the room quieted down enough for several persons to answer, "Yes." . . . "*Sí*." . . . "*Oui*."

"Come up here," he urged, and jumped up on a table. Three passengers came up to him. "What other languages do you speak?" he asked.

"Spanish," said one, "and some Italiano."

Another said, "French."

And a third said, "Gaelic—Irish, you know."

"Good. Now I want you to repeat everything I say, every word, each of you one at a time, loud, in your own native language, so everyone can hear."

The three nodded.

He addressed the crowd in a loud voice. "The *Titanic* is sinking. It hit an iceberg. It is sinking. I must talk to you." Only a few people stirred, but the noise level increased as they talked among themselves. He repeated the warning and nodded to the three interpreters.

Each of the three repeated his words, first in Spanish, next in Italian, then French, and finally Gaelic. After each new language announcement, the babble and din of the crowd reached a higher crescendo. Women screamed, and their children cried in response. Each time, the interpreter would have to shout more loudly. The crowd moved forward, surrounding the table tightly. More and more shouted after the announcements, until Darnell felt it was like waves on a shore, cresting, dying down, cresting.

He shouted again. "Put on your life jackets. You must wear them. Tell the others." Darnell shouted it. His interpreters repeated it, one by one. Some shoved their way desperately out of the room. Some stood in place, still looking confused and afraid. A few ran into the hallways, knocking others down in the rush, heading for their cabins.

Darnell called out, "Wait! Hear this! Get your children together. Find life jackets for all of you. Go through the second-class area, or break through the barriers. Get up to the boat deck. Get to the lifeboats." Darnell shouted it twice, although he knew few understood him. But the interpreters repeated it in their native tongues, and others moved out the doorways. But many stood and talked excitedly with each other.

From his position atop the table, he watched the growing pandemonium, satisfied he had done all he could. He could see many would not move. With the help of interpreters he gathered up two dozen women and led them upward, through second class.

His message in the steerage took hold slowly. Stewards and passengers pounded on cabin doors, to notify others. Some went into their cabins and pulled on their life jackets, and put them on their children. Many gathered up their meager belongings. Some refused to leave their cabins. But gradually a migration of steerage passengers toward the upper decks took form. They found the second-class route, broke down barriers, and struggled upward with their children and baggage. They left their comfortable haven in the ship's bowels with an expectation of safety above.

Meanwhile, Darnell reached the boat deck with his small contingent of women. He placed them in the care of an officer who was congregating women from the first and second class for boarding boats, smiled, and said, "*Arrivederci,*" and "*Vaya con Dios.*" As he walked away, his mind still swirled with images of the crowds of haggard, frightened, trusting people below. He would never forget the sight of them, huddled together with their families and small, precious possessions, not knowing quite what to do, or who or what to trust. Now at least this small group could see the sky once more. He hoped more would arrive soon.

While he elbowed his way through the crowds on the boat deck toward the lifeboats, a rocket flared into the sky again. He clicked the case of his watch open and saw it was 1:30 a.m. Darnell knew the ship did not have much longer. He wondered how many lifeboats remained, how many minutes the helpless souls on deck had left before being plunged into the icy ocean. He realized, thinking of them in that detached way, that he, too, was one of them.

Chapter Eighteen

Monday morning, April 15

The images of the immigrants in steerage that Darnell brought up with him to the boat deck contrasted sharply with those he confronted as he made his way through the now teeming and more desperate masses of passengers. They were still almost all first-class, with a smattering of second class, mostly those he had seen in the dining room, enjoying the fine crystal and vintage wine, listening to the Captain's tales at his table, and sharing their own stories of high finance and high fashion with each other. They were the chosen few.

Earlier he had glimpsed the millionaire Guggenheim on deck in a long coat and life jacket. Now he saw him again, dressed in full evening clothes, just as his valet was. Darnell thought, He's lived this way all his life, dressed in tuxedos and dinner jackets, and he'll die the same way. The millionaire's way.

Bruce Ismay still looked disheveled, seemingly unaware of his appearance, but now wore a life jacket. He was trying to help, but intruded himself into the duties of the officers. He paced back and forth between the lifeboats shouting, "Get them loaded quickly. You must lower the boats. There isn't much time."

He tried to order officers to lower boats only partially filled, but they resisted. Darnell saw it as panic, although he knew there was truth in the feeling that time was slipping away.

Finally, in exasperation, one officer told Ismay, "Let us do our work, sir, dammit. You're not helping us, you're hurting." Scowling, Ismay stomped off in another direction, perhaps, Darnell thought, to the far side of the ship to find other officers he might find more amenable.

Darnell spotted a passenger sitting quietly in a deck chair, observing the procedures in a detached manner, petting his dog. The little dog appeared as complacent amid all the din as did his owner, who continually stroked the dog's head.

At one lifeboat, Darnell saw John Jacob Astor with his young wife, who had formed such a close attachment to Penny. The thought of her, carrying the millionaire's child, and the parting the newlyweds were facing at this moment, seared his thoughts.

Astor was speaking to his wife. "Madeleine, you must listen to me. I can't go in this boat with you, not this one. Women and children are being taken off first. That's the way of it."

As Darnell walked up to them, Astor turned to him eagerly. "I'm trying to explain the procedure to my wife, Professor. Maybe you can help." He turned to his wife. "Listen to Professor Darnell, Madeleine. You remember him."

Madeleine Astor looked at Darnell and asked, "Did Penny get off the ship? Into a lifeboat?"

Darnell nodded. "Yes, Madeleine. I put her in a while ago. It's a precaution we must take, so there'll be no danger to women and children while they're doing repairs. We'll no doubt find space in a later boat. Perhaps everyone in lifeboats will even be brought back and reboarded."

"You see, dear? Now you must believe me."

"Yes," Darnell said. "You must trust your husband, the one man on this ship, the one man in the world I'm sure you place your greatest trust in."

Astor nodded and gripped his wife's two hands. "You see? And we have to think of our child that you're carrying. You know I'll follow later if need be. And if we're separated, and get picked up by different ships, I'll see you in New York."

Astor took her in his arms and embraced her. They kissed tenderly. Then his tone became firmer. "Now we must get you on board this boat." He took her arm and edged her forward, toward the officer in charge.

"Step right in, madam," the officer said. He held her arm and helped her make the large step across and down into the lifeboat, virtually lifting her into the boat. Madeleine Astor seated herself and looked back at her husband. She raised one hand in a farewell gesture. John Jacob Astor smiled and waved a good-bye. His lips formed the words silently, "I love you."

As the ship lowered, Astor took Darnell's hand and said, "I can never thank you enough." Astor walked away toward the smoking lounge. Darnell wondered if he would ever see him again.

Familiar faces reminded Darnell of the vast wealth and prestige of the mostly American first-class passengers. Major Archie Butt, President Taft's military aide, standing with Colonel Archibald Gracie, a military historian. An American mystery-story writer, Jacques Futrelle, talking seriously with his wife.

Darnell came up to Isidor Straus, the founder of a vast department store empire, and his wife, whom he'd met at the Captain's table. They glanced at Darnell. Mrs. Straus was speaking to an officer. "I won't leave my husband."

Mr. Straus pleaded, "Please, dear, you must go. All the women are going."

She shook her head defiantly. "You waste your breath, Isidor. I simply will not leave you. Can you help, Professor?"

Darnell spoke to the officer. "Look here, he's an old man—can't they go into the boat together? There's room."

"It is women and children only," Straus said.

The officer stiffened. "And I have my orders. I can't go against them."

"Then it's settled. I stay," Mrs. Straus said. She entwined her arm in her husband's. "Let's go into the lounge, dear, where we can sit and talk. A lot of people are waiting there."

Darnell moved on, shaking his head. He'd heard that some men were going into half-filled boats on the other side of the ship. But he was beginning to see that first-class passengers, and a few second-class, by the nature of early notification and their status, and being near the top decks, were getting first priority. Not many steerage passengers had yet reached the boat deck. The crew below still worked to keep the ship operative for the Marconigram messages, and for lighting. And the band still played lively tunes at their post, on deck, trying to cheer up the forlorn passengers with their music.

Officers loading boats dealt with a multitude of problems. They had difficulty persuading passengers to leave the giant ship and enter the small lifeboats. They called out to the crowd, seeking crewmen to row the boats, asking, "Does anyone have experience on the sea?" Some stepped forward, saying they did, and they were placed in the boats.

Still, boats were far from full to capacity. Darnell watched three of them being lowered and estimated they were only half full, on the average. He wondered if Ismay had sent boats down that could have been filled.

Suddenly, a surge of people swept onto the deck, and Darnell could tell by their clothing they were from steerage. They rushed to the boat-loading area and clamored for seats. A few were able to convince officers, who seemed to be giving preference to first class, to load them, too. One girl said, "My mother's in that boat," and they allowed her to take a seat.

The crew of the *Titanic* seemed to have no chance at all to enter a boat. They stood, watching the proceedings, as if they had a duty to wait, to let passengers board first. But gradually, as the minutes wore on, more crewmen and staff entered the boats.

Darnell needed a sense of purpose and headed for Officer Lightoller to see if he could help the officers in any way. If he could keep busy, it would keep his mind away from the tragedy he knew would be the fate of most of the passengers surging about the decks, searching for some security or salvation. As Darnell worked his way through the crowds, a sharp blow on the back of his head sent him crashing to the deck, striking his forehead on the hard wood. His world went black.

Cold water pouring onto his face brought Darnell back to consciousness. A worried-looking Sung stood over him. He said, "Professor, Professor."

Darnell opened his eyes. His head throbbed as he sat up and brushed the water from his eyes. "God." He winced, dizzy and nauseous. He touched the back of his head and his forehead gingerly, feeling swelling but no blood.

"Must've been Burton. Did you see him, Sung?"

"Not sure. I hear shouts, 'Man down.' I see you, lying here. Many men, women running."

"Thanks for getting the water."

Darnell tried to stand but thought better of it. "Dizzy," he said.

"I help you," Sung said. He gripped Darnell's right arm and brought him to his feet, leaning Darnell against the wall. "Stay there for a moment."

Darnell nodded. He didn't feel like moving. "So Burton's still aboard, and still dangerous. Have to find him."

"Crowd is getting dangerous, too," Sung said. "They are worried, fighting over boats."

Darnell checked his pocket and found the cold, steely assurance of his revolver there. "Let's see what we can do."

Darnell and Sung struggled through the growing masses of passengers milling about, some seeming not to know what to do. Women obediently lined up by boats. Darnell was amazed at the orderliness of the crowd. But he heard the impact of their fears in the words of the passengers—in their good-byes, in their voices: "Hold Mommie's hand." . . . "I'll see you in New York, my dear." . . . "Give this ring to my wife, if, you know, I don't make it."

Some without life jackets ran back toward the cabins to get them and came out, strapping them on.

A small girl of three or four years stood against the wall, crying. Darnell bent down. "Where's your mommie?" he asked.

"I don't know." The little voice interrupted her sobs. "She went away."

Darnell picked her up and carried her to the nearest officer. "This child has lost her mother. Take care of her, will you?"

At last Darnell and Sung reached the area of the forward lifeboats. Darnell came up to Second Officer Lightoller, who was supervising the loading of a boat. He asked him, "How many boats left, Herbert?"

Lightoller frowned. "Not many. Two on this side. One or two on the other. Of course, there're four collapsibles, but they're harder to deal with. We'll get to them last."

Four burly men, looking like blacksmiths or farmworkers, approached the crowd from the rear. One called out to Lightoller in a gruff, accented voice, "Make way, we're getting on that boat. You try to stop us, it's your funeral."

Lightoller raised his hands and shouted back, "Men, listen to me—it's women and children only. Would you take the place of a child?"

Darnell had worked his way through the crowd, behind Lightoller. He pulled out his revolver and fired it into the air, once, twice. The explosions shocked everyone nearby, and the four men stopped. Darnell shouted at them, "This boat is for women and children. If you're a woman, a child, or have a child with you, step forward. Anyone else will have to get by me, and this." He brandished the gun.

The four men retreated several steps, then turned and walked away from the boat. One of them looked back and shouted angrily at Darnell, "I'll remember your face, Mr. Dandy."

Lightoller gave Darnell a grim smile. "Thanks. That saved this boat, but we're losing valuable time." He hurried the women along into the boat.

Darnell stood to one side and watched several

women step into the lifeboat. He thought of Penny out on the dark sea in her lifeboat. Was a lifeboat as safe as the officers said? Or could it capsize and drown its passengers if the seas became rougher? But there wasn't much choice—the *Titanic* had little time left.

He shivered with the thought. To Lightoller he said, "I'll see what else I can help with. I'll be back to give you a hand with the collapsibles." Darnell knew he needed to stay busy to keep his mind off the inevitable calamity.

He watched the crew throw overboard anything that could float—wooden steamer chairs, barrels, tables—to give passengers something to cling to after the ship went down, and helped them toss the wooden material over. Not many men would get into boats, he thought. Maybe it would help them.

Aware of Burton's renewed presence, he stayed alert, searching the deck about him, knowing Burton was aggressive now, and not afraid to show himself. Sung stayed close to him.

Passing the wireless room, Darnell pulled open the door and asked Phillips and Bride, "Any news, Sparks?"

"We're sending, sending," Phillips said. He looked up at Darnell. "Most ships are too far away. We reached one ship, the *Carpathia*. It's not too close, either, but it changed course, and it's steaming toward us as fast as it can travel, considering the ice floes. We've told the captain, we keep him informed."

"How long will it take?" Darnell asked, guessing the answer to his question.

"Not soon enough, I'm afraid," Phillips said. "At least not before we . . . go down. The *Carpathia*'s at least four hours away."

As Phillips spoke, Darnell watched the blue

sparks underneath his finger fly at the telegraph key. Thank God for Marconi, he thought, and this new technology. "What signal are you sending?"

"Morse—CQD. And our call letters."

Darnell said, "Why don't you send that new signal? What is it—SOS? 'Save our souls,' they say. It's supposed to be easier to send and identify."

Harold Bride nodded. "I was thinking of that. Do it, Jack. It's the new international rule. And we may never have another chance to send one—" Bride bit his lip. "I didn't really mean it that way."

As Darnell listened, he heard the telegraph take on a different rhythm—three short, three long, three short, then switching to a different sequence for the *Titanic's* call letters, then back again, the pattern repeated, with SOS, and the call letters again. It went on and on several times, as he stood there.

"I'll move on now," he said. "Thanks, men. We all appreciate your devotion." He closed the door and stepped out on the deck where Sung waited. "We have to help with the boats, soon," he said. "But there's a killer still on board, and I have to do everything I can to find him."

"Let him drown."

Darnell shook his head. "He may drown, and we all may. But I've got a duty to try to capture him if I can. And I guess I take it personally when someone tries to kill me."

Chapter Nineteen

Monday morning, April 15

As Darnell and Sung edged through the crowds, they came to a haggard-looking Captain Smith, walking in the opposite direction.

"Darnell," Captain Smith said, grasping his hand. "I heard what you did in third class to help them. I am in your debt."

"I'm glad I could help. How much time do we have left, Captain?"

"A half hour, or a little more. The ship's list to the bow is getting worse by the minute. When the time comes, lad—well, good luck." Smith put his hand out again and took Darnell's in his. "God be with you."

Darnell and Sung moved along the deck and ducked inside the smoking lounge, to cut across to a little-used service stairwell. The ship's architect, Andrews, sat by himself, away from groups of other passengers who sat at tables. He wore his dinner jacket, collar loose, no life jacket or outer coat. He stared off into space. He had a drink in his hand and looked like he'd had several already.

Darnell walked up to him, while Sung held back several paces. "Aren't you coming up on deck, Mr. Andrews?" he asked.

Andrews shook his head. "No. But good luck to you, sir." His eyes were bleary, but his voice steady. "Much of this was my fault." He sighed. "For me— well, I'll never reach New York, never salute the Statue of Liberty. Always wanted to . . ." His voice trailed off and he took a large swallow of his drink.

Darnell wished him good luck but received no reply, just a nod of his head. He could see the man would not try to save himself. Was it guilt— punishing himself for a bad ship design? They shook hands, and Darnell and Sung left the architect sitting alone, with his own dark thoughts.

They took the stairwell down to D deck, splashed along a watery hallway to the glassed-in infirmary and hospital rooms, and Burton's offices. The floors slanted sharply forward, more noticeably down there below decks, with inch-deep seawater. Darnell knew the water was filling so fast now that this deck would be fully underwater soon.

"If Burton's hiding anywhere, he'll be here," Darnell said. He entered the infirmary rooms cautiously, revolver in hand. They sloshed through the water in the reception area and into the receiving and examination rooms. Sung stayed several feet back.

Darnell checked first one side of the darkened room, then the other, and behind them, as they walked. Their shadows wavered on the walls in front of them from the one reception desk lamp which still burned brightly.

Sung whispered, "Professor?"

"Yes?"

"You think he is here?"

Preoccupied, Darnell gave no answer. He examined Burton's desk. His stethoscope, a black bag, and gloves lay on the desk. Two photographs rested on it. Darnell picked up the larger photo—Burton, with a middle-aged woman, her arm linked with his, standing in front of a modest home. The second, a smaller oval photograph in a glass frame, was the one he had seen when he interviewed Burton. He shook his head as he looked at it more closely—a winsome young girl with a delicate smile and wispy blond hair, standing next to Burton. Each had an arm around the other. His daughter.

"He's not here," Darnell said. "I'd say he never came back here. If he had, he wouldn't have left these pictures." He thrust the oval photo into his coat pocket, wondering whether Burton's twisted mind had blocked his memory of the precious photos, or whether the man was simply desperate to escape capture.

Feeling the water creep higher around his shoes, he knew it was time to give up the search. He said abruptly, "We need to get back on deck."

He hurried through the door, Sung following. The water was at least an inch higher than when they began their search. Darnell and Sung retraced their route, slogging through the water as the ship listed more dangerously toward the bow, making their passage more difficult. He felt an eeriness about it, almost a dizziness, walking at what seemed an angle just to stay upright.

They reached the lounge, finding Andrews still sitting, still drinking. They exited to the deck without speaking to him, and Darnell led the way to the boat deck.

As they walked up the outer stairs to the boat deck, a collapsible boat was being lowered, almost full of women and children. Darnell saw "collapsible" meant the boat was smaller, with canvas sides that fastened upright, making it lighter, able to be uprighted and floated, without mechanical devices.

As it reached a level six feet below the deck on its way down to the ocean, a large woman clothed in an ankle-length flouncy dress, a hat, and a full veil climbed over the railing and jumped into the boat. He was surprised at her daring to make the jump.

But as he watched, Darnell realized it wasn't a woman. Below the hemline of the dress showed a man's trousers and shoes—it was a man dressed as a woman. Darnell shouted, "Stop him!" But it was too late. The boat was already twelve to fifteen feet down, dropping fast. The man in women's clothes looked up at Darnell from his seat, lifted the veil, and bared his teeth.

"Damn, it's Burton!" Darnell shouted. He pulled out his revolver, trained it on Burton, but saw that women were crowded too closely on both sides of the doctor. He couldn't take the chance. He watched with frustration as the boat touched the water.

The two sailors in it quickly pulled away with boat oars, apparently anxious to move away from the expected undertow of the ship when it would sink. Darnell glared at the boat and Burton's smirking face until they faded into the gloom of the night.

"Not much left to do now, Sung," he told his valet. "Let's find Lightoller."

As they walked toward the bridge, Darnell heard the strains of music coming from the stern—the ship's band still playing, duty-bound, it seemed, to perform right to the end. They played sprightly songs to provide comfort to those who had no boats to go to, for those who had resigned themselves to their fate, standing at the rail, holding on to it, with its false security.

The band was playing a lively ragtime tune, but Darnell found no cheer in it. The music stopped, and, when it resumed, the sound of an old hymn, solemn but uplifting, wafted above the hubbub of the crowds of passengers.

Another surge of steerage passengers swept out onto the deck, frantic, anxious now to enter lifeboats, but found they had all been lowered. A few stokers came on deck, their duty done below. They could see their fate, also, was bleak, with no means of survival other than their life jackets.

The ship's list was extremely pronounced now, some of its cabin lights at the bow already submerged underwater, and Darnell and Sung struggled in their efforts to move in that direction, toward the collapsibles. Any remaining collapsible boats would be above the wheelhouse at the bow, ahead. Darnell and Sung kept a balance holding to the rail and pushed forward.

Water poured steadily over the bow toward them now, flooding the deck with a foot of water. As Darnell reached the bow, a collapsible was about to be lowered, quite full with passengers now, as they understood the danger. He watched as Director Bruce Ismay stepped up to the boat and asked whether he could board it. The officer in charge nodded, and Ismay stepped into the boat, taking the last empty seat, and it was lowered away. Only one collapsible remained now, secured on the top of the bridge house.

Passengers surged in the opposite direction, toward the stern, urged and shoved along by the throngs around them, a moving, heaving mass of humanity. Some fell and were trampled on, and women's screams filled the air. Those who reached the stern, with its deceptive feeling of greater safety, crowded together, awaiting the final flood. Darnell and Sung pushed forward, finding room to squeeze by, sometimes being jabbed or shoved by passengers going the other way.

A number of dogs ran about the deck, and Darnell realized the kennels must have been opened and the dogs brought out. He saw Captain Smith standing near the bridge speaking to several officers. "Men," he said, "I'm discharging you now. You've served your ship well. You've done all you can, above and beyond your call of duty, and you've helped to save our passengers. Now, lads—if you can—try to save yourselves. And God be with you." That has the sound, Darnell thought, of an epitaph.

He watched Captain Smith go back to the bridge. The man's shoulders were bent, as he seemed to suffer from his years and the burden of the last hours. What images and memories and regrets must be filling the Captain's mind, Darnell thought. After years of uneventful service, perhaps looking forward to his retirement and resting in his final years, now he must face the ultimate calamity of a sea captain—losing his ship.

And, rightly or wrongly, would Smith take the responsibility on himself for the loss—not taking ice warnings seriously enough, going too fast, not being on the bridge himself when it happened to give better orders? Darnell knew enough of the dedication of the man to feel that Smith would indeed take that burden and responsibility. And perhaps take it with him, at the end, to his sea grave, unable to share it with anyone. It was the tradition, wasn't it, Darnell thought—the captain going down with his ship?

Chapter Twenty

Captain Smith's final words to his officers—*"Save yourselves. And God be with you."*—rang in Darnell's head as he neared the bridge. He found Second Officer Lightoller struggling along with some crewmen to remove the last collapsible boat from its moorings, positioned atop the officers' quarters. Darnell clambered up the ten feet to where they were, Sung alongside him. "Grab that oarlock," he called out to Sung, his voice strident, louder than the noises of the crowd below and the men working on the boat. "Hang on, and push when they push."

"All together now," Lightoller shouted. Six men, three on a side, fixed handholds on the oars, the oarlocks, or the canvas, and pushed in unison. As the boat became free, a huge wave crashed over the bow toward them and flipped the boat upside down to the deck. The men jumped down, but moments later the waves swept the boat into the sea.

The boat dragged the men along—shouting and cursing, tumbling backward, as it took them into the maelstrom of swirling water. The force of it flushed them down into the depths of the sea. Some, such as Harold Bride, clung to the boat, while others were thrown loose. As he hit the water, Darnell took a last, deep breath and held it as he was pushed below the surface of the freezing water. The cold shocked his body, and he was afraid he would lose the precious air in his lungs.

The ship's bow angled sharply down, foundering, with ocean waves seeming to rush back toward the stern as the bow sunk forward. The ship now sloped into the ocean at a forty-five-degree angle, seeming almost fixed in that position, but imperceptibly inching more and more into the water. Terrified screams from passengers at the stern racked the air as the waves swamped them. Some jumped over the side into the ocean as others dived straight into the water, trying to swim into the waves.

The waves engulfed them and scattered them irresistibly in all directions. Some were able to grab deck chairs and tables that were floating by or within swimming distance. The sea sucked others into the depths. Those who lived floundered, stunned, adrift in the unforgiving icy sea, their clothes soaked, nothing between them and a freezing death except their life jackets and a will to live.

The waves held Darnell downward, a dozen feet under the surface, in the freezing cold of the sea. He thought his lungs would burst until suddenly he was thrust upward to the surface by a force emanating from the ship. Maybe it's air, he thought, blasted from one of the ship's huge funnels. Gasping and choking, he tried to keep his head above the water and discover where he was.

He struck his head on an obstacle and found himself in a dark airspace, bumping another unseen person. His teeth chattered and the cold salt water he swallowed gagged him, made his throat sore and his stomach nauseous. Darnell struggled to breathe as he flailed about in the water.

Someone in the dark next to him gasped also, and cried out, "Help, help!" Darnell recognized Sung's anguished voice, with a panic he had never heard in it before.

"It's me, Sung. I'm here," he answered, and at that moment Darnell's fogged mind cleared and he realized they were in an air pocket under the upside-down collapsible boat. He knew they must get out, and on top of the boat.

He reached out and grasped Sung's arm and held him up, flailing in the water with his other arm. "We're under a boat, Sung, and we have to get out of here. I know you can't swim, but do your best. Take your deepest breath. Duck under the edge, and then come back up again. Kick hard with your legs—it'll help keep you on the surface now, and bring you up when you go under. I'll be there to help you. All right?"

Sung coughed and sputtered from the seawater he inhaled. "Yes. I try."

"I'll go first, and you go immediately after me. I'll catch you when you surface."

Darnell took a deep breath, submerged several feet, pushed outward and upward through the water. He kicked and pulled his arms up toward the surface and emerged two feet from the edge of the boat. He grasped the flat canvas side of the boat, which had not been raised, and held tight. He watched for Sung to appear, but was afraid of the worst, that Sung might not make it.

He dove down a few feet and bumped against Sung's body. He grabbed him by the life jacket and hauled him to the surface. Sung gasped for air, spit and sputtered and coughed, and beat the water with his arms. Darnell stroked back the few feet toward the boat with one arm, holding Sung with the other.

When they reached the edge he told Sung, "Hang on here." He climbed on the topside of the capsized boat, where a number of men, mostly crew, already sat or lay, exhausted by their experience, some hurt and groaning in pain. He recognized wireless operators Bride and Phillips.

Phillips lay still, eyes closed, his legs dangled in such a way Darnell suspected they were broken. Bride's legs were caught under the body of a crewman. With difficulty, his own body and Sung's both slippery and wet, Darnell pulled Sung aboard, and they, too, lay silent except for coughing and sputtering as they tried to catch their breath. Darnell spit out seawater, tasting the bitter salt on his lips. He patted Sung on the back and smiled. "So far, so good."

Darnell sat up and looked about the boat. At least ten other men were on it. He was glad to see Officer Lightoller at the bow of the boat. Lightoller looked bedraggled and water-soaked himself but seemed in charge of the craft. Darnell raised his hand in greeting, and Lightoller gave a short salute in return.

All around them, passengers floated in the dark ocean, crying out for help from the lifeboats. Few of the boats had lights, and there was little ambient light. To Darnell, it seemed the steady wailing of the unfortunate victims blended into one stark, heart-piercing composite scream in the dark. Sung covered his ears.

Darnell stared at the *Titanic*, far into the sea at the bow, slipping gently but inexorably below the waves. A creaking, groaning sound came from the ship, and Darnell watched, awestruck, as the *Titanic* moved deeper and deeper into the ocean. Smoke and sparks rushed out of the funnels. Portholes disappeared from sight, one by one, as the great ship moved below the surface.

A thunderous sound came from the ship. Darnell caught his breath at the sound. He wondered if it could be the huge boilers exploding and crashing through the entire vessel. He suspected the ship was cracking apart. The ship's lights burned brightly to the last second. Then suddenly the lights totally blacked out, flickered on briefly once more, then went out again, plunging the ship and the ocean around it into complete darkness.

The *Titanic*'s bow was poised in a virtually motionless posture, at a bizarre angle, the stern seemingly broken off. Then began its relentless slide beneath the surface, inch by inch, foot by foot. Whether the ship was in one piece or two, Darnell wasn't sure, but it was all soon swallowed up by the sea.

A short dead silence among the floating, wailing passengers and those fortunate enough to be in lifeboats followed the stunning, awesome, unthinkable sight of the sinking of the huge vessel. What once dominated the seascape was gone, nothing but ripples on the water and a vapor of smoke to mark her departure.

But after a few moments, the stark cries of those in the ocean quickly resumed in an even greater crescendo of wails and screams. Some called out, "Help me!" Some cried uncontrollably. Others screamed, "God save me!" The sounds of their plaintive voices cut straight into Darnell's heart. He closed his eyes to block out the sounds, but it didn't help.

The largest ship in the world, an unsinkable giant, had lived less than three hours after it had struck the iceberg. What chance did they have in their relatively tiny lifeboats?

Darnell asked Lightoller, "How soon do you think the rescue ship will arrive?"

"The wireless boys reached the *Carpathia* about midnight. They were four hours away then."

"Right. So it could be soon?"

"God help us, I hope so."

What the night ahead held for them, Darnell could not predict. The moonless night offered no comfort, and only the stars provided cold light. Nothing but the flickering lights in the distance from the few lifeboats with lanterns aboard gave any sense of man having any hope or control over his destiny. The sea was calm as a pond at that point, but Darnell was concerned a rising squall in the dawn could end that and swamp their unstable, capsized boat.

The collapsible was listing heavily to one side. Too many men were on one edge. Lightoller blew his whistle to get the survivors' attention. "Spread out," he ordered. "Balance the boat."

The survivors moved painstakingly and slowly into new positions. Darnell positioned himself near Officer Lightoller and next to Sung, to offer his valet whatever protection he could. Gradually the stability of the boat improved enough that the men settled into fixed places. The one woman survivor with them was now in the center of the craft, the safest spot, surrounded by the men.

Disembodied voices floated eerily across the water from nearby boats. A woman's high-pitched voice pierced the air, saying, "Let's go back—we can save some." Angry sounds of arguments disputed what to do. A man's gruff voice said, "We'll capsize."

Gradually, the lifeboats drifted farther and farther apart in the dark. Darnell heard a few boats circle back and pick up a handful of survivors. Lightoller shouted encouragement to one boat that came near. "Go after them. More can be saved."

Minutes passed. An hour. Voices from passengers floating in the sea weakened, and fewer cries for help from the passengers could be heard as they succumbed to the freezing temperature of the sea. Darnell knew the icy cold ocean would claim them all, even some of those in lifeboats, if help didn't arrive in time. Those in the ocean could never last until a rescue ship found them.

Chilled, wet to the skin, shivering, Darnell was nauseous with the sense of death in the sea all around them. Several more men swam to the boat and others pulled them aboard, until men covered every inch of the hull. They clung to the edge and underside of the boat, the only handholds.

Waves splashed onto the overturned hull, warning constantly that rougher seas could completely engulf the small lifeboat, and toss it and the men on it into the ocean. If that were to happen, he had to accept the certainty of an icy death. The unstable craft rocked back and forth dangerously in the quickening sea. There was no way for even an experienced officer like Lightoller to steer it.

Darnell caught a glimpse in the dark of a man who looked like Captain Smith floating in the sea thirty yards away. He wore no cap, but Darnell saw a flash of familiar white beard. The man called, "Ahoy, ahoy." Darnell called back, "Captain?" But the man slipped away, moving in another direction or slipping under the waves, and Darnell lost sight of him.

Darnell swore under his breath at being separated from Penny in the freezing Atlantic, with even death in the sea something each might face, separately and alone. The irony was agonizing, as he thought of how he had fallen in love with her after his years of bachelorhood and had then been torn away from her by this calamity.

He kept an eye on Sung, next to him, to make sure he held on to the edge of the hull. If the boat sunk, Darnell realized he could not save his valet again, probably not even himself. He thought, also, with bitterness that Burton, the killer, sat safely in a lifeboat, while stalwart men had stayed on the *Titanic* and were now lost to their wives and children in the undiscriminating sea.

Darnell yearned to see Penny again. The only hope at this point was the *Carpathia*, the only ship receiving the *Titanic*'s distress call close enough to help. The wireless men had said the ship was steaming toward them at its top speed. But the sea could rise and toss the lifeboats about just like the deck chairs and other broken wreckage from the *Titanic* that floated by in the ghostly night.

Chapter Twenty-one

Monday morning, April 15

Penny Winters shivered, pulled her coat around her, and looked about her lifeboat. It was only half full, with thirty or so women and three male passengers, plus two crew, serving as oarsmen. There was plenty of room to pick up survivors, and she could hear faint cries in the distance. Why didn't they go back?

A woman next to Penny said, "You would think they'd have a lamp on each boat, so we could see better."

The man next to her, apparently her husband, said, "Yeah, and a pot of hot coffee, I suppose? We're lucky to be alive."

Penny's thoughts were all of John. Is he out there in the water, freezing, with only a life jacket to save him? John, dear John—where are you? She bit her lip. He had to be alive—she would never admit otherwise. Somehow they would be together again.

"Those poor people in the water," Penny said. "Can't we do something?"

A woman on the other side of her grabbed her arm, sobbing, "We have to go back. My husband's out there—they wouldn't let him get into the lifeboat—and these seats are empty. Oh, Jim!"

"We must go back," Penny called to the oarsmen. "Turn back, we can pick up survivors."

The woman next to her echoed her cry, saying, "We could find my husband—all of our husbands." She turned to the other women, urging them to say something. Soon, a chorus of voices saying, "Go back," filled the air.

"No, wait," one of the male passengers called. "If we go back, there are so many of them they'll capsize the boat climbing on. We'll all drown."

The officer in charge of the oarsmen turned to him and said, "Sir, you're lucky to be here. Now shut your mouth! We're going back."

The crewmen handling the oars turned the boat around in a wide arc and pulled strongly toward the spot where the *Titanic* had sunk. As the men rowed feverishly, the women looked ahead on the sea for survivors, Penny watching for John. They had drawn so far away, Penny could see it would take much time to reach the area, and she hoped it would not be too late.

In the distance, she saw another lifeboat with a lamp on its bow also heading toward the spot from a different direction, but, in the dark, she could see none of the other lifeboats or collapsibles. She hoped all the boats would turn back. Maybe one of them could pick up John.

The cries of the remaining survivors in the sea grew louder as they approached the area where the ship went under. "Look, there's a man!" Penny shouted, and the oarsmen turned and pulled up to him. Two of the men on the boat hauled him aboard, shivering, teeth chattering, soaked through with the icy seawater.

"Th-thank G-God," he said as he collapsed on the

floor of the boat. "I—I thought I was a g-goner." By his clothes, they could see he was a stoker.

The oarsmen pulled on forward and another man was found in their path, and the maneuver was again repeated, bringing the man aboard. It was a man Penny had seen promenading the first-class deck but had never met.

The cries were fainter, as Penny peered anxiously into the dark, hoping to see John Darnell. In a few minutes, another man was found and hauled aboard, and then another, and one last survivor, a woman who told them that she had worked in the ship's kitchen.

Penny could hear sounds in the distance but heard no other lifeboats returning to search. Her worst fears began to be realized as survivors' cries in the dark sea became fainter and fainter. It had been an hour since the ship went down, and those in the ocean had succumbed to the cold, had drifted too far away to be heard, or had died in the unrelenting sea. Soon, her heart sank at the awesome, final silence.

She continued to pray for John's safety, never giving up. She helped administer to the men and the one woman they had saved. It gave her something to do. She and the other women provided the few blankets and wraps they had brought with them to keep the survivors from the sea as warm as possible, and some offered their sweaters or scarfs.

But finally Penny could do nothing but sit in her place, huddled within her coat against the cold air, her shoes and feet soaked with icy water that had sloshed into the boat several inches deep. She waited for the dawn, for a possible rescue, for some sight of other boats, and thought of John.

* * *

The struggle to stay alive aboard the capsized collapsible boat that Darnell and Sung clung to during the long night increased with each minute. The men huddled together atop the outer hull of the overturned boat. Their wet coats adhered to their bodies, their teeth chattered uncontrollably, and they could not stop shivering. It was not like being in a lifeboat, which Darnell would have considered a luxury at that point. It was being half in the ocean and half out, with the ocean greedily wanting more of their bodies.

Some men succumbed to the numbing cold, falling unconscious. Some lost their hold on the boat's side and slipped silently into the ocean, while the rest watched helplessly, too exhausted to save them.

Darnell spoke to Sung, partly to keep Sung's spirits up, partly just to hear a voice. "Stay alert, Sung," he said. "We have to hold on until the other ship arrives. Then we'll be all right."

Sung said little. "Yes. Hope it is soon."

"Tell me, Sung—your family—I don't know much about them. You said you have a mother and father in China?"

"Yes, and a son."

"A son! I never knew that. How old is he?"

Sung brushed a quick tear away from his eye and looked down. "Sorry," he said. "Thinking of him . . ."

"I know."

"He is ten now . . . I haven't seen him for five years, since I took that one trip."

"I remember."

"I may never see him again. . . ." He lowered his eyes again, and Darnell knew they were filling with tears.

"Of course you will. You'll see him again, if I have

anything to do with it. The sea is quite calm, still, and our trusty boat, here, seems to be holding up."

Sung nodded. "Must have faith."

"Exactly. It will be all right." Darnell put his arm around Sung's shoulder.

As Darnell surveyed their makeshift craft, he gradually focused on some of the survivors clinging to the boat. There was Colonel Gracie. Chief wireless operator Jack Phillips looked seriously hurt. Harold Bride's legs were still caught under a heavy crew member, and his face now showed pain. He saw that one young man who had helped free the collapsible was there, and one lone woman pulled in from the sea had held on.

"Hello, Sparks," Darnell said to Bride, on the opposite side of the hull. "Glad you're here."

"Yes, sir. I am, too. But my legs are killing me."

"How is your partner?"

"I'm afraid for him, sir. I think one of his legs was broken in the sinking, and he is not taking the cold well. He's like frozen almost, through and through."

Darnell shook his head, doubting the ability of Phillips to survive. There was no way to assist him, given the unstable condition of their makeshift boat.

Most of the men aboard had been pulled in by those who first reached the boat, and the group gradually grew to twenty, then thirty, including one woman. The growing weight of the men pressed the craft several inches deeper into the ocean as air escaped from the airspace beneath the surface. Two prostrate men, one of them Phillips, became half-submerged.

"Stand up, men," Lightoller called out. "You'll keep warmer, and this thing may not kill us all. But do it slowly, carefully." One by one, the men stood up in the ankle-deep water, holding to each other for stability, back to back, shoulder to shoulder, ankle to ankle.

Lightoller confided in Darnell, "I can't navigate this with just the one oar we have. We're lucky it's held up this long. And we may not last the night."

"We need to get onto another lifeboat somehow," Darnell agreed.

A man suggested they pray aloud. One began, "The Lord is my shepherd . . ." Another looked up to the sky and said, "Our Father who art in heaven . . ." Others joined in with hoarse, solemn voices which carried across the water.

Lightoller had been periodically calling, "Ahoy!" to other distant boats, knowing they needed to be picked up by one. After an hour, a lifeboat drifted within sight in the dark. Lightoller shouted to the seaman in charge of the boat. "Ahoy, mate—heave to." The sailor obeyed and pulled the boat alongside.

The boat was only half-filled with passengers, almost all women. Darnell looked at each passenger anxiously, holding his breath. He soon saw that neither Penny Winters nor Doctor Burton was aboard.

Lightoller told the sailor, "We'll transfer to your boat." When the man hesitated, Lightoller ordered, "Look lively, man. Give us a hand."

"Yes, sir," the sailor said, grabbing the canvas side of the boat. "I'll hold your craft here, best as I can."

Lightoller ordered other sailors to help hold the two boats close together. "One at a time, lads, and carefully," Lightoller told the men.

He and Darnell helped them into the other lifeboat, one by one, first the woman, then the wireless operator, Phillips, his legs dangling, the man appearing lifeless. They laid him as gently as they could in the other boat. "Easy now," Lightoller cautioned. Phillips made no sound, and his eyes were closed. If alive, he was barely clinging to life.

The other men stepped over to the other lifeboat, trying not to disturb the delicate balance of their overturned craft. Stepping across the gap between the two boats, one man without a life jacket slipped into the ocean. He made no cry, and before anyone could grab him, he sank deep below the surface.

"Shall I go after him, sir?" one sailor asked Lightoller.

"Move, man, get in the boat—I'm afraid he's a goner. We'd just lose you, too."

Darnell felt the pangs of frustration and pain to see a man die in front of his eyes. One more poor soul was lost, added to the hundreds who had already perished in the night.

After the exhausted sailors and stokers boarded, Darnell helped Sung aboard, and stepped in himself. Captain-like, Lightoller boarded last. The boat was filled to capacity. Lightoller took over the navigation of it and assigned two sailors to the oars to draw them closer to the other boats.

Most of the men seemed to collapse in their seats, sighing with relief, holding their head in their hands, or leaning against one another. Some had tears in their eyes. Some closed their eyes now, for the first time since they were swept off the ship. The sole woman sobbed softly.

This lifeboat had a lantern at the bow. Wondering how soon the *Carpathia* would arrive, Darnell pulled out his watch and clicked it open. Waterlogged, it had stopped at 2:12 a.m., when he was swept off the *Titanic* into the ocean.

Penny was on his mind constantly. She was his main concern. He realized then the only possessions he had saved were his watch and his revolver. In one pocket, he also found the waterlogged photograph of Burton and his daughter which he had taken from the doctor's office. He'd need that for positive identification by the *Carpathia*'s officers, if Burton were found aboard.

He was relieved to be aboard a more stable boat. What a difference, he thought, that the four days since he left his comfortable flat in London could make in his life. His toes had no feeling, and his fingers, stuffed deep into his coat pockets, felt just as numb. As he shivered on the wet board seat, he realized that just clinging to life itself was something. But he swore he would gladly give ten pounds for a glass of sherry just then—better yet, a large, stiff whiskey.

The lifeboat pulled away from the collapsible heading toward distant lifeboats in the growing light of the predawn. Darnell was consumed with worry about Penny, in her lifeboat, somewhere out there on the sea. He thought also with anger of Burton, safe in a lifeboat, in his woman's disguise. Despite the desperate tragedy of this night, he knew his danger wasn't over, and that he still had a duty to capture Burton before he killed again.

The sea lapped against the sides of the boat. The steady clank of the oars in the oarlocks as the sailors pulled the boat forward gave out a rhythmic, eerie sound on the otherwise silent sea. And the smell of the wet clothes of the passengers next to him filled his nostrils.

Occasionally, Lightoller would call encouragement to a lifeboat within hailing distance. Some passengers told their harrowing tales of rescue to others. Others sat, stunned—shivering, silent, and staring at the sea.

Lightoller warned Darnell, "We're safer now; the

sea is still calm. But a choppy ocean in the morning could capsize these boats. These little craft weren't meant to be out here very long. So be prepared for anything."

Nothing mattered but the arrival of the *Carpathia*, their one chance at survival. They were hundreds of miles from the Grand Banks of Newfoundland, and farther, to America beyond. Their only salvation lay in the hope of being picked up by the other liner, if it could, in fact, find them, before the sea rose and tried to claim them.

A faint light in the distant sky flickered just above the horizon, and passengers turned their heads to stare at it, until it died. "A shooting star," a woman said. "Maybe it's a sign," another said.

But several minutes later another white flash blazed up into the night sky. Cheers and yells went up from the passengers in the far-flung lifeboats as they realized it was a flare shot from another ship—a rescue ship.

The cheers and shouts of "Thank God!" and "Hallelujah!" were far different sounds from the heart-rending cries and screams of those drowning in the sea two hours earlier. The *Carpathia* was coming, signaling her arrival. A distant lifeboat also shot off a flare, and other cheers rang across the water.

"A boat comes," Sung said.

"Yes, Sung. A big ship. Big enough to save us all."

Lightoller said, "They're sending flares to light up the sea, not just to let us know they're coming. They'll need that light to find our boats." The small, dark lifeboats had drifted wide apart, and were scattered, by that time, over more than a mile's radius around the point at which the *Titanic* sank, some two or more miles apart.

Darnell watched the horizon and saw the outline

of the ship clearly now. Voices of the passengers aboard their lifeboat buzzed with happy words. He heard laughter for the first time since the night before on the *Titanic*. As the ship grew larger, approaching them, he put his arm around Sung's shoulders. His voice choked as he said, "We're going to make it, old boy."

But Darnell knew their ordeal wasn't over yet—the rescue operation would be hazardous, and could increase, if the sea were to swell. Then, after they were taken aboard the *Carpathia*, he would face a final, fatal confrontation with the killer. But at this moment, his main thought was, I'll be seeing Penny again.

Chapter Twenty-two

Monday morning, April 15

The shivering, exhausted passengers in the lifeboats called out in tearful, joyful tones to each other, and laughter carried across the sea from one boat to the next. The chorus of cheers, in that remote piece of ocean, was like nothing Darnell had ever heard before. A lifeboat sent up an answering flare, and, as if in response, the *Carpathia*'s deep horn blasted, drowning out their voices, and the ship sent another flare into the night sky. Soon it was close enough to some lifeboats to pick up survivors, at what Darnell estimated was about four a.m. His only thought was to see Penny again, and he realized she did not even know he was alive, and, in fact, had every reason to believe him dead.

"This boarding process will be dangerous, and slow," Darnell said to Sung as they watched the first lifeboat passengers being picked up. The lifeboat, dwarfed by the large liner, rocked gently next to it. The *Carpathia*'s deckhands lowered a rope ladder which sailors in the boat grasped, steadying it on each side.

"Jacob's ladder," a crewman said. "Takin' us to heaven."

One by one, passengers, mostly women and children, all still wet to the skin, feet slipping, labori-
ously climbed up the shaky ladder onto the safety of
the ship's deck. Those too feeble to climb were
hauled up in canvas slings. Climbing up, and when
they reached the deck, women sobbed with relief,
their first emotional release after the long ordeal.

A second lifeboat rowed to the side of the ship
after the first passengers were taken aboard, and
the laborious procedure was repeated. Then another
followed. And another. Each empty lifeboat was
hauled aboard by *Carpathia's* deckhands.

Three hours passed, the longest hours Darnell
could remember, until their turn came. The passengers in the boat Darnell was on climbed the rope ladder up to the *Carpathia's* deck. Phillips' body was
hauled up by two sailors.

When Darnell stepped onto the *Carpathia's* deck
he learned Phillips had been pronounced dead, officially, when brought aboard. On the lifeboat, they
had known it for some time. His body was taken to
the infirmary to be held there, along with other bodies from other boats, until buried at sea. Darnell
closed his eyes and said a silent prayer for the brave
young man who had sent distress calls right up to
the last minute.

Bundled in a wool blanket, Sung sat on the deck,
leaning against the rail, drinking from a cup. He
looked up at Darnell as he approached.

A sailor placed a blanket around Darnell's shoulders, and a woman handed him a steaming cup.
"Tea?" she asked.

"Thank you," Darnell said, surprised he could still
speak at all. He took a large gulp of the tea, burning
his tongue but not caring. He stood next to Sung.

"Well, Sung, we made it." Darnell patted Sung on the back. "You can write your family when we reach New York, tell them you're going to come for your son."

"I should do that?"

"Tell them you're going to bring him to London, to live with us. We'll convert that alcove into a small bedroom for him."

A broad smile transformed Sung's face. "I write him. Yes, and I will go." He looked at Darnell quizzically. "But Miss Penny—would that be all right with her?" He put his hand over his mouth. "Oh, sorry."

Darnell smiled. "It's all right . . . yes, I know she wouldn't mind." He stood up. "And I have to find her now, Sung. You stay here, and I'll be back soon."

"Yes, Professor. I stay here."

The deck was crowded with the rescued passengers from the *Titanic*, bundled up in green or brown wool stateroom blankets. Some drank hot tea or coffee, some stood by the rail or against a wall, but most sat huddled together against the walls of cabins. Stewards and sailors circulated about busily, taking care of the passengers. They made sure each one had the small comforts of a blanket and a hot drink, and gave first aid to those who were injured.

As Darnell hurried along the deck, searching for Penny, he peered into the face of every woman he passed. It was lighter now, in the early dawn hours. He recognized some of the women, wives of famous men like Mrs. Rothschild, a widow now, like many women, their millionaire husbands having gone down with the ship.

With the heavy crowds and few feet of uncluttered deck space to pass by, and the many faces to examine, precious minutes passed, and Darnell grew desperate to find Penny. At last he heard Penny's voice calling, "John! Over here!" and his heart leaped. Bundled in a dark green blanket, she sat among a long row of women leaning against cabin walls. As he ran to her, she jumped up, and her blanket fell to the deck.

He swept her into his arms and held her tight. After a moment, their lips met in a fervent kiss. "Penny—thank God we're together again."

"You're alive!" Tears streamed from her eyes. "It's a miracle." She smiled through the tears and touched his face with her hand.

"Out there, all night, I wondered whether I'd ever see you again, in this life," Darnell said. He retrieved her blanket and pulled it around her again. Motioning to a place along the walls of the cabins, he said, "There's a spot." They sat down on the cold deck, their blankets draped about them both now, arms around each other, holding hands as if they would never let go.

"How did you get off the ship?" Penny held on to him like he might vanish again.

"A bunch of us were unhooking a collapsible boat, on top of the bridge. The waves surged over us, and we were all swept overboard. I was pushed down under the sea. I don't know how I surfaced, but suddenly I was under the capsized boat. Then we were able to climb up on top of it."

"Sung, too?"

"Yes, he's safe."

Darnell told of being picked up by the other boat, and of Phillips dying, but omitted his sighting of Doctor Burton leaving the *Titanic* in women's clothes. As he finished his story, he realized Penny knew nothing about cabin 13, the murders on other ships, and Burton's attempt to poison him. He frowned, realizing now was the time for him to tell her that entire story. Her safety and his own would be at risk if Burton was aboard the *Carpathia*.

Darnell took both of Penny's hands in his for a moment. "There's something I have to tell you."

"About your reason for the trip?"

"Yes. The investigation I told you about."

"I know—the ghosts."

He kept his voice low so only Penny could hear. "White Star Line employed me to break a jinx on their ocean liners. There were three apparent suicides in cabin thirteen on three other ships within the past few months. They had heard I investigated paranormal experiences."

She whispered, "You scared away castle ghosts and church ghosts. So they said, 'Get rid of our ship's ghost.' "

"Something like that. Ismay, the chairman, called it a jinx, although Captain Smith had doubts of that. So I agreed to take cabin thirteen on the *Titanic*, make myself bait. I was convinced the suicides were really murders. I don't believe in jinxes—to me, the number thirteen is just the one that comes after twelve."

"What did you find out?"

He held her hands tight. "The killer of the three passengers on the other ships was the *Titanic*'s ship's doctor, Gareth Burton. And . . . I have to tell you this, Penny, he tried to kill me, too."

"John!" Her eyes widened.

"He poisoned the sherry bottle in my room—but I thought something like that was coming, and noticed it in time. Sung and I fought with him, and captured him. But he escaped and jumped into a lifeboat."

Penny looked around nervously. "You mean . . . ?"

Darnell nodded. "Yes, he's probably on this ship—

I think he is. That puts you and Sung in danger, too. He's a vengeful man."

She pulled her coat around her tighter. "What can we do?"

"He was dressed like a woman. At least he was when he leaped into the lifeboat. I saw his pant legs and shoes under the long woman's dress. He wore a veil."

"So we'll be searching for a woman in a long dress with a veil?" She glanced at the women directly across from her and next to her.

"Not we, Penny. I'll do the searching. This man's a murderer."

"But you know you can count on me."

Darnell nodded. He had to protect Penny and Sung. And even though the tragedy of the hundreds of passengers lost in the disaster dominated these past hours, he still had to follow through with his duty. The three poor souls on the other ships had been murdered. Darnell must keep his commitment to White Star Line. He was obligated under his contract with Ismay, even if Captain Smith had died. And it was personal now. The man had tried to kill him, too. He clenched his fists. If Burton was on the ship, Darnell was determined he'd pay for his crimes.

"Let's walk over to see Sung. And I have to talk with Lightoller about a search party." He entwined her arm in his. "You're staying with me now."

As they wound their way through the crowds of survivors and the rescue ship's regular passengers, Darnell was glad to notice familiar faces of people he'd known or seen on the *Titanic*. They passed the two elderly ladies he had interviewed in the library room of the ship; Carrie and Marybelle Trent were safely aboard. "Hello, ladies," he said. "I'm glad to see you both made it."

Marybelle nodded. "Another one of our adventurous trips."

Carrie added, "It was a nightmare. I think we'll dream about it . . ." She sobbed and her eyes filled.

Marybelle finished it for her, ". . . all our lives."

Darnell noticed the survivors were not all women and children. Seeing Lightoller, he and Penny stopped to talk.

Lightoller tipped his hat and asked, "Are you all right, Miss Winters?"

Penny nodded. "Yes, and I want to thank you for helping save John. If you hadn't been on that raft, I don't know what would have happened."

"Part of the job, miss."

Darnell said, "I'm surprised at the number of men. I thought it was women and children first." He gestured around at the mixed crowd of men and women.

Lightoller said, "Some of those men are crew members, over twenty on our collapsible boat, some had to man oars in lifeboats."

"That wouldn't account for this many men."

"I know. I tried to hold to 'women and children first' on the port side, but on the starboard side—sad to say—some boats were lowered too quickly, less than half full. And they didn't follow that rule. Men—even crewmen—were allowed aboard."

He shook his head. "But it was a problem either way. Some women just wouldn't leave their husbands. They thought it was safer to stay aboard the *Titanic* than go out on the sea in lifeboats, and we couldn't send the boats down without someone aboard. There wasn't time to waste. We lost too many women, even young boys wanting to be brave, like men, staying on board with their fathers." The irony and immensity of the tragedy showed in Lightoller's eyes and voice.

"Were any other officers saved?"

"Fourth Officer Boxhall, Fifth Officer Harold Lowe, and Third Officer Herbert Pitman. The rest went down with the ship." He shook his head in obvious disbelief and dismay. "The Captain, Chief Wilde, First Officer Murdoch, Sixth Officer Moody—they're all gone. I'm the only Senior Officer alive. I'd be a goner, too, except for my lucky break being near that collapsible." He scowled. "But Chairman Ismay made it. They put him in a private cabin."

Darnell could see Lightoller's resentment of the Chairman's good fortune. He had lost men he worked with side by side and was close to every day. The loss of half the officers, Darnell knew, was not in the tradition of the sea. It was just that there weren't enough boats to go around. Bride, the junior wireless operator, survived only because he climbed atop the overturned collapsible boat as Darnell and the others had done.

"Where is Bride?"

"In the wireless room sending messages from survivors to the mainland. His feet were so frostbitten they carried him in."

Darnell and Penny walked on, nodding to people they knew. From the size of the crowds, Darnell doubted even half of the passengers and crew had been saved. The women's faces he saw bore stark expressions of shock and grief, not yet fully realizing, perhaps, the enormity of what had happened. Most had lost their husbands in the undiscriminating sea.

Stewards offered hot food, but few women ate. "My husband's dead," Darnell heard one say in a choked-up voice as he passed.

"I'm so sorry. But just drink this tea, ma'am," the steward told her. "You need to have something hot."

She said, "I can't eat anything. I couldn't keep it down."

Penny was startled at the voice. "Madeleine! It's Penny."

The woman looked up at Penny through her tears and threw herself into Penny's arms, sobbing on her shoulder. Her cries racked her body for moments until she pulled herself together. "I'm, I'm sorry," she said, "I didn't mean to burden you. . . ."

"Oh, Madeleine, I'm so sorry for you—you lost your husband?"

"Yes. He died in the sea. They wouldn't let him into the lifeboat."

"But there were empty seats, in my boat, in every boat. I saw how it was when they took survivors aboard here."

"I know—I know. But what can be done? Nothing." She dried her eyes with her sleeve. "I just have to go on somehow. Me . . . and my baby."

Penny held her hands in hers. "Is everything—all right?"

"Yes. Thank God. I have something of him to always remind me of him."

After promising to come and see her later on at her estate, Penny took Darnell's arm and walked along with him. She held his arm tight.

"Sung should be along here soon," Darnell said. "He was sitting next to the rail."

A blast of a ship's horn shattered the air, and passengers rushed to the rail to see another liner approaching.

"It's the *Californian*," Darnell said. "I can't believe it. Phillips tried to reach them for two hours, and now they show up when it's all over. That's ironic."

Apparently the captains of the two ships communicated by wireless, because after picking up some remnants from the *Titanic*, the *Californian* stayed in place, seeming to wait for the *Carpathia* to move on.

Sung came to their side at the rail. "Saw you arrive here," he said. "So glad you are safe, Miss Penny."

"Thank you."

The three stood at the rail, also wondering what would happen next. The *Carpathia* cruised over the *Titanic*'s burial area and back, searching a last time for survivors, finding none.

Darnell and Penny stepped over to the rail and watched the proceedings. The crew hauled aboard the last of the now empty lifeboats. Darnell pointed at the waterlogged flotsam and jetsam of the *Titanic*'s wreckage, deck chairs, a life preserver, bits and desolate pieces of the ship, floating by in the sea. "That's all that's left of her, Penny. The greatest ship in the world."

She held his arm tight. "All those poor people. And we have each other . . . we're so lucky."

The ship's sirens blasted, signaling its departure for New York, and a cheer went up from the crowd. The mixed sound of the sirens and cheers rang across the decks. A short, acknowledging blast came from the *Californian*. It was mid-morning, and the rescue ship was on its way.

"Our night of terror is over, Penny," Darnell said. "In only four days, we'll be in New York."

Chapter Twenty-three

Monday morning, April 15

Huddled among a crowd of rescued crew and passengers sitting along the rail of the *Carpathia*, dressed in his crew uniform, Doctor Gareth Burton kept himself as unobtrusive as possible. One among many, he felt, was his best security.

The events of the night still rumbled through his mind. Before jumping into the lifeboat from the *Titanic*, he had dressed in the crew clothing he had grabbed from his closet, and covered with the stolen long woman's dress and coat. But after he was safe in the boat and it pulled away, he doffed the woman's dress and coat, then appearing as a crew member. The passengers on the lifeboat would not speak to him, sickened at his deception.

Now he found himself accepting tea from a steward. He pulled the stocking cap down over his ears, trying to further disguise himself. He had removed his gold-rimmed glasses earlier, and kept them in his inside pocket.

Burton worried that if the damned professor and his valet had been saved they could identify him, even with his somewhat changed appearance. He hoped they had died in the seas. Should he search for Darnell and his man to see if they were aboard, and attempt to dispose of them with the element of surprise, or wait for Darnell to come to him? He was torn—either choice was perilous. He would have to take a chance on revealing his identity. But it was them or him, and he had no doubt he'd have to kill one or both of them. The thought of it excited him.

Two hours had passed since Burton climbed up the rope ladder from his lifeboat. The gray midmorning light made him aware he was more likely, at his unusual height of well over six feet, to be discovered by Darnell in the daylight if he walked about the ship. He decided to move about and search for Darnell only after nightfall. For now, he'd blend in with the other survivors, huddled under a blanket—that was the best course—and wait for the protective cover of darkness.

Gradually, in watching the activities of other passengers, he noticed a small scene a hundred yards away on the other side of the deck. It was the professor, taking his lady friend in his arms. Damn them. He gritted his teeth—so the damned meddler was alive. Well, he wouldn't be for long. He watched, seething, as Darnell and the woman embraced, sat down on the deck, and talked. Dark thoughts raged in his fevered mind, although his face—the tip of his personal iceberg—showed none of the danger ready to explode.

Burton resisted the impulse to jump up now and attack them. With great restraint, he controlled the urge. But he noted their exact position in his mind, rose and moved slowly away from them farther toward the bow, where injured men lay on makeshift cots. He lay down on an empty cot and pulled the blanket up around him. He'd wait there until nightfall.

During the long hours of the day, Burton's

thoughts of the terrible past year raced again through his muddled mind. His life had been ruined, that much he knew. He remembered, with regret, his former good life. Born in London, attending prep schools, graduate of its finest medical school, a ship's doctor for White Star Line for many years, he had enjoyed a privileged, respected position. He sailed on larger ships, associating with and taking care of the health needs of wealthy, first-class passengers. He often dined at the Captain's table on other ocean liners—although, he thought with a scowl, Captain Smith had never invited him to his table. But then his wife had died, and he suffered the tragic death also of his daughter. As he thought of it all, Burton's temples pounded, his head hurt, and his eyes filled with tears.

His thoughts were interrupted by a steward walking by, hearing his soft sobbing. "Are you all right?" the steward asked with concern.

Coming to his senses, Burton nodded, answering, "I'm sorry. It's all right." He realized the man thought he was crying because of the calamity of the *Titanic*, the tragedy of it all, perhaps for having lost a family member or fellow crewman. But, ironically, his grief now was for his wife and daughter who had died months before. Once again, he felt blind rage, the urge to jump up, run back, find Darnell, and slit his throat. Instead, Burton pulled the wool blanket around him tighter, curled his legs up into a fetal position, and closed his eyes. He must control himself. Revenge—the word seared his brain. The twisted thought of that was all that sustained him.

With his gloved hand, he felt down into the pocket of his wool coat. Yes, his small carrying case was where he'd stored it, with his scalpel inside—

razor-sharp and waiting. It would be his weapon this night, silent and deadly.

That night on the *Carpathia* was darker than it had ever been on the *Titanic*. No gaiety here, no bright lights or sparkling music. The rescued passengers took as much comfort as they could find, kept somewhat warmer by blankets, sitting on the deck. Soon, they were moved into the dining room and other common rooms for the night. Luckier ones were given vacant bunks in passenger cabins. Every bed in every cabin was filled with either passengers or survivors. The *Carpathia*'s crew took needed rest at night also, and the forlorn and haggard lot of rescued passengers were left to sleep as best they could.

One person who did not sleep was Doctor Gareth Burton. It was another moonless night, dark and quiet, the sky lit only by the brilliant stars. He rose and stealthily made his way back toward the stern to the place where he had seen Darnell and his lady friend. Arriving there, he was angered to see both of them had disappeared. He swore under his breath. He walked up and down the deck in both directions, inspecting closely the passengers who remained on deck, but Darnell and his lady friend were nowhere to be found.

At last, Burton gave it up and slowly threaded his way through the maze of blanket-covered passengers lying on the deck or in deck chairs until he reached the cot he'd vacated. Only as he lay down again on the cot with the blanket over him, calmer then, did he surmise what had happened. They'd probably been given a cabin. He'd heard the Chairman and others had been given that comfort. That was a complication. It would make it harder to find them.

But Burton's determination remained firm. They must die. Tomorrow he would find them. He knew, also, he would need a better hiding place, because they would come looking for him. His breathing was short and rapid, and his eyes wide, staring ahead. A red haze filled his mind. He lapsed into a nightmarish sleep.

John Darnell lay in bed in the dark in the second-class cabin bed. Darnell had been provided by the *Carpathia*'s captain with cabin space for himself and Sung, and another shared cabin for Penny. It was almost two a.m., but he couldn't sleep. A rescued *Titanic* purser snored heavily in the other bed.

During the day, Penny had spent several hours with Madeleine Astor, comforting her, keeping her company.

Darnell had taken Lightoller into his confidence about his true cabin 13 assignment and his attempted murder at the hands of Burton.

"A murderer?" Lightoller showed his astonishment. "If that's true, we have to find him."

"Tomorrow morning would be best. Today, all the crew is involved in helping the survivors. Too much turmoil. It'll settle down tomorrow."

"So we'll do a search, then?"

"I'll need your help in convincing Captain Rostron. And getting help from him."

Lightoller shook Darnell's hand as they parted. "Tomorrow, then."

Darnell and Sung had talked, sitting a short distance from where Penny and Mrs. Astor were together, so he could watch her. Even in the light of day, Burton could possibly do something to attempt to harm Penny. Darnell tried to recall whether Burton had ever seen him with Penny. If he had, the danger to her was even greater.

In the late afternoon, the four of them ate the dinner provided by the cooks and waiters of the rescue ship, and recounted all the things that had happened in the past twenty-four hours.

Darnell stopped by to see Bride, in the wireless room, and found him at his Marconi switch, a pile of messages in front of him to send. "How are your legs, Sparks?" he asked.

"Very sore. May need some medical treatment."

"But can you work?"

"Must do it. Those other operators would never get these all out," he said, pointing at the stack of messages. "These poor people want to tell someone they're alive. That's what this all is."

Darnell also talked with Colonel Archibald Gracie about their experiences on the overturned collapsible boat. "It's something none of us will ever forget," the Colonel said. "I'll write a book about it, for others to remember."

Now, as he tossed and turned in his bed, Darnell wondered about Penny, sharing the next cabin with two other rescued women. Was she still awake, comfortable, sleeping, dreaming? And he worried about her safety, although she was just one wall away.

He heard Sung's rhythmic breathing as the valet lay on a portable cot placed on the floor between the two beds. Darnell thought of Sung's ten-year-old son, approaching his vital years of growth, thousands of miles away in China. Darnell reproached himself for not learning about the boy before. Why hadn't Sung told him? Had he been so busy or unapproachable his valet was afraid to even mention it? If so, that would change.

A night and day none of them would ever forget

had ended. Darnell was thankful they were at last steaming toward New York, each hour bringing them closer to land, and still feeling the exhaustion of the ordeal. But sleep would not come, and when it did he knew it would be fitful, reliving the images of the dark ocean, the bright flares across the sky, the *Titanic*'s sinking, and the passengers' unheeded cries for help. He had no desire for sleep of that kind.

Instead, his mind swirled with questions. How to find Burton and capture him? Would the ship's captain believe Darnell's story and offer help in a search? One thing was sure: He had to find Burton before he killed again, out of desperation. And he must find him tomorrow.

Chapter Twenty-four

Darnell woke in a cold sweat. He pulled on clothes a *Carpathia* steward had provided, and took Penny and Sung to the dining room. A long line led from the hallway into the dining room, and they took places at the end of it. The ship's staff offered hot coffee and tea, crumpets, and toast with orange marmalade.

Penny held Darnell's arm as they wound their way through the line to the serving tables.

Penny said, "It's amazing how they're able to handle another seven hundred passengers, along with their own."

Darnell nodded. "They're probably working double shifts."

"I could help them," Sung said.

Darnell studied him. "I don't know . . . are you able?"

"Yes. I will see the cook, right after we eat."

"All right, Sung. I'm sure they could use your help, just don't overtax yourself. Will you cook your special cuisine?"

Sung smiled. "Chinese fish-and-chips."

Darnell turned to Penny. "Sung's son is coming

from China to live with us ... uh, Sung and me, that is."

Penny smiled. "I know what you mean. I think that would be really nice." She avoided his eyes as a small smile played about her lips. "I like children."

They stood against the wall along with other passengers.

Penny sipped her hot coffee. "When will we reach New York?"

"I'd say three days," Darnell said.

Sung touched Darnell's arm. "Something to tell you."

"Yes, Sung?"

"Spoke to cook friend that last night on *Titanic*, before fight with doctor. Couldn't tell you before now."

"You found out more about the fourth death?"

"Girl, fifteen, sixteen, raped, as cook said." He lowered his voice. "Cook also say, girl thrown overboard by the men."

Darnell thought at once, Could she have been Burton's daughter? "Did he say anything about her mother or father?"

Sung nodded. "Father was White Star ship's officer. Called accident, hushed up. Ship captain didn't know crew did it."

"That's important, Sung. That puts it all together."

Penny said, "I heard. What will you do now about the—murderer?" She shivered saying the word.

"We'll search for him. I'll take you to your cabin, and you can lock yourself in. I'll see Lightoller and the Captain. I have something new to tell them now."

Penny studied his face. "You'll be careful, won't you? I just got you back from the dead." Her eyes were moist.

"Don't worry, Penny. We'll have armed men."

"I go, too?" Sung asked.

"No, you'll stay here and do some nice, safe cooking."

Penny glanced around the room. "He could even be here."

"Right, anywhere. We'll have to inspect everyone on deck, every cabin. He could still be disguised as a woman, so we can't overlook them." His face was grim. "But we'll find him."

"He's dangerous, John. Maybe more than you know."

"I have my friend here." He patted his overcoat pocket holding his .38 special. He'd have to clean and oil the waterlogged gun. He'd be sure others searching would have weapons.

Darnell didn't deceive himself. He was the only one knowing the full extent of Burton's crimes, and would be the man's first target. Burton, now a hunted, desperate criminal, would do anything to avoid capture—a cornered animal fights to the death.

Following breakfast, Sung went looking for the head cook, to volunteer. Darnell took Penny to her cabin, made sure she locked her door securely, and headed up to the bridge to find Herbert Lightoller. He found him there with the *Carpathia*'s Captain Arthur Rostron, hero of their rescue. Rostron was saying, "I've never steamed through ice that fast before. Full speed. It may not have been prudent—we could have hit ice ourselves."

"You won't find anyone to question that," Lightoller said. As Darnell walked up, he turned to him. "Good morning—I know you want to talk with the Captain."

"And with you, too."

Darnell hoped the *Titanic*'s Second Officer could support what he would say to the Captain. To Rostron, he said, "I need some help on something very important."

"Lightoller mentioned there was a serious issue but didn't go into detail," Rostron said. "Go ahead."

"Can we go to your cabin, Captain? Others shouldn't overhear this."

Rostron said, "Of course." He turned and headed past the bridge, followed by Lightoller and Darnell. "My cabin's just around the corner."

When they were all seated in Rostron's cabin, door closed, Darnell glanced around the room, taking in the seafaring artifacts—a model ship, a compass and sextant, books on sea lore and maps—filling every spot on the captain's dressers and desk and bookcase. A cabin of a man who loved the sea.

Rostron came to the point. "Now, Professor Darnell . . . something important, you said." He fixed his gaze on Darnell.

"We have a murderer aboard, Captain."

"A murderer?"

"Chairman Ismay can confirm parts of what I'm going to tell you. Could you send for him to come to your cabin? He should be part of this."

Rostron looked puzzled, but stepping outside his door, he gave instructions to a steward to find Ismay and bring him there. He returned to his seat.

Darnell said, "As background, there were three deaths, all apparent suicides, one on each of three different ships of the White Star Line."

Rostron interrupted, "I heard rumors of the deaths—it's bizarre . . . sorry, go on."

Darnell told of the visit of Ismay and Captain Smith to his London flat, explained how they had hired him to take cabin 13 on the *Titanic* to investigate.

A rap on the door came, and Rostron let in Chairman Ismay.

Ismay stared at Darnell as he stepped through the doorway. "Professor. Glad you survived, man. . . . I'm afraid our friend Captain Smith was not so fortunate."

"I know. When we met in my flat in London, none of us could have predicted anything like this tragedy."

Ismay nodded and seated himself in a straight desk chair.

"I've filled Captain Rostron in on the cabin thirteen deaths . . . of course I knew from the first there was no jinx on the cabin, despite the unlucky number. I don't tolerate superstition in my work. The deaths were murders. The important thing is that I've uncovered the reason for the cabin thirteen deaths, Chairman. They were murders, and the murderer is aboard the *Carpathia*."

Ismay took in a breath sharply. "Murderer? But who?"

"It's your ship's doctor, Gareth Burton. I told Smith."

"How do you know it was Burton?"

"He tried to kill me, too, with poison, just like he poisoned your cabin thirteen passenger. Sung and I fought with him, but he escaped and jumped into a lifeboat. I'm sure he was picked up with other survivors and is hiding out on this ship."

"I . . . I don't think I understand all this. Why would a doctor, our ship's doctor . . . ?"

"We all know he was drinking heavily. His wife and daughter died last year—he'd been distraught, and I felt their deaths and the cabin thirteen deaths were somehow connected."

Rostron said, "Losing your wife and daughter's enough to make a man crazy, for sure. I can't imagine the grief."

Ismay broke in. "But the doctor was back to work. Why blame White Star? And why kill three innocent passengers?"

Darnell said, "I just discovered the reason for that a few minutes ago. The killings were a form of revenge against your line—misguided, of course, but very logical in his twisted mind. His young daughter, a girl in her teens, was brutally raped, repeatedly, by two White Star ship crewmen, then she was thrown overboard. She was raped and murdered."

"My God!" Ismay's eyes were wide.

"It was hushed up, but Burton must have found out that the crewmen did it from other crew members. His mind warped by hatred and despair, he decided to take revenge. For his first murder, he threw the woman overboard, just like his daughter was killed. That was his first revenge, and he followed with the other two murders. He was able to fake them as suicides. Remember, he examined both bodies of the second and third victims—the poisoning and the shooting—and called them suicides."

Ismay said, "Burton's murders echoed his daughter's death."

Darnell looked at Ismay. "I think we'll find, Chairman, when we investigate his daughter's death, that the poor, unfortunate girl had sailed in cabin thirteen. That gave us your cabin thirteen jinx—the other victims simply had the bad luck of booking the cabin whose number Burton made part of his hate."

Ismay sat silent, stunned. Darnell saw fear in the man's eyes—perhaps for himself, perhaps for the horrible publicity.

Darnell went on, urgently now. "We must find him without delay. He's dangerous and could kill again. He has absolutely nothing to lose. And with his crazed mind, he may not realize that anything he's done is wrong."

"Are we sure he's alive?" Ismay asked. "On the *Carpathia*?"

"Anyone who was alive and in a lifeboat is aboard the *Carpathia* now," Rostron said. "No question about it. If he was in a lifeboat, he's here somewhere. What now?"

"We need an armed search party," Darnell said. He pushed hair strands back from his forehead. "We need to scour the ship. Four search teams of two men each could do it. Director Ismay, Second Officer Lightoller, Fourth Officer Boxhall, and I could each lead a team. We know Burton and can identify him. Captain, if you can assign an officer or reliable crewman to work with each of us, we could get four teams started within the hour."

Darnell turned to Ismay and Lightoller. "Are you willing?"

Ismay said, "Of course."

When Lightoller nodded, Darnell asked him, "Can you speak for Boxhall? Will he join us?"

"He will, out of duty, when he knows what's involved."

Rostron nodded. "I'll ask my Chief to appoint four men to the teams, and we'll meet back here in my cabin in a half hour. We'll go over plans of the ship and begin the search at once."

Ismay scowled. "A murderer. Dammit! Haven't we had enough deaths in the past thirty-six hours to last a lifetime?"

Darnell said, "The lives lost with the *Titanic* weren't within our control—at least, after the iceberg was struck. But in Burton's mental state, he could kill again, and we have to prevent that. There are innocent lives at stake now."

* * *

At eleven a.m., eight men sat where they could in Rostron's cabin, on a few chairs, on the edges of the desk, with their eyes fixed on the Captain. Rostron cleared his throat and spoke to the group. "Men, we're here because we must look for a murderer."

The word brought looks of astonishment to the faces of the *Carpathia* officers, and one repeated the word, "Murderer."

Rostron went on. "We'll have four teams of two, led by Professor Darnell, Director Ismay, and Officers Lightoller and Boxhall, each teamed up with one of you officers. Stemple, you'll go with Darnell. Williams, with Ismay. Johnstone, with Lightoller. Polardi, with Boxhall. I'll be on the bridge.

"Professor Darnell will explain how we go about this."

Darnell held up the photograph of Burton and his daughter. "What does a murderer look like? Our man looks like this." Darnell handed the photograph to the man next to him.

"Take a good look, Williams, and pass it on. It's Gareth Burton, the ship's doctor from the *Titanic*. He looks very ordinary. And don't be deceived by his profession—now he takes lives instead of saving them. He killed three people in the past three months." He quickly told the story of the deaths in cabin 13, his own attempted murder by Burton, and Burton's escape.

Third Officer Stemple whistled. "Not half a mystery, is it? He kills innocent people to revenge his daughter. Many men could go crazy after what he went through, I suppose."

"But Burton can kill an innocent person again, if we don't find him and stop him." Darnell turned to the Captain's map table. "Let's go over these blue-prints of the *Carpathia*. Now, he could be on any deck, because survivors have been spread about on the lower decks as well. Right, Captain?" The men gathered around the chart.

Rostron nodded, gestured at the chart. "He could be on any deck, might be in a cabin, wherever we had vacant cabins or a space for someone to share one."

"Survivors sharing with regular passengers."

Rostron said, "But we kept no track of who went where. We didn't know their names, except for a few, like the director." He glanced at the Chairman. "But others, well, we'll just have to check every cabin. He could be anywhere."

Darnell considered that. "Four teams, four decks. I suggest we work our way up, sweeping upward, starting with E deck, D deck, C, and B. If we don't find him as we sweep through the four lower decks, then we'll converge all four teams on deck A and on up to the boat deck." He made a rough estimation. "We must finish this today, and reach deck A before it gets dark. If we start now, we can do it."

"If—I mean, when—when we find him, then what?" Officer Johnstone looked at his Captain and at Darnell.

Darnell answered. "He'll be armed, I'm sure of that. And he's desperate. It may take two to over-power him. You all have the handguns the Captain issued you?"

The men nodded, some saying, "aye," one saying, "We're ready for him."

Fifth Officer Polardi added, as if for the group, "I've had experience with his kind in Sicily." He nudged Boxhall in the ribs with his elbow. "Let him try to get by us, eh, Boxhall?"

Fourth Officer Boxhall frowned. Darnell saw the concern in the young officer's face and realized these men hadn't bargained for this kind of duty. "Don't do anything foolhardy," he said, "and if you find him, act quickly, before he does."

Captain Rostron echoed his words. "Act at once. But only use your weapons in emergency. We want him alive, if possible."

"One final thing," Darnell said. "When I saw him last, as he jumped into that lifeboat, he was dressed as a woman."

Stemple whistled. "Bloody coward."

Darnell continued, "When I last saw him, he had on a flowery woman's dress and a long, dark cloth coat over that. And a veil. He's tall, though, and would appear larger than a woman."

Boxhall blurted out, "So that's how he got away."

"But I caution you," Darnell went on. "He may look very different now. He may not have those woman's clothes on anymore, may have ditched them. But the clothes are only part of it. Remember his face, his height, the dark bushy hair, the deep-set eyes in that photograph. Study that photo. He can't change that. When you see him, you'll know him."

There were no responses. The officers looked at each other, silently, awaiting orders now. "Any other questions?" Darnell asked, giving them time to consider.

He realized how dangerous this operation would be, and wondered momentarily if they should wait until they reached port, let the police search the ship. But he dismissed the idea, realizing the chaos there would be in New York when they docked. The police would never find him. And in Burton's demented state, he was a bomb, ready to go off, a danger to any luckless passenger who might be in his way if he lost control, and especially to Sung, and even Penny, as well as himself. No, they had to find him, and soon.

"All right, then," Darnell said. "Captain Rostron, Director Ismay, I'll ask you to give your men their orders." He stepped back.

Ismay nodded at Captain Rostron. "You do it, Captain. My men will do their duty."

"Officers Boxhall and Polardi, deck E; Lightoller and Johnstone, deck D; Director Ismay and Williams, deck C; Professor Darnell and Stemple, deck B. I'll post two stewards or pursers at each stairwell, to watch for him going up or down, so he can't slip by you. I'll be on the bridge. Let me know at once if you learn anything."

The men nodded, looked at each other with anticipation and uneasiness in their eyes. "We're ready, Captain," Polardi said.

Rostron turned to Ismay. "Are you still game to be part of this, Director? There's mortal danger here."

"Of course I am. It's my responsibility, after all." Ismay rested his hand on Darnell's shoulder. "Thank God you were on the *Titanic*, Darnell. He could have claimed another victim." Ismay jumped to his feet. "God, I just thought of something. To get revenge on White Star, Burton could have come after me."

Darnell said, "As long as he's at large, you're in danger now, too. What better revenge on your company than to kill its Chairman?"

Darnell touched his coat pocket containing his .38 special, giving him assurance it was there. He hoped the oiling he'd given it between the two meetings that morning had brought it back to operating condition, but had no way to fire it without creating an incident.

"All right, Captain," Darnell said. He stepped over to the passageway door. "Let's find the killer."

Chapter Twenty-five

The four search teams dispersed quickly down the stairs to the lower decks, each team peeling off as they reached their assigned deck.

Darnell and Third Officer Stemple began their search of deck B from the bow.

"I know a little about how that doctor feels," Stemple said to Darnell. "He wanted revenge . . . I did, too, when I lost my son."

"What?"

"My son was killed. Oh, it was different, of course. He was just a bystander in a pub fight. A drunk hit him. His head struck a sharp corner. Dead. Just like that. And only nineteen. It's three years ago, and I still dream of it." Stemple's eyes reddened. "I don't know if I'm any better than the man we're looking for."

"But you didn't avenge him," Darnell said. "You didn't kill innocent people."

"No. But I felt that need for justice. I was at sea when it happened, but if I'd known the name of the other man, the one who caused his death . . . I don't know what I'd have done."

Darnell scowled. "This one's different. Burton took the lives of three people he didn't even know.

The best that could be said is that he's out of his mind. He's dangerous."

"I know what we're facing." Stemple stopped as they reached the end of the passageway. "We should start here. There are a few service rooms along the way. They should be locked, but my master key will open them, and the cabins."

"I can identify Burton more easily, so I'll go into the cabins first," Darnell said. "You stay behind me, for backup."

"Are we looking for a man, or a man dressed like a woman?"

"Either. Just be alert. He's very tall."

They approached the first cabin, and Stemple knocked on its door. "Officer Stemple," he announced. "Open up, please."

They heard a rustling inside, and in moments the lock clicked and the door opened six inches. "Yes? I haven't been feeling well."

"We'd like to inspect your cabin, ma'am," Stemple said. "Just take a minute."

The woman opened the door wider, and Darnell stepped through the doorway, his handgun gripped in his side pocket. He looked about, while Stemple followed him in, a few steps behind.

"Thank you, ma'am," Stemple said when they had finished.

Darnell pulled the door closed behind them as they stepped out of the room. "Let's move on."

Across the way, Stemple opened a service closet and quickly determined it simply had the usual mops and cleaning supplies. But Darnell knew each time they opened a door, he could be there.

They went on to the next cabin, and the next, Stemple announcing them, Darnell searching, moving as rapidly as they could. They checked all storage and service rooms along the way. Stewards and pursers at the stairwells assured them the wells were cleared to the next deck. Stemple searched the unoccupied public rest rooms, gun drawn.

The fourth cabin revealed a tall, heavy woman, wearing a black veil over her face. Darnell was startled at first, but seeing her face close, tears streaming down it, realized it was not Burton. He entered the cabin, his hand in his coat pocket still holding his .38 special. A second woman sat in a chair, staring at the wall.

"I'm sorry about your loss, ma'am," Darnell said to the veiled woman. "Your husband?"

"Yes. It was terrible. To say good-bye, knowing it could be good-bye forever. And it was." She touched a handkerchief to her eyes. "We'd been married twenty years."

Darnell made a quick search, offered his hand to the woman, and said, "Thank you. We won't disturb you further."

In the hall, Darnell looked at Stemple. "We're going to see a lot of this. Be prepared for it."

"How can you prepare yourself? These poor women."

Five cabins, then ten, many with *Titanic* survivors, some of whom Darnell recognized, doubled up with *Carpathia* passengers. Some cabins held grieving widows and children, and the same scene seemed to be repeated over and over. Some seemed occupied, but with no answer to their knock, Stemple used his passkey to enter. In these cases, both Darnell and the officer had their handguns drawn and ready. The passengers were apparently on deck.

The time approached two p.m. "We're half done," Stemple said. He removed his cap and blotted the inside of it with a handkerchief. "Don't know why I'm sweating."

Darnell nodded. "Nerves. With each door we open, we could find him waiting for us."

As they continued, Darnell found in the next cabin the two elderly ladies he had interviewed in the library of the *Titanic* three days earlier and had spoken to on deck the day before.

"Hello, ladies," he said, pleased to see their ancient cherub faces again. "Marybelle and Carrie."

"I'm Carrie."

"And I'm, well, of course, I'm Marybelle." She looked about and gestured. "Officer Lightoller helped us . . ."

Carrie finished her sentence, ". . . get these quarters."

"We'll have a lot to tell them in New York." Marybelle's moist eyes glistened. "We were just talking . . ."

". . . about all those poor people who died," Carrie said.

"It could have been us," Marybelle said.

Darnell said, "Ladies, we're searching for a desperate criminal. I'd advise you to stay in your cabin. That's the safest place for you. At least until dinnertime, when you're in a crowd."

Their eyes widened. They looked at each other.

"Desperate?" Carrie questioned.

Marybelle pulled her shawl about her. "A criminal? How exciting, I mean . . ."

"This is serious, ladies. Be careful." Darnell touched Marybelle's arm lightly. "Don't open your door to any stranger. Keep it locked."

"Oh, we will," they chorused.

"We've already had our tea," Carrie said.

Darnell searched the cabin, just to be sure Burton

was not concealed in a closet where the two ladies would have been unaware of his presence. Satisfied, he stepped out of the room, Stemple following. He listened to hear the lock click shut before he and Stemple moved on.

"On one of the ships, they were in a cabin next to one of the so-called 'suicide' cabins. They told me they were convinced the man in that cabin was not the type to take his own life. Now we know they were right."

Stemple called the bridge to check in with the Captain, and learned all the teams were about an hour away from completion of their respective decks. No trace of Burton had been found. Darnell and Stemple moved on methodically with their search.

Penny Winters paced back and forth in her cabin. "I can't take this any longer. Four hours, and not a word." She spoke to Carolyn Maddux, a second-class *Titanic* passenger who had been in the lifeboat with her and now shared the cabin with her.

"You're worried about John, your friend, aren't you?" Carolyn placed her hands on Penny's shoulders. "Worrying doesn't help, all your walking back and forth."

Penny stopped her pacing. "You're right. I have to do something besides worry."

"What? Go up and help search for a killer? Leave that to the men." She frowned deeply.

Penny shrugged. "Maybe I shouldn't have told you about all this, but I had to tell someone."

"I know. But I won't tell anyone else. I know we can't panic the passengers."

Penny spoke with decision. "Well, at least I'm going on deck. I can look for John, see if he's all right."

She whirled and grabbed her long coat from the closet.

"Penny, please. Think what you're doing."

"I am thinking. Maybe I can help in some way. I'm worried about him, and I just can't stand it down here anymore."

"You could put yourself in danger." Carolyn blocked the door. "Don't go, Penny."

"I'm going. Let me by."

Carolyn frowned. "All right, I tried. Then I'm going with you." She pulled on her own coat.

The two women headed down the C deck passageway toward a stairway and took the two flights up to the door to the main deck. They noticed the pursers standing at the bottom and top of the stairs. They pushed through the double doors out onto the A deck and edged their way through the throngs of passengers over to the railing.

"Look at that ocean. Breathe that air. It makes you feel alive again," Penny exclaimed. She took a deep breath. "That cabin's a prison." The air was cold and brisk, and the ship threw high furrows in the waves up from its path against the side of the ship, with fine sprays of it reaching the two women.

Carolyn looked at her. "Now what?"

"I don't know. But I feel alive again, being out here. Let's just walk about. Maybe I'll see John."

"And if that man sees you?" Carolyn looked around them to see if anyone was listening to them.

"He doesn't know me. He's never seen me." She eyed the other woman. "Are you afraid? You don't have to come with me."

Carolyn sputtered, "I'm not afraid."

The two women picked their way through the crowds. Penny heard the sobbing of women nearby, suffering the aftershock of the tragedy, reliving their last moments with their husbands, sharing their experiences now with other bereaved widows. Stewards brought out trays of hot soup, coffee and tea, and passed them around, serving those who were able to be on deck and unable to stay in their cabins.

"I don't know what I would have done if John hadn't survived," Penny said. "Until we found each other on deck, I was suffering just like these poor women."

Stewards offered Penny and Carolyn hot tea, and they took mugs of it and drank it, standing at the rail. Penny brushed back her long, soft hair as the wind tossed it about.

"Let's go up to the boat deck," Penny said. "Maybe John's there."

Darnell and Stemple reached the last B deck cabin at just after four p.m. "He's not on this deck," Stemple said as he closed the door to the last cabin. "Not in any cabin, service room, restaurant, or smoking room." He leaned against the wall and lit a cigarette. "It's against the rules, but Captain Rostron won't mind." He took a few deep puffs on his cigarette, then stamped it out. "What now?"

"See the Captain."

They wound their way forward and up to the boat deck, to the bridge, where the Captain stood talking with Ismay and three other officers.

The Captain turned to Darnell. "Three decks complete," he said. "We're waiting for the last team, then, if that deck's clear, we'll cover deck A and finally the boat deck."

Darnell squinted at the sky. "We'll have light for a while."

The Captain said, "We should take him without harming him, if we can. He deserves a trial."

Ismay snorted. "He's caused our line enough trouble. Killed three people, disrupted our organization. He's dangerous."

Darnell wondered if Ismay was thinking of his own safety now.

"He's entitled to a fair trial," Rostron cautioned. "Justice."

"Of course, of course," Ismay replied. He turned his back on the group and stared out at the sea. "Justice," he grumbled.

The last team, Boxhall and Polardi, stepped into the room. "Not a sign of him, Captain," Boxhall said.

"All right," Darnell said. "We'll go through deck A and come back up here to finish. We've narrowed it down to these two decks. Be on your guard."

The men filed out of the room. Darnell wanted to see Penny, to make sure she was all right but knew there wasn't time. He pushed through the swinging doors to the stairwell down to A deck, the others following.

At the far end of the ship, Penny and Carolyn stepped from the A deck stairs onto the boat deck.

Penny said, "Let's go see if he's on the bridge."

Carolyn stopped. "I don't know why I'm here, Penny. You'll probably want to be alone with John, if you find him."

"What will you do?"

"I'll be around, somewhere on deck. You'll find me if you need me."

Penny nodded and watched as Carolyn walked away. She turned and made her way through the thick assembly of passengers. Some sat in deck chairs with blankets pulled around them. Others stood at the rail, facing the cold breeze created by the ship's twenty-knot speed and the natural wind currents.

Most were first-class passengers, still dressed in their fine clothes. Others were obviously second-class, and some, although far fewer, the poorly dressed steerage passengers, some still carrying their canvas bags of belongings. One thing the survivors all had in common was their stunned expressions, their grief and pain, the tears the women blotted from their eyes. Some held each other for comfort of a friend, or someone who had shared the horrible experience. Others sat in chairs, with their eyes closed, apparently trying to forget the events of the day before. Still others stood at the rail, breathing in the sharp, fresh air, trying to clear their minds, perhaps, of their ordeal.

As she came to the bridge and saw officers moving about behind the windows, Penny decided to see the Captain and ask about John. She walked up the stairs and found Captain Rostron, who told her Darnell was on A deck but advised her to stay there with him.

Ignoring the advice, Penny left the bridge and hurried back toward the stairwell. The cold, late afternoon wind sent a chill down her spine and brought a sudden sense of foreboding to her. She yearned to be with John, to hold him close.

Chapter Twenty-six

Tuesday, April 16

Gareth Burton pulled the tarpaulin cover back down over the area of the lifeboat where he had entered it, but left a crack for visibility. Earlier that morning, he had moved from his cot up to the boat deck and secreted himself in the boat.

Now he huddled, stiff and sore, in the boat, seething with anger. Me, he thought, forced to hide like a pursued animal, like a common criminal. Me, one of the best physicians on the line. But they can't take away my revenge. They'll never forget cabin 13. I even caused the *Titanic* to sink. What a sweet revenge! And yet, he thought, there were children lost—young boys, even girls, like my own daughter. He frowned, his thoughts jumbled and confused. Tears came into his eyes. His fevered forehead beaded with perspiration. His mind whirled, and his main thought always came back to him—what is there to live for now?

Occasionally, Burton inched up the flap of the tarpaulin and peered out at passengers passing by on the deck. Mostly he lay back, hands under his head, and stared at the tarpaulin ceiling in the semi-darkness, with thoughts, memories, churning in his mind. He heard the voices of passengers as they walked by, and bits of their conversation about losing husbands, their suffering in the lifeboat. But the words only lightly penetrated the haze of his consciousness.

He had to force himself to concentrate. He must remember his main goal now, his only goal, to kill Darnell and anyone who stood in the way of that. If he could find Ismay, and take him also, that would be even better. But if he showed himself, he'd be captured, he knew that. He'd wait for something to happen, something that would tell him what to do.

As Penny Winters hurried along the promenade toward the stairs to A deck she looked about her in frustration, thinking Darnell might have come back up already, but she saw no sign of him or any search crew.

"Where is he?" she said to herself and bit her lip. She straightened up and continued her march along the starboard side, past the lifeboats, toward the stern. She decided to look over this deck before going down one level.

Penny felt a sense of aloneness and weariness as she threaded her way through the milling crowds of passengers. She watched for John, and was so concentrated on trying to find him that she failed to notice the man following her now, only a dozen feet back.

Burton wore *Titanic* crew clothing, a black coat, and a stocking cap pulled down over his ears and hair. His glasses were in one coat pocket. In the other he clutched the handle of his scalpel.

He had seen Penny Winters walk by through the slight opening in the tarpaulin cover, and recognized her as Darnell's friend. This was his chance. Circumstances were telling him what to do. He climbed out of the boat, appearing to any passenger's casual look as if he were a *Carpathia* seaman engaged in some kind of duty.

He fell in behind Penny, a dozen or more feet back, and saw that she was heading for the stern. She was apparently looking for someone, her head turning this way and that, her gaze moving back and forth. He realized at once that it was Darnell she was seeking. They had become separated somehow, and she wanted to find him. Perfect. A few more strides and she'd be opposite the stairwell door. He saw his chance to grab her.

He lengthened his stride until he was only a few feet behind her as she reached the stairwell. Couldn't be better—she's near the door. A disturbance was occurring near the rail, a child was crying, a woman ran in that direction, and all eyes focused on the confusion. It was his chance.

Burton was about to reach Penny, when another woman called to her from behind him.

"Penny," Carolyn called, and walked rapidly past him to catch up to her. "I've found out something."

Penny stopped and turned to her. "What is it?"

"I saw the search crews down on A deck. You can find John there."

Burton, frustrated, stood apart, looking away from them, but close enough to hear some of the conversation as they talked. The two women had finished talking now, and the one called Carolyn returned in the direction from which she had come. Penny now turned and headed for the next stairwell.

When she reached the doors, Burton grabbed her around the throat with one hand and stifled her voice. He pulled her through the swinging doors into the stairwell. He pressed his scalpel against her neck. "If you scream, lady, you're dead."

He released his hold on her throat enough for her to talk, but she had trouble saying the words. "What—what do you want?"

"John Darnell. The professor. Your professor. Where is he?" Burton pressed the scalpel tighter against her skin. A drop of blood formed at the juncture of the blade and her throat.

"I—I—don't know."

"It won't help to lie. I heard what your friend said—A deck, right? Searching for me." Burton laughed. He pulled her down the steps to a small landing between decks where they could not be seen from either the boat deck or the A deck below. He stood behind her, holding her around the body with one arm now, keeping the blade at her throat.

Burton lowered his voice. "I just want to talk with him, to tell him my story. I won't harm him."

As she looked over her shoulder at him, his eyes bore into hers. Burton knew he could deceive her, knew she could easily be manipulated by his superior intellect.

"He's looking for you," Penny said.

"How many men are searching?"

"I don't know."

"Are they armed?" He pressed the knife harder on her throat, and another drop of blood formed. "They're on the A deck, I know that." He glanced down at the door below.

"I can't tell you anything. Just let me go—I'll tell John to come here."

Burton laughed again. "Don't play innocent with me. We both know what's going on here. They want to kill me. As soon as they see me, I'm a dead man."

"No, no. They'll take you to America, give you a trial."

"I'm going to put on my own trial. Your precious Professor Darnell—he's the defendant. And White Star Line, and Chairman Ismay—they're defendants, too." He paused, and his lips turned up in a snarl as he said, "And I'm the prosecutor, the jury, and the judge." Beads of perspiration began to form on his forehead.

Suddenly he pulled her down the rest of the stairs and over to windowed double doors leading out to the A deck. "Time to hold court," he said. He held Penny to one side, out of view from the windows, and looked out of them onto the deck. "We'll just watch for him here, for a while. For your professor."

John Darnell and Officer Stemple moved slowly along the deck on the starboard side, in a loose team of two, but fifteen feet apart. They scoured the face of every passenger as they passed them. The other three teams checked cabins, the smoking lounge, the dining room, and the deck on the port side.

As he and Stemple approached the stern, Darnell wondered if Burton had been missed somewhere below decks. He could have hidden in a closet. Or could he have gone down to the boiler rooms or machine rooms, farther below? He began to doubt they would find him at all. They might have to go down to the boiler and machine areas.

The air was getting cooler, and the sun was low in the sky, behind gray clouds. Many passengers who had cabins were retreating to them, and others bundled up tighter with their coats and blankets.

The voice came from Darnell's right—not loud, but strident and full of emotion. "Darnell. Over here."

He turned and saw the face of Gareth Burton looking out at him through a glass in the partially open stairwell door. He was about to call to Stemple, but Burton called, "Just you."

Darnell caught a glimpse of Penny's face through the glass. A glint of metal at her throat told him everything—Burton had taken her as a hostage. Darnell grabbed his .38 in his pocket as he walked to the door. He'd be ready for Burton, if he could use it safely. Now it was Penny he was worried about again. When Darnell reached the entrance, Burton pulled the door open, inward, and Darnell stepped through the doorway.

"Nice and easy now, Professor," Burton warned, his eyes glittering. "You can see your mistress here is one inch away from a severed jugular. Her life is in your hands. And I'll take your gun if you value her life."

Darnell took in the situation. Burton was right. He couldn't risk her life by attacking him. He'd have to go along with him until he could see his chance.

"Slow and easy. I know you have a gun. Hand it over by the barrel."

Darnell did as Burton said, watching the man's eyes for any weakness, any distraction that might give him a chance. But he couldn't risk anything happening to Penny.

"Now, just put your hands up, Professor, put them on top of your head, please . . . that's right." Burton sneered as Darnell followed his instructions. "Now, we're just going up these stairs to the boat deck. But first—you'll call off your dogs." He pointed to the door window, and Darnell saw Stemple approaching. "Tell him, if you want your mistress and yourself to stay alive, the search teams stay down here on

A, in one spot at the stern, where I can see them from the deck above. Do it."

Darnell stepped quickly to the door and pushed it open an inch. Stemple was within distance of his voice. Darnell urged, "Burton's got us. Penny Winters is a hostage. He's taking us to the boat deck. Spread the word to the teams—stay down here at the stern. Don't come up to the boat deck. Tell the Captain."

Darnell let the swinging door flap shut, as Stemple ran in the other direction.

Burton said, "That's a nice boy, Professor. You take orders very well."

Darnell said, "It's your move, Doctor. What next?" He continued to be alert to any opportunity to overturn the situation.

Burton laughed. "We're going up, to the top. You go in front. We'll follow. Up the stairs, now."

Darnell led the way up, Burton following with his blade at Penny's throat, his arm around her body, clasping her other arm tightly with his hand. As they stepped through the upper doorway onto the boat deck, Burton said sharply, "To the stern."

Darnell assumed Burton chose that route because there were fewer passengers there. Most who had not returned to their cabins were closer to the bow, along the rail. They looked ahead into the ship's path, wanting to be the first to see land, although it was still hundreds of miles away.

As they reached the rail at the stern, Burton pressed both of them against it, his scalpel still on Penny's throat. A few passengers saw them, saw the knife, and a hubbub of talk began, but none came close to them. One man ran off, as if to seek official help. When any of the few who watched caught his eye, Darnell shook his head, hoping they would understand that meant it would be dangerous to interfere with Burton.

"Can you swim, Professor?" Burton's smile seemed more evil and demented than ever to Darnell. He wondered what dark thoughts must be whirling through the man's head.

"You see," Burton was going on, "I had a careful plan, to execute anyone in cabin thirteen, where my daughter was murdered. The penalty for interference in my plans is death. Unless you can swim for it." He laughed. "But I told your friend here," he nodded at Penny, "I'd have a trial first. I'll give you that."

"You'll be the one on trial," Darnell said. "Why don't you surrender now, turn your knife over to me. We'll keep you safe and turn you over to the authorities in New York."

Burton ignored the words. "The charge against you is interference, and if Ismay was here, I'd add rape and murder of my daughter as a charge. But you'll do. You work for White Star, too, so you can take his place, and the place of those men who killed my daughter and ruined my life." Burton's eyes were wild.

Darnell said, "I'm sorry about what happened to your daughter. I'm sure you loved her very much."

At the unexpected gesture of sympathy, Burton's eyes filled with tears, which he brushed away quickly with a coat sleeve. He answered, "Yes, I loved her, but more than you could ever know. What do you know of a father and daughter's love, you and your dry books? What do you know of a pretty, freckle-faced child—not even a young woman yet—and never to be one now. What do you know of those White Star Line crewmen—those beasts—who violated her, took her young life, and ruined mine?" His face was flushed, and his forehead now glistened with sweat.

Darnell slowly lowered his hands an inch, testing whether Burton would notice. "It's true. I don't have a daughter. But I have Miss Winters—Penny—and I love her as much as you loved your daughter. I know what love is."

"This woman wasn't raped like an animal, thrown overboard like garbage." Burton's eyes glared.

"Nothing any of us can do could ever change that. But people will understand how you felt. They'll help you. There are facilities . . ."

"Hah! I know what you're saying. An institution? I've seen that kind of help. The poor people that aren't crazy when they get there, they drive crazy."

Darnell tentatively lowered his hands slightly. If he could reach out . . .

Burton broke off his thought. "Get those hands back up!" He stepped back, putting more distance between himself and Darnell. "Do you want me to give your woman a sample, a little slice on the cheek, perhaps? This scalpel has a razor edge, I can assure you."

Darnell put his hands higher again. This was not the time to take action.

Burton said, "Defend yourself. You're on trial now."

Darnell could see keeping Burton talking might be his only way to distract him, to give him an opening and a way to overpower him when he became less vigilant. He tried to put himself in Burton's mind, to find the weaknesses there, something that could give him an edge over the man.

Chapter Twenty-seven

Tuesday, April 16

J. Bruce Ismay fumed and walked back and forth in front of the other search team officers. "What are we going to do, just stand here? We could overpower that one man. I know him—he's a drunk and a weakling."

Stemple spoke up. "Darnell told me they were hostages, not to go up. The man had a knife to the woman's throat."

"One woman. But we have the whole ship at risk here. He could even try to kill me."

"We're armed," Lightoller said. "Little chance he could do that. But you're right, we have to do something."

"He's not watching us," Stemple said. "If we can't see him up there, he can't see us."

Lightoller said, "The three of us—let's go up a port side stairwell, come up behind his back, if we can, and surprise him."

Ismay nodded, and Stemple said, "I'm ready."

The three backtracked, passed through the main dining room to the port side, and approached the stern stairwell. Lightoller led the way up the stairs. "Don't show yourselves yet, just stay back on the landing. I'll size up where he is, and what is happening. Then we'll see if there's anything we can do."

At the boat deck level, Lightoller peered out through the glass window. The deck area he could see was deserted. They were apparently around the corner to the left of the structure. He motioned to the others to follow, and walked softly to the corner and peered around it. Burton's back was toward him. He held Penny Winters, the knife still at her throat. Darnell faced him, his hands in the air. A half dozen passengers watched in a huddle, from a distance beyond.

"I might be able to approach him from here without being seen," Lightoller said to Ismay. "But I'm worried about the woman. If he sees me, he could kill her in an instant."

"But then he loses his insurance," Ismay said. "Without her, he knows he's a dead man." He held out his revolver. "I could hit him from here—maybe I should just do that."

Lightoller shook his head. "Unless you're a marksman, you could easily hit her. That won't work." He watched as Burton and Darnell talked but could not make out their words. "We'll wait a bit."

In his peripheral vision, Darnell saw Lightoller's head and shoulders appear beyond the corner of the wall, but he made no movement at all, keeping his gaze fixed on Burton.

"Defend yourself," Burton demanded. "You're on trial."

"All right. Your daughter wasn't murdered by White Star Line, or by Ismay, or by me. The men who did it were simply cruel, heartless men who happened to work on that ship. They'd have done the same thing anywhere, under similar conditions."

Burton smirked. "Very fancy talk. But a ship shouldn't hire people like that. They shouldn't hire animals."

"You've killed, too," Darnell pressed him. "Three innocent people, two men and a woman who did you no harm."

"It was a message to White Star. My revenge—letting the line know they had committed a crime and had to pay for it." He paused. "I had nothing against those people. They were just pawns, nameless passengers."

To Darnell, Burton seemed tired, and even more confused and distraught. If he could get him angry and disturbed enough, he'd make a move.

Burton shook his head as if to clear it. "Your defense is lacking, Professor. The jury will have to decide—and I'm the jury. You're guilty, and you must die."

"And your guilt?" Darnell pressed. "How will you pay?"

"I've already paid, in advance—with my own daughter." Burton's feverish face took on a sly grin. "There's something you should know. I've had a greater revenge than anyone realizes, the greatest revenge anyone has ever had."

"What do you mean?"

"I caused the ship's crash with the iceberg," Burton said.

"The binoculars, the stolen charts. That was your doing."

"How did you know that?"

Darnell kept him talking, keeping him off balance. "I saw the binoculars box in your office when we talked. Later, I knew you'd taken them. And the charts—you were the logical one to do that."

"Here's one you don't know—I damaged the wireless."

"I suspected that. Now it's clear. But nothing you did had any effect—they had other charts, they repaired the wireless."

Burton spoke desperately now. "If they'd had the binoculars, they could have seen the iceberg. Tell the world that, Darnell—tell them what a genius I am, a genius for revenge." His mouth formed into a twisted leer.

"You couldn't have known the ship would sink. It was fate. And if you want people to know your part in this, you'll have to tell them yourself. If you turn yourself in, maybe you'll get the glory you want. Otherwise you'll soon be just another casualty of the shipwreck. And that's how I'll tell it. Because you're going to die, Burton—that's how your story will end."

Darnell saw the man grow more angry with each word he spoke, and he repeated his words. "Just another casualty. A footnote."

Burton's eyes bulged. "How dare you—I'll show you what I'll do!"

He jumped for Darnell, forgetting his hostage, reaching out, swinging with his scalpel, missing Darnell's face by an inch. Penny squirmed away from his grasp. Darnell dropped his hands and sidestepped the charging man. He called to Penny, "Run! Get away from here!"

Darnell grabbed Burton's right arm as the man missed him, twisting the arm backwards with all the strength he could muster against the larger man. He had felt Burton's strong hands once before when they struggled in his cabin. Burton cried out and the scalpel fell from his hand. Darnell kicked it, and it slid away on the deck to the edge of the ship and out into the ocean.

Penny ducked under a guide rope and ran toward the port side. Lightoller stepped out from around the corner of the structure and called to her, "This way."

As she reached him, she said, "John needs help!" But Lightoller was already running toward the struggling men.

She turned and ran back after Lightoller, toward the two men, who were fighting more fiercely now. Ismay and Stemple followed her, guns drawn.

Darnell and Burton traded heavy blows on the face and head, half wrestling, half fighting. Darnell's face was bloody. Burton's eye was puffed and bruised, and his coat torn.

Their struggle had propelled the two men close to the stern rail now, in a death grip. Burton had both of his big hands on Darnell's neck, throttling him. Darnell gasped for breath. He threw his arms upward in one desperate stroke and broke the hold.

Darnell saw now that he could get the better of the man, and struck Burton again and again in the face. Burton fought back viciously, flailing wildly, and hit Darnell with first one hand, then the other, on the jaw, in the eye, in the stomach. But the two days without food and Burton's confinement had taken its toll on him, and he began to falter, as he felt the effects of the fight.

Lightoller crouched a few feet away now, his revolver out, trying for a clear shot at the doctor. But with the men weaving back and forth, there was danger of hitting the wrong one.

Running up beside him, Ismay said, "Shoot, shoot!" But, his own gun out, he did nothing himself.

Stemple ran up now, gave his gun to Ismay, and

said, "Hold this. I'll help him." He ran toward the two men.

Burton bled profusely now from his nose and a cut above his eye. He stumbled backward, trying to catch his breath, wiping the blood away from his eyes with his torn sleeve. Darnell struck another vicious blow, and Burton fell against the rail. Seeing Stemple approaching, Burton climbed up on the rail and shouted, "Stay back!"

Darnell and Stemple halted in mid-stride and stared at Burton. "Don't do it, man!" Darnell shouted.

"What have I got to live for?" Burton turned and looked down at the ocean. "I'll go the way Emily did."

"No, wait!" Darnell shouted and rushed forward.

Burton closed his eyes and stepped over the rail just as Darnell reached it. Darnell watched him fall. Burton's scream of rage and terror resounded upward. Burton opened his eyes once more, looking upward, and Darnell stared into them one last time as the man's body reached the waves. Burton's cries stopped suddenly as he hit the water, just above the giant propellors of the ship, and he was sucked down into the depths.

Darnell stared down at the sea, as Penny came up to him and put her arm around him. An angry stain of bright red blood rose to the sea's surface, then quickly dissipated, washed away in the powerful wake of the ship. "A terrible way to die," Darnell said to Penny and pulled her close.

Ismay stood at the rail staring at the sea, and the wake of the ship. "No more than he deserved," he said. "And no less."

Stempled walked toward the other officers who

had charged up the stairs. "It's all over. He's dead," he said.

Penny shuddered. "What a horrible man, John . . . but what a poor man, too. His life ended so miserably."

"Yes." Darnell stared at the sea, darker now, blacker in the growing nightfall. "But his pain is over now, forever."

Ismay, a triumphant smile on his face, said to Darnell, "The man got the justice he deserved."

Darnell glared at him. "You're the last man who should speak of justice, Ismay. What justice was there in the cabin thirteen murders, Burton's revenge for a horrible crime your own men caused? What justice for the rape and murder of Burton's daughter by your crewmen? What justice is there for the *Titanic* tragedy and the men, women, and children at the bottom of the sea, and for Captain Smith, and your officers and crew? All dead—when better ship construction, more lifeboats, and boat drills might have saved them."

He could see Ismay cringing before his words as his voice rose with his emotion.

"So what was it, Ismay? Did you trade bulkheads and lifeboats for deck space and cabins? Did you trade speed for safety, and sacrifice your magnificent ship in a search for glory? Burton paid his price, and you'll find yourself before the public's own bar of justice. But no justice can come to the hundreds of men, women, and children whose graves are in the sea. For them, and for the *Titanic*—the rest is silence."

Darnell took Penny's hand and pushed by Ismay. He pulled her quickly through the gathering throngs, striding forward to the bow, wanting to get as far away as he could get from the scene of the struggle and the last bitter chapter of Burton's life.

As they walked, Darnell touched his handkerchief to Penny's neck and drew it away with drops of blood. "That was too close," he said. He blotted blood from the corner of his mouth.

At the bow, they joined the other rescued passengers, the weary refugees from the great *Titanic*, as they searched the gray, hazy horizon for any sign of land. But that welcome sight would not greet their eyes for two more long days at sea.

Chapter Twenty-eight

New York City, Thursday night, April 18, 1912

The *Carpathia* steamed into New York harbor thirty-six hours after the *Titanic* would have arrived, in the dark of night and a light fog. It was first sighted by those on land at 8:30 p.m.

The ship was greeted by a huge crowd of over 30,000 people who braved driving rainstorms to come down and meet it. Throngs of relatives, reporters, and curiosity-seekers, held back by police, lined the docks in a turmoil of confusion, emotion, and fear.

Near panic and pandemonium was created by small boats crowding the water on either side of the ship as it steamed slowly into the harbor. Darnell and Penny, and Sung nearby, watched in amazement from the rail, which was lined with survivors from the *Titanic*, who stared at the dock, hoping to see their families.

Passengers on the decks of the small crafts alongside the rescue ship waved at those aboard. Some were relatives who had secured passage on the little boats to get as close to the *Carpathia* as possible. Others were officials of the city and the port. Reporters swarmed over the decks of the small boats shooting photographs, making notes for their newspaper and magazine articles of what they saw of the passengers lining the *Carpathia*'s rails. It was a sight that would be reported over and over again in newspapers for days and months to come.

As the *Carpathia* reached the White Star Line pier, survivors watched from the deck in awe as *Titanic* lifeboats reclaimed from the sea, their refuge for several hours on that terrible night, were lowered to the water. Darnell could imagine workmen removing from the sides of the boats the brass plates bearing the name *Titanic*. After unloading the boats, the *Carpathia* pulled in slowly, with tugboat help, to the Cunard Line dock, for passenger disembarkation.

Tugboats nudged the *Carpathia* into Pier 54, and the laborious procedures of tying it down and putting out gangplanks took place. The passengers soon found that they and the other survivors could not be easily disembarked in all the turmoil. They were kept on the ship for "official reasons," primarily for an official inventory of those aboard, and inspection of proof of citizenship and passport documents. Many survivors had no such identification or documents. Many women explained, in tears, "My husband was carrying it." An hour passed after the ship's arrival before the first passengers disembarked.

The delays built a sense of hysteria among the survivors on deck almost equal to that of the anguished families on the dock, who were desperate to know whether their loved ones were among those saved or had been lost in the tragic sinking. Not enough information had been passed along over the wireless, although the operators, including the *Titanic*'s wireless man, Harold Bride, had worked night and day sending messages to anxious relatives.

Herbert Lightoller came up to Darnell and Penny. "I'll say good-bye now. I wish you both the best."

Darnell took Lightoller's hand. "We thank you for everything—even for our lives."

Penny kissed Lightoller on the cheek, saying, "Good-bye," and he seemed more flustered than at any time during their harrowing trip.

When unloading finally began, Darnell watched as Chairman J. Bruce Ismay, ironically, exercised his privilege of rank by being the first survivor to leave the ship. Ismay was immediately surrounded by reporters, and Darnell could imagine the grandiose stories that he would tell.

Amid the confusion, Darnell watched a man holding a camera, apparently a newspaper reporter, in a black slicker and a fedora hat that dripped rainwater, scramble up a gangway to a lower deck. The man feverishly began to interview passengers and crew as they passed by, any who would talk with him, reaching out and grabbing at the coats of people to stop them.

Darnell grimaced. "Now I suppose they'll be searching for me, those reporters, to talk about the wireless reports I sent ahead about Burton and the three murders," he said to Penny, "although it's small news by comparison to the *Titanic* tragedy. I hope it gets lost in all the other reporting. I'm not looking forward to it."

"Do you have to see them?"

"Only if they want an explanation about Burton. But I have to clear the record, and let the families of the victims know what really happened, that their relatives didn't commit suicide. I'll get their names and addresses, and at least write them."

"And White Star Line? How will they come out of all this?"

"They'll pay a penalty, at least in the press, for the murder of Burton's daughter, the murders by Burton, and even Burton's own life. These may be lost, among the deaths of a thousand, five hundred victims of the ship's sinking. But there will be investigations and hearings. Everything will come out."

Darnell held Penny's hand as they stared out at the crowds swarming on the docks and the passengers leaving. "The lines will have to make changes."

"They need new laws," Penny said. "Making ships carry enough lifeboats for everyone."

"So many things. Lifeboat drills, solid watertight compartments, wireless rooms operating twenty-four hours a day, and changing sea-lane routes—going farther south in the spring when icebergs are moving. And carrying spare binoculars. I hope they do these things. They're the lessons to be learned, perhaps the only positive things history will point to out of this tragic voyage."

"Hundreds of people wouldn't have died if we'd had those laws." She held his arm tightly. "We're the lucky ones, John. We have each other."

He looked in her eyes. "One good thing from this terrible trip, Penny, was meeting you, and falling in love with you."

Penny said, "We have each other. But think of Madeleine Astor losing her husband, in her honeymoon year."

"And a thousand other tragedies, as sad as hers."

Darnell held her tight as they looked down at the tearful, frantic people on the dock. He thought of the lives destroyed, the widows, the steerage children who never had a chance.

"I'm going to do what I can to help change the laws," Darnell said. "I'll write letters and testify about what I saw in steerage, trying to help those unfortunates. I want to tell them how the ship's officers, like Captain Smith, and Phillips, and Moody, who heard the first iceberg call, stayed at their posts until it was too late for them."

Penny shivered and put her cold hands into her coat pockets. She felt some paper in one pocket and brought out an envelope Darnell had thrust into her coat pocket just before she boarded the lifeboat. She opened it. Inside was a single sheet of *Titanic* stationery. She read the words on the sheet aloud:

"Dearest Penny,
When you read these words, I may have perished, along with many others on the Titanic, *which surely will sink before this night is over. I want you to know I love you dearly, and I give you all my possessions in London, most particularly 5,000 pounds being held in trust for me by my solicitors, Pringle and James, on Kensington Road, in Knightsbridge, near Hyde Park. They can direct you to my flat. This is my last will and testament, signed this 15th day of April, 1912. I also leave to you, my darling Penny, all of my love—for all time.*
John F. Darnell."

Penny pulled him to her and kissed him with all the compassion and passion of her being. "I won't need this note, John. I have you. But keep it for me, as a memory of that terrible night." She put the sheet into his coat pocket.

Darnell took a deep breath, and when he breathed out seemed to expel with it, at last, the tenseness that had been in him for days. "I'm glad this trip is over."

He saw that the crowds of passengers rushing from the ship had thinned down enough to make it possible to leave. "What do you say, Penny, my love? Shall we go ashore? Come on, Sung."

Darnell hooked his arms through Penny's arm on one side and Sung's on the other, and headed for the gangplank, walking briskly between them. His face relaxed into a soft smile as he thought of their future in England together—especially their country retreat in the Cotswolds White Star's fee would buy.

"I want to see what it feels like to walk on dry land again for a while," Darnell said. "Then we'll sail back to England."

Penny looked up at him, her eyes teasing. "John, I was, oh, just wondering . . . which cabin we will book when we go back?"

Passengers they passed frowned at Darnell's deep laughter. He returned Penny's look, and they shared a very private secret. "I think you know," he said, smiling into her eyes, "which cabin we *won't* take."

John and Penny Darnell return in . . .

The Case of Compartment 7
by Sam McCarver

Join them for another adventure of

murder and intrigue,

this time aboard

the exotic Orient Express!

Coming from Signet in February 2000!